Massacre in the Seine

Tom Sommers

EuroCanals Publishing LLC

Massacre in the Seine is a work of fiction. All characters, with the exception of historical and public figures involved in events which have been widely reported, are products of the author's imagination. Any resemblance to persons living or dead is entirely coincidental. All references to the Airbus factory and the A380 aircraft are purely a creation of the author and have no basis in fact.

Cover Photograph & Design by the author

Published by EuroCanals Publishing LLC
www.eurocanals.com
facebook: EuroCanals

Additional copies can be obtained from:
www.eurocanals.com
orders@eurocanals.com

About the Author

Tom Sommers, an American, began his canal-cruising avocation with a trip in 1966 aboard a classic wooden motorboat from Cayuga Lake, in the Finger Lakes of Central New York, through the New York State Barge Canal (Erie Canal) and the Oswego Canal to Lake Ontario and the St Lawrence River. Later canal trips included one across the length of the Erie Canal and down the Hudson River to the Statue of Liberty.

After early retirement from an engineering career, Tom moved to coastal North Carolina where he boated on the IntraCoastal Waterway and worked as a boat broker and as an advertising sales representative for a boating magazine.

In early 2000 Tom and his wife Carol acted on a longtime desire to live in Europe and cruise the canals and rivers. Their first year was in Paris, on the Canal St Martin, then on the river Seine near Conflans-Ste-Honorine, and later on the northern coast of Brittany. During these years they have traveled extensively along the waterways and visited France, Belgium, Germany, The Netherlands, Luxembourg, Switzerland, Italy and England.

Beginning with the monthly newsletter "Cruising the Canals & Rivers of Europe" in September 2000, Tom currently offers forty e-book waterway guides, as well as an extensive website describing the inland waterways of Europe.

Other books by Tom Sommers:

Cruising the Canals & Rivers of the Netherlands on ORION (2010)

Cruising the Canals & Rivers of the Netherlands (2011)

Cruising the Canals & Rivers of France (2013)

For more information:eurocanals.com/Order/orderbooks.html

Table of Contents

For Carol –
I'll meet you in Toulouse!

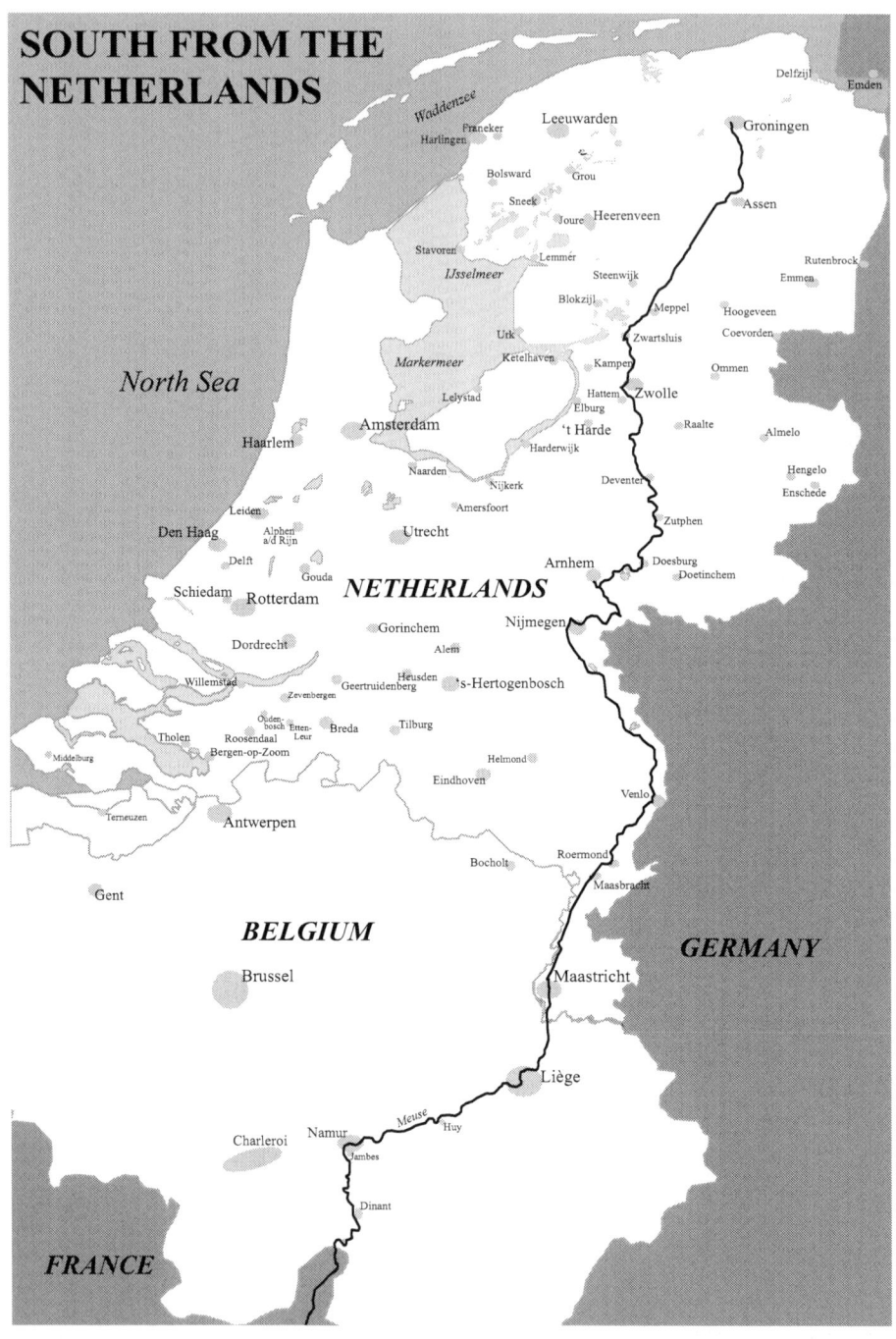

SOUTH FROM THE NETHERLANDS

Waddenzee

Delfzijl

Emden

Leeuwarden

Groningen

Franeker
Harlingen

Bolsward

Grou

Assen

Sneek

Joure

Heerenveen

Rutenbrock

Stavoren

Lemmer

Emmen

IJsselmeer

Steenwijk

Blokzijl

Meppel

Hoogeveen

Urk

Zwartsluis

Coevorden

Markermeer

Ketelhaven

Kampen

Ommen

Lelystad

Hattem
Elburg

Zwolle

North Sea

Amsterdam

't Harde

Raalte

Almelo

Haarlem

Harderwijk

Naarden

Nijkerk

Deventer

Hengelo

Enschede

Amersfoort

Leiden

Zutphen

Alphen
a/d Rijn

Utrecht

Den Haag

Delft

Arnhem

Doesburg
Doetinchem

Gouda

Schiedam

Rotterdam

NETHERLANDS

Nijmegen

Gorinchem

Dordrecht

Alem

Willemstad

Heusden
Geertruidenberg

's-Hertogenbosch

Zevenbergen

Ouden-
bosch

Etten-
Leur

Breda

Tilburg

Tholen

Roosendaal

Helmond

Middelburg

Bergen-op-Zoom

Eindhoven

Venlo

Terneuzen

Antwerpen

Roermond

Bocholt

Gent

Maasbracht

BELGIUM

GERMANY

Brussel

Maastricht

Liège

Meuse

Charleroi

Namur

Huy

Jambes

Dinant

FRANCE

Er valt geen peil op te trekken - there is no knowing what will happen

The expression stems from the shipping trade where a *peil* is a known fixed point that one can use to determine location and determine the course (*geen* means none). You can also use the phrase for people, e.g. *op hem valt geen peil te trekken*: he is unpredictable.

Dutch Word of the Day dwotd.nl

"Air France 990 Super, taxi into position and hold, runway two-six right".

That's the one, thought Piet. Paris CDG to Johannesburg. 11:37PM and it's stopped at the end of the runway, right on time. The plane had pushed back from the gate right at the scheduled 11:30 departure. The biggest Airbus, A380-800, "Super" size in air-traffic jargon. Hundreds of passengers, probably, and the goal is to spread bodies all over Paris. Perhaps some would drop into the Seine, that would be perfect. This flight was picked because it has the necessary flight path, when taking off to the west on runway 26R, to turn directly over the center of Paris.

Piet was at the *Hotel Les Relais Bleus* on Route de l'Europe near Gonesse, 6.2 kilometers from takeoff. It was the site, and now the home of a memorial, of the Concorde crash a dozen years before. He calmly, and alone, had dinner at the *Grille du Relais* steakhouse on the south side of the hotel, then walked across the parking lot to a recently-plowed field on the north side of the hotel. The open field to the northeast gave an clear view toward CDG; at his back was the bright glow of lights from Paris. Piet looked straight up into the dark sky and was surprised that he could see so many stars, this close to Paris.

He had rented a car at Gare du Nord and driven north on the A1, stopping at *Le Bourget* airfield to purchase a scanner radio from an aircraft electronics shop. He set the radio to the tower frequency and set another channel to scan for ramp service communications. The radio jumped between channels. At 11:17PM he had heard Kassa, the baggage handler, say the key words: "Okay, all bags are in the right place." On his mobile phone, Piet called Jamel and said "The box is in place." "D'accord," Jamel replied.

Kassa had placed the trigger box on the inside of the plane's hull and connected the two wires, just as Jamel had instructed him. He found the tiny steel wires near the corner of the baggage compartment door; they were almost impossible to see unless you knew just where to look. Kassa used the width of his closed fist as a measure from the edge of the door opening, 45 degrees up to the left. Contact adhesive held the box tight to the skin of the aircraft.

Inside the box was a sensor for atmospheric pressure; by pushing the button on the trigger box Kassa had zeroed the altitude setting to the altitude of *Charles De Gaulle* airport. The trigger was preset at 1,500 meters (5,000 feet). Jamel had worked out the distances and estimated altitude of the flight as it climbed out: 6 kilometers to Gonesse, 17 km to Stade de France, 20 km to the Boulevard Périphérique on the northern edge of Paris.
That would be the desired explosion point; the proper altitude setting when the plane would be near that point was estimated to be 1,500 meters.

"Air France 990 Super, cleared for takeoff".

"990 rolling".

Soon Piet could see the flashing lights rise above a row of trees; ninety seconds later the huge airplane passed directly overhead. He turned to follow it as it swung through to southbound, while calling Jamel again, to say 'It's in the air'. The bright glow of stadium lights for a football game at *Stade de France* gave him a point to judge distance; as expected, three minutes later the plane appeared to be right over the stadium. In less than a minute after that, it should be at the explosion altitude, flying toward the center of Paris.

Piet wondered if he had successfully thwarted the explosion, or would pieces of aircraft, and pieces of bodies, be scattered across Paris?

Part I

South from the Netherlands

Piet Roefs' second life began at age 52, on the morning of April 18, 2011. He said a brief goodbye to his wife Matje, slid a backpack over his shoulders and rode his bicycle the six kilometers from Matje's apartment at Korte Haven 52A in Schiedam to the rail station in Rotterdam. His last day as an officer with the Rotterdam Seaport Police was just the past Friday.

In the previous months he had already traveled twice to Groningen, in the far northeastern corner of the Netherlands, to inspect a boat named *Margriet* and to purchase it for a long journey. He wasn't yet sure where that journey would lead, but he had decided to go south on the inland canals and rivers of Europe to the south of France and the Mediterranean Sea. He wanted to be far away from Schiedam; it's an attractive town, part of the Rotterdam metropolis, an historic center ringed with canals, but after three decades Piet was through with it, and with Matje. "No more Matje, now I'm off with Margriet instead," Piet said to himself, with a laugh.

The train trip to Groningen was fast enough, just over three hours, but because of construction on the rails it required a section by bus from 't Harde to Meppel. No bicycles were allowed on the bus so he had made his preliminary trips without his primary means of transportation, using the local bus to get around in Groningen.

But he wanted his own favorite bike on the boat, so he made a practical decision: to travel by rail to the stop at 't Harde then ride on the bike from there to Groningen. More than 100 kilometers, but that was a distance that he rode almost every Sunday with his cycling club. Four or five hours, just the afternoon. It would be a good feeling, riding alone into new countryside to begin his new life.

He had made the final payment to own the boat so it was ready for him to spend his first night onboard, on the south side of Groningen. The waterway there is the Noord-Willemskanaal, a canal used by commercial barges and occasional pleasure boats traveling between Groningen and Assen, and further south to Belgium, Germany and France. In the morning Piet would be southbound on that route. His plan was to set off for southern France, with no particular schedule or final destination in mind.

It was after 6PM when he rode across the grass to his new home on the water. The boat was locked, as he expected; the previous owner, Ben Baartman, had told him to pick up the key from Jan Blok, a stone sculptor with a home and workshop on a nearby side channel. Following Ben's instructions, Piet easily found the dirt lane into the sculptor's property.

Riding along one of the parallel dirt ruts into the woods, he came upon a large clearing with two crude sheds and scattered blocks of stone, some finished into sculptures: spirals, male and female torsos, abstracts. A shaggy little black dog with white chin whiskers ran around the yard, barking at his every movement.

One of the sheds backed up into the woods, a steel structure with arched translucent roof panels, open on three sides: the sculptor's workshop. A large block of stone stood four feet tall in the middle of the shed; a tall, lean man, his hair and clothes covered in dust, used a heavy electric grinder to cut vertical grooves down from the top of the stone, 10 or 12 inches long. A nearby wooden chair serves as a portable workbench; he put the grinder down on the chair seat and, with a hammer and chisel, knocked the corners off of the stone, throwing chips for a long distance; Piet stepped back to stay clear and in doing so was noticed.

"Hallo, I am Piet Roefs. I've come for the key for the boat."

"Yes, Ben said you would be here today. I'm Jan Blok. Sorry, my hands are covered in dust." He put down the tools and walked over to Piet, extending his hand.

Jan wears plastic earmuffs, a breathing mask and safety glasses but his hair collects grit like a dust-mop. When he stops to speak and takes off the mask and glasses, hanging them on the knobs of the straight-back chair, the only clean area is the triangle of his nose and mouth. Cheeks, eyebrows, forehead are covered with white stone dust. The lines and creases in his face show him to be older than Piet, probably in his sixties. His wild brown hair is streaked with blond, thinning from the front and from the back; the spot on the back is like a monk's. A tall handsome man with narrow face and piercing blue eyes, a cheerful, friendly smile. Women must melt when he smiles at them, Piet thought; I wouldn't mind looking like that.

"I have your boxes inside my barge, they arrived just a few hours ago," Jan said as he pointed the way, across the clearing.

"Thanks for receiving my shipment," Piet replied. "Just some clothes, books and bedding. Margriet is already well fitted with kitchen and sailing gear. I won't need much."

A narrow footpath leads from the yard through bushes and flowers to a wooden gangplank attached to the deck of a huge ex-commercial barge. Walking onto the deck, Piet stopped to enjoy the view: a still, narrow waterway enclosed by a jungle of greenery. The brush grows wildly on both banks, not unlike Jan's hair, Piet thought. He appears to not use a hairbrush or comb, but his wild hair style is perfect for him.

The ladder down into the barge is steep but a handrail on each side helps during the descent. At the foot of the stairs Piet looked around to take in the surprisingly-large space. Around the perimeter of the main room, obviously an all-purpose room used for sitting, dining and sleeping, are natural-wood cabinets and shelves, arranged randomly. Everywhere in the room, on the tables, shelves and cabinets, are many small sculptures made from clay or stone; gray, black, brown, purple, lime green and alabaster.

Four tall narrow chairs with high backs, the seats covered in pink vinyl, are at a dining table made of a pine-plank top set on two steel sawhorses. A pair of well-used work boots sit next to the table, on an oriental rug. Nearby are two stacks of rough firewood for the furnace, one of them 4 feet high and 8 feet long, incongruously set among the bookshelves and at the foot of a bed. The bed is a handsome pine frame of antique style, a wide single with white duvet. There is no indication of a resident companion.

Round ship's portholes open to provide air but most of the light comes from the large overhead hatch-cover skylight. Charcoal sketches are hung on the walls; art books, paperbacks, CDs and a Scrabble game are piled randomly on shelves built-in around the room. A comfortable black leather couch with sheepskin throw separates a sitting area from the dining table. On a table behind the couch is a tall white Noguchi lamp. Some sculptures sit on the floor, on rectangular stone bases. The overall effect of this room is one that has been created over the years, not from a specific design plan.

Piet thought, this is a guy who knows how to set his own style; I could learn a lot from him.

Piet saw his boxes and picked them up, eager to get on to his own boat. There was no food onboard Margriet for dinner but that problem was solved by Jan, who invited him to return for beer and dinner. Piet agreed to come right back after a quick look around his new boat but refused any help from Jan with the boxes. He could leave his bike and walk to the boat, carrying the boxes.

Piet returned within the hour, stepping onto to the deck of the barge and stopping again to look around in wonderment at this idyllic setting, so close to the modern world but also so private. Jan came up the ladder with a cool bottle of Heineken for each of them and motioned Piet to take a seat.

The evening went late, but Piet was in no rush to leave early. Jan was too entertaining, with stories about his stone works. Sitting in the large living space, Piet told him "This is a place a man can live in and be comfortable - not worrying about whether the neighbors approve of the 'display' lamp in the center of the front window."

"What do you mean? I have a display lamp, the Noguchi. But I don't have a window to put it in," Jan said.

"That's the point. You have the Noguchi because it gives you pleasure, it's a piece of art. It's not to show to the neighbors, obviously you don't live like that. You don't even have any neighbors!"

"Yes, and that's the way I like it."

"I have, just this week, left my wife of 26 years because of things like that lamp," Piet said. "I started thinking about it on our 25th wedding anniversary: why am I living like this? I didn't want to live in Matje's apartment any longer. It is her apartment, she lived there first for several years before we got married and I moved in. She works as an assistant to a decorator, a job that she started even while still in school, at a shop named *Versailles*. That's how the apartment became filled with frilly, overdone lamps, tables, pillows and who-knows-what. She could buy these things at a deep discount, or better yet get them free when they had been replaced with newer objects by the rich ladies of the town. The name of the shop explains everything, she got to thinking that she was Marie Antoinette, for chris'sake!

"Now she can just pile up all of those goddamn frilly pillows on my side of the bed, she'll never know the difference, except I guess the pillows won't snore. Now she can sit there alone, with the fancy drapes across the front window, the ugly lamp in the middle, all the passers-by can think how nice, and how old-fashioned, it looks. I want my own life, and my own style."

"Oh, well, I see!" said Jan, a bit taken aback by this rant. "Now it's just you and your boat, you can make your life as you want it."

"Yes, just as you have done, and I'm starting it tomorrow!... Sorry for dumping all of that on you. I've enjoyed meeting you, I hope you don't mind if I stay in touch?"

"Please do, I would like to hear how you are making out on your adventure."

In the morning Piet rode his bike to shop for groceries, north along the canal path to the second bridge then west, as Jan had told him. At 11:00 he said his thanks and goodbye, cast off and soon became a tourist: on the east bank of the canal was the striking sight of the *Witte Molen*, the 'White Windmill'. Piet had of course seen thousands of windmills in his lifetime, but this was the most beautiful of all, an all-white structure on a red brick base, with graceful curves in the vertical panels, quite like a slim lady's 19th century corset. The sight of it made him think about what he was leaving behind, the culture and traditions of Holland, a country that he had never left before, even for a holiday. But that is what he had decided on, a new life.

The first stop of the trip was a planned overnight at the village of De Punt and an afternoon appointment at the *Beuving De Punt* boatyard for service on the diesel engine. Injectors and filters were to be replaced, the boat filled with diesel fuel and with fresh oil in the engine, making it ready for a long trip.

Piet was interested in De Punt because, even though it was just a tiny and seemingly insignificant village, it had been the scene of an event which had caught the national interest, and his as well. In May 1977 nine armed South Moluccan (Indonesian) youths hijacked a train (reported in the media as a *treinkaping*) on the rail line just 1.5 kilometers east of the village and held 45 hostages there for twenty days. The infamous liberation siege by Dutch marines took the lives of two hostages and six hijackers.

The South Moluccans had come in 1951 for a temporary residence in the Netherlands, with the promise of the Dutch government in the Moluccas that they could establish their own state. They stayed in camps, at Vught and Schattenberg, usually under moderate to poor conditions. After a generation - 25 years - they had still been waiting for the fulfillment of the promises of the Dutch government; some of the younger generation could no longer accept their situation and went on to radical actions.

Piet had recently turned 18 at the time. He avidly followed the daily news reports for his first glimpse of the problems of immigrants, or refugees, in a much different foreign culture. The camp at Vught was only 16 kilometers north of Piet's home, about the distance that he rode his bike to school each day, but he knew nothing of the camp or the people in it until he saw it on the news broadcasts. Then he learned that it had been an SS concentration camp during the Nazi occupation. The displacement of people from another part of the world to a 'concentration' camp near his own home had been difficult for him to understand.

Piet spoke to the owner of the boatyard, who told him how to get to the isolated location of the hijacking on foot. It was a short bike ride east along a highway until he came to the bridge over the Drentsche Aa river, which he remembered seeing on news reports; the curious had stopped their cars at the bridge to look toward the hijacked train. It was too far to be seen through the trees along the river, but occasionally they could have seen helicopters circling over the site. He locked his bike in some brush and walked along the dike of an irrigation canal. He had been told to walk south until the canal is directly alongside the rail tracks. There he was able to identify the exact spot by the bullet strikes still evident in a steel electrical pole on the rail line.

He spent some time there thinking about the past, and about the minds of the immigrant boys who were about his age at the time, while they were in this situation for three weeks. It was difficult for him to comprehend their drive and their situation in taking hostages and then dying in a siege. He couldn't imagine himself ever having the nerve to do such a thing. He thought, "Look how long it's taken me to get a backbone."

Piet grew up in Oirschot, Noord Brabant; he thought it was probably the most boring town, in the most boring province, in the country. His father was a mathematics teacher while his mother did the cooking, cleaning and ironing, including the ironing of the white tee shirts and blue jeans that Piet wore just about every day. He cycled to high school or to the movies in Eindhoven, 13 kilometers each way. In the evenings and on weekends he cycled alone on the Wilhelminakanaal towpath to Tilburg or sometimes as far as the Amer river, a 100 km round trip.

He reflected now about those days over three decades earlier, when he was perfectly protected and comfortable, free to mostly do as he pleased, as long as he got good marks in school. That wasn't hard, he was the type of student who didn't have to study a lot to be able to pass exams with ease. He thought that some of those boys in the hijacking team were not too different from him, except that they couldn't ride a bicycle anywhere they wanted, if in fact they had one, and if they studied and got good grades it would lead them nowhere. Well, that was the way of the post-WWII world, with millions of people displaced. He remembered them being labeled DP officially, much worse unofficially.

Returning to the boatyard, Piet stopped at the edge of the parking lot to read a stone memorial, for three firefighters killed on May 9, 2008 fighting a building fire at this same boatyard. Although that was another national sorrow, an event known throughout the Netherlands, he had not remembered the name of the boatyard, or even the town. Now he was stunned at the coincidence of him being at this spot as he thought about those public servants, with the camaraderie of police and firefighters worldwide. Some of his friends are on the seaport fire team.

It was a small fire in the beginning, probably a car on fire inside the building, then polyurethane insulation panels on the walls and ceiling overheated. Combustible gases collected in the high point of the roof and the gases exploded; the explosion turned a routine big fire into a disaster. The building has now been removed, with just the concrete floor used as part of the open storage area for boats on trailers. Piet told himself not to bring up this disaster with the men at the boatyard, it was too recent.

These events remained on his mind as he rode on to the village, stopping to view the *sluis* (lock) that he would pass through the next morning, his first lock of many at the helm of Margriet. First he will pass through a lifting bridge and then into the upstream-facing lock, where it may be a little bit difficult to operate the boat single-handed when the lock fills, sometimes with turbulence, to lift the boat. But he could see that there were vertical tubes set in the lock walls, an easy place to loop his line through from bow to stern and hold the boat steady.

He saw another surprising sight, two identical full-sized statues of a man, in a smooth, simple style, each perched atop a pier, facing each other on the east and west sides of the entrance to the lock. At first he thought they might be the work of his new friend Jan, because of the proximity of his studio, but no, these are bronze, while he works only in stone. There was no plaque or sign to explain the significance or the sculptor of these handsome artworks, but just the sight of them gave him pleasure. He was glad to have lived in a country where things like this are done, adding culture to a utilitarian structure, for no apparent reason.

The boat was ready when he arrived back at the boatyard. He motored 500 meters south on the canal, just enough to make sure that there were no oil leaks, then tied up for the night at a spot near the lock but separated from the village by a grove of trees. He made his first meal on the boat: knockwurst and sauerkraut on buns. Not too adventurous, plenty of time for fancier cooking as time goes by. Other than a few cars passing by on the road until midnight, there was hardly a sound all night. On the first night of his trip he was happy to be alone.

The next two days were a good time for Piet to get started on learning his boat and how to handle it in locks by himself. Also plenty of time to think things over, while slowly traveling across a large and relatively unpopulated section of northeastern Holland. He entertained himself by listening to his library of songs on an iPod; with earbuds in, he blocked out the steady drone of the diesel engine.

The Noord-Willemskanaal is a pleasant, calm route, it is narrow and curves a bit but widens occasionally, with open views of flat green fields and flocks of sheep. The highway which parallels the canal is often some distance away and behind the trees. There are locks and low bridges to be operated, so the passage can't be done in a hurry. It was early in the season so there were no pleasure boats on the canal except Margriet, and just a few commercial barges passing by northbound. It took almost three hours to arrive at the west side of the city of Assen, 15 kilometers from De Punt.

Piet saw no need to stop at Assen; he continued south on the Drentsche Hoofdvaart. This is one of the longest straight-line waterways in the Netherlands, with the most locks and bridges as well. Some people dread this trip, but Piet found it not as boring as it might seem. The canal is lined by poplar trees and many farmhouses, as well as occasional villages and towns, so there is always something to be seen.

Piet often thought about his visit with Jan; "…a very attractive guy to women, much more so than me. But I guess I'm still okay, I'm fit enough and not bad looking."

Piet is on the tall side and no belly yet. Sandy hair turning gray, cut short, blue eyes. No beard until retirement but he had always hated to shave every day, so now he shaves cheeks and neck only, every four or five days, when it begins to itch. It didn't take long to grow a seaman's gray-black full beard.

"I don't look all that different than I did when I was in my twenties. Just kind of average, not someone to draw looks from women. I'll have to get my nerve up and not be afraid to speak to them, maybe I'll score once in a while." He was already feeling that he needed female companionship occasionally.

After a day at the helm of Margriet, Piet had gotten the feel of steering the boat. He was traveling at the speed of a jogger, about 6 to 8 kilometers per hour. The slight nudges of the wheel, needed every few seconds to correct a drift towards one bank or the other, were now embedded in his subconscious. No navigational skills or electronic equipment were necessary, not even a compass, although the boat was well-enough equipped. There was no place to go other than straight ahead on the dark line of water between the green banks.

He did have to watch for approaching barges, but that meant only moving closer to the right-side bank, then correcting against the pull of the barge's wake as it passed by. He kept track of his progress with a coin on a paper chart, anticipating his arrival at a lock or bridge. The boat could pass under many of the bridges; others lifted for passage, often sensing the boat's arrival and opening automatically. Because of the small amount of traffic, usually the locks were open and ready for entry without delay; the Dutch system is to operate the locks and bridges remotely, using sensors and video cameras, so the operator would usually have the lock gates or the bridge opened before the boat arrived.

Piet had selected this particular boat because, along with suiting his limited needs of space and his ideas of style, it would be able to go almost anywhere. Margriet's water draft of 0.7 meter is about as shallow as it can be on a boat meant for cruising. The *doorvaarthoogte*, the clearance required to pass beneath bridges, is 2.4 meters, again very low for a live-aboard boat.

Margriet was built in 1965, at the Blom boatyard in Hindeloopen, as a *Waddenzee sleepboot*, a steel-hull tugboat designed for work on the shallow, tidal northern sea of the Netherlands, between the Frisian islands and the mainland of Friesland and Groningen provinces. The broker's listing document described it as 'in fine original condition, being a tugboat it is resilient, robust'.

It is a purposeful-looking boat, but elegant in its simple lines. The bow and stern are both blunt, flat sheets of steel which slope back under to the waterline; the low, choppy waves of the Waddenzee were not parted by this hull shape, they were pushed down under the boat. It is a good hull for the canals, where there are no significant waves except the wake of larger and faster boats sweeping across, to be knocked down by the high bow.

The hull has been painted glossy dark green; a white rubbing rail along the widest part of the hull sweeps from the corner of the bow, nearly two meters above the water, through a deep curve toward the waterline before rising again to the stern corner, half as tall as the bow. High gunwales angle in from the rub-rail, protecting a wide walking deck on each side of the cabin. The shapes of this hull are much different than most of the thousands of motorboats in Holland; the unique look is one of purpose and confidence rather than stylishness. Some might even describe it as goofy-looking.

The red, white and blue bars of the flag of the Netherlands fly from a staff at the stern. The aft one-third of the boat is an open cockpit with benches along each side for seating. There is an engine throttle control, but no wheel, on the port side of the cockpit, for handling the boat in a lock or when docking. The large cockpit and easy access along the side decks made the boat attractive to Piet for his expected single-handed travels; he could quickly move about to handle the locking and mooring lines.

The wheelhouse at the back of the bright-white cabin is entered from the cockpit, through two varnished doors with just a low step up from the aft deck. The short wheelhouse makes it easy for the skipper to move from the inside helm out to the exterior, from either a standing position or from the tall helm stool. Both the wheelhouse and the main cabin two steps down offer enough headroom for Piet at 1.90 meter (about 6 feet 3 inches), even though he is almost six feet tall.

There is a hand-pumped toilet in a tiny closet, but no shower; the galley sink is used for personal washing as well as kitchen service. In the bow are vee-bunks; the one on the port side is the larger. It's fine for Piet alone, he found a comfortable bed there and he uses the smaller bunk for clothes storage. Guests, which Piet expects will be rare, can sleep on the convertible dining-table bench. The galley is basic, a portable 4-burner gas stove (no oven) and a tiny gas-powered refrigerator. Piet's assessment: for me and my needs, it will do just fine. Matje would hate it, way too simple and straightforward; she would at least have to have frilly curtains on the wheelhouse windows.

At the end of a long day, after passing through five locks and twenty opening bridges, Piet stopped at the visitor's quay in the town of Dieverbrug and noticed a Vietnamese restaurant, *Hui Mao*. That would be a common sight in Rotterdam but it was strange to see it out here in the open fields of the Dutch countryside. He thought that it would probably provide him with a better meal than he could make for himself, and he was right.

Another day brought him into Meppel by late afternoon, to a mooring on the quay of a short dead-end canal, across the water from a long block of newly-constructed shops and apartments, the modern facades finished in a variety of shapes and pastel colors. It was a change from the usual Dutch brick buildings with stepped rooflines. Other than that, he didn't have any interest in the town and made dinner onboard, after a brief bike ride for exercise.

It was an easy ten kilometers the next morning to Zwartsluis, no locks or bridges and just a couple of commercial barges to avoid, with no trouble. Piet tied up on the town quay at 10:00 and walked around the corner to an outdoor table at *Horeca Centrum De Albatros* for coffee and pastry. He wanted some new ropes and other hardware, which he found in a nearby chandlery.

Soon back underway, he circled back around an island and through the floodgate to the Zwarte Water, the 17km river route into Zwolle. He docked on the town quay at *Rodetorenplein*. Zwolle is a medium-sized city with lots of shops so Piet shopped for groceries; he took note of the banner over one of the shopping streets warning, in Dutch and English: *Zakkenrollers Actief*, 'Beware of Pickpockets'. Reminds me of Rotterdam, he thought.

Jamel always takes the same route to work at AIRBUS. It isn't the shortest or the most direct - it's the one that allows him to go fast, very fast, for a short period. His daily goal is to achieve the autoroute speed limit of 130 km/hour (about 80 miles per hour) on the city streets.

His *deux roue* (two-wheel) vehicle, a Yamaha FZ8 Fazer motorcycle, is not allowed on the limited-access highway, the *péripherique*, which would be the obvious route for a high-speed commute from the east side of Toulouse to the airport at its northwestern suburb, Blagnac. So over time Jamel found a route that suited him.

From his apartment in the neighborhood of Côte Pavée, at 33 rue Julien Cassange, he turns away from the direct route, instead heading southeast out of the city. He rides at the speed limit, 50 km/hr, on narrow, tree-lined residential streets to bypass around the old city center, eventually turning to the west and crossing first the Canal du Midi and then two wide channels of the river Garonne, separated by an island.

The island between is the home of various sports facilities, including the Stadium de Toulouse. It is there on the Boulevard des Récollets that Jamel can make his speed run, for the street is wide, four lanes, elevated above the surroundings and has no intersections for a straight one-kilometer section. Early in the morning the street is often empty, just waiting for use as a speed course.

Jamel crosses the bridge over the east branch of the Garonne at 80 km/hr, watching the intersection ahead, at the end of the bridge, carefully. If it is clear, he goes for maximum acceleration. He sometimes does reach his goal, but only by taking the chance that the intersection on the west side of the island will also be clear. He then has to brake hard, for on the other side of the western branch is a *rond-point* which almost always has heavy traffic.

Why does he play this game? It's the thrill of course, but also the feeling of freedom and the control of power. Jamel controls the acceleration with his right hand, twisting the throttle open. Then he controls the deceleration, a more difficult task, with both hands and both feet, downshifting and braking hard. He is in total control of the machine, and of his life, at least

ments. And there is the feeling of defying the authority of the
if only by making a mockery of their speed limits.

The electric-blue Fazer moto is a good commuter but it is also a road-eater
on Saturdays, when Jamel rides the narrow, twisting roads of the Pyrénées
with five or six friends. They ride south into the foothills, generally
following the Garonne river upstream toward its source. The hills get taller
and the valley gets narrower, with jagged peaks of bare rock breaking out
above the trees. During much of the year those peaks are snow-covered;
patches of fog hanging above the road are common. The town of Fos, a
gray ensemble of stone walls and tile roofs, marks the end of the valley and
the beginning of the climb up to the high peaks.

The N125 *route nationale* passes a dam and alongside the shore of a small
lake; a short bridge, *Pont de Roi*, marks the actual border with Spain; a
modern concrete bridge has replaced the older, more beautiful arched
bridge made of hexagonal stones, which still stands nearby. Above the
bridge a hydroelectric station has been carved into the mountainside,
utilizing the flow of the Garona river. A sign announces that they are now
in the *Val d'Aran*, on the Spanish highway N230.

At the town of Les, the *Ostau Dera Nheu* restaurant/pension is their usual
stop for lunch. Then, 5 km south, they take the road to the west, turning
back into France, on one of the famous roads of the Pyrenees mountains,
the Col de Portillon. The road ascends from the Spanish town of Bossost
through four tight 180-degree switchbacks and then a series of sweeping
curves to the wooded summit, which is again the French-Spanish border.

On the French side there are ten switchbacks and three 90-degree turns as
the road descends into Bagnères de Luchon, a thermal spa village in the
heart of the central Pyrenees. It's the junction for several famous Tour de
France climbs including the Peyresourde, Col de Mente, Portet d'Aspet and
the Port de Bales.

Jamel and his buddies ride this downhill route single file, sweeping through
the wide curves at high speed and braking for the tight turns, laying the
machines over on the entrance and accelerating with full power on the exit.
A brief burst of speed and then hard braking for the next turn, again and
again. It's only for twenty minutes or so, but it is always the highlight of the
day's ride.

From Luchon it is a slow ride north past towns along the valley to rejoin the route across the fields to Toulouse. The day always ends at *Le Toubkal*, a Moroccan restaurant on Place Perchcpinte in the St Étienne quarter of Toulouse. Jamel's usual dinner is *Couscous à la kefta* and red French wine.

The river Gelderse IJssel, named for the province of Gelderland but commonly called just the IJssel (pronounced eye-sel), was Piet's next waterway after Zwolle. An Englishman whose boat was moored nearby had just come down the river (in this case "down" means northbound, toward the North Sea); he told Piet to expect an opposing current of 3 to 4 km/hr. There are no locks and the few bridges are high, so the trip is a slow, steady run. Piet had picked Deventer as the stop for the next night; it is necessary to do some planning as you can't just stop anywhere on the river, the current is too fast and the banks offer few good mooring spots.

It was a day of wide open skies on a broad river. Because of seasonal flooding the river plain is wide and flat; most of the towns are far back from the river, only the church steeples show their existence. There was more traffic than before, commercial barges and an occasional pleasure boat, as this is a major connecting route, a primary north-south waterway. The day was uneventful, however, and he felt very alone in his small boat on this wide river.

When he was alone on those long boring stretches of water he often listened to his large library of music. Piet wasn't much connected with the new technology of computers and MP3 players, but in preparation for this trip he had purchased an Apple iPod Touch and a friend on the seaport police had converted Piet's collection of vinyl records and cassette tapes and loaded them onto the iPod.

Piet had felt very alone for years, except when he was at his job or cycling with his team. Now, in this empty countryside, his companion was his iPod, playing mostly Bob Dylan songs. He had begun collecting Dylan albums when he was 17. The well-known Dylan albums and songs were popular a decade earlier, he had heard some of them played on the radio when he was a teenager. But he bought his first Dylan album, "Desire", only in 1976. He didn't know then that it wasn't considered a good album, that people thought it was an irregular collection with no central theme or style. Piet liked it anyway and played it over and over. Hearing it now it took him back to those days and thoughts about how his life had turned out to be like it was.

As the music scrolled through the range of his collection, one pop song stuck in his head, by the Welsh singer/songwriter Bonnie Tyler. He turned off the iPod, repeating in his head just one line from the song: …"turn around, bright eyes…"

That's what Piet called Matje right from the start, 'bright eyes'. In his first year on the seaport police he was cycling home, still in uniform, through the city center and saw a car coming at him, driving the wrong way on a one-way street. He waved it down and stopped at the driver's window. He was startled by her bright eyes, blue as the sky, surrounded by blonde curls. Sweet, innocent and beautiful.

"Don't you know this is a one-way street, the other way?"

"No, I'm not from here, I live in Schiedam."

"Well, where are you headed now?"

"I'm looking for the HEMA store."

"There's their red sign, down there on the left, but you should come in from Hoogstraat. Anyway, there must be a HEMA in Schiedam, they're everywhere."

"Yes, but I just got my driving license and I want to go somewhere in my father's car. My nearest branch in Schiedam is old and, I think, slightly depressed. It has most of the stuff that other HEMAS have but no amount of giant pictures of brightly colored clothes pegs and cork-screws will make it cheer up. Sometimes it doesn't even have apple tart. I go there out of pity."

"All right, I'll walk ahead of you around the corner in case any cars come, you can park there. But I'll have to get your name and phone number for the records." Of course he had no authority for that, but he was in uniform and anyway it was his duty, if you stretch it some.

18

After that he could think of nothing else but her. He used the phone number to call her later in the week and make a date for a dance night. Two years later they married and he moved into Matje's apartment in Schiedam. Soon a baby boy was born, with a serious heart defect. Matje cared for the baby night and day, giving up her work at the decorator's shop *Versailles*.

For six years Matje's full-time work was caring for the boy Jan, in hospitals and at home. Piet no longer existed for Matje, she was too busy and too focused on Jan. The love affair was over, along with any type of sex. It took a long time but eventually Piet looked elsewhere for sex and then decided to make a new life alone, long after Jan had died.

He turned into the jachthaven at Deventer at a little past 16:00; it had taken him almost 8 hours to travel just 34 kilometers: 4.25 km/hour, even without any lock or bridge delays. He could have walked the distance just as fast, or done it on his bicycle in a little more than an hour.

A second full day on the river brought him to Doesburg, again an easy day with no locks or bridges to wait for. He was hoping to reach Arnhem by noon on the next day. Arnhem is the city at the southern end of the river IJssel, after the junction with the fast westbound flow of the Neder-Rijn river. When he made the sharp 180-degree turn to the west, Piet immediately thought that this felt more like his familiar river at Rotterdam; it is in fact the same, despite being named the Lek for some distance before becoming the Nieuwe Maas as it passes through the middle of Rotterdam.

He arrived at Arnhem just after noon and first ate lunch onboard, then walked west along the riverfront Rijnkade to the John Frost bridge, the "Bridge Too Far", the prized bridge over the Rhine that the allies could not take from the Germans in September 1944. Operation Market Garden was meant to end the war quickly, after the Normandy invasion and the liberation of Paris. It failed due to the disregarding by the Allies of intelligence from the local Dutch people and by technical failures. Piet had always been interested in the events, as his home city of Eindhoven was the beginning point for the troops marching north to Arnhem and the history was well-known by his parents' generation.

Piet was curious to see the actual site of the major battle. The best way to see this, he had been told, would be from the *Sint-Eusebiuskerk* church tower, 93 meters high, a short distance northwest of the bridge. A glass-enclosed elevator inside the church lifts visitors to an observation level in the tower, *Het hoogtepunt*, the high point of Arnhem. There the view showed clearly all of the significant locations of troops and activity. With the help of a battle map that he had brought with him, he could envision the troop movements, their river crossing and the final failure on the bridge.

Back at ground level, Piet bought a postcard with a photo of the church and sent it to Jan with a simple greeting and a brief listing of his stops so far. He walked halfway across the John Frost bridge before returning to the shelter of the boat as rainstorms hit the region. He holed-up inside the place he now considered his home.

After his high-speed run in the middle of the city, Jamel is forced to ride the rest of the way to work at AIRBUS along with slow traffic, for six kilometers on city streets. It's quite a disappointment to him to be just like the other commuters, shuffling along in traffic.

The AIRBUS factory is a mixture of large and small buildings on the southwestern side of the Toulouse-Blagnac airport; two parallel runways, laid out northwest-southeast, separate the complex from the passenger terminal on the northeastern side, closer to the suburb of Blagnac and the city of Toulouse.

The last turn on Jamel's route, and the official address of AIRBUS, is Rond-Point de la Crabe. If there is a break in the traffic, which there usually isn't, Jamel uses that 270-degree arc to accelerate and lay the motorcycle over for a quick blast on his approach to the main boulevard of the plant, Chemin de l'Espeissière. Then he slows again and winds through the parking lots to the electrical wiring shop near the A380 assembly building.

Jamel is an electrical wiring installer; he started at AIRBUS a decade earlier, first on the smaller aircraft and now on the giant A380. He was hired on the basis of his Master Electrician certificate, gained after years of experience in wiring homes and commercial buildings, but he has shown himself to be even more adept at the complexities of aircraft wiring.

His usual assignment is to work alone at a long steel table, grouping wires into a bundle and binding them together, for later installation as part of the wiring harness inside the aircraft. There are from 8 to 24 wires in a bundle; the entire assembly, laid out on the table, can be as long as the circumference of the A380 fuselage, 34 meters. The drawings and specifications that he works from call for connector plugs and terminals at certain distances along the wire bundle.

Jamel draws each wire from a spool, laying it out as called for by the drawing. He carefully measures the along the wire, terminating it at the specified length. The wires make a colorful mélange on the table, as each wire is identified by a basic color along with other colors in stripes, and with identifying text printed on the wire. Following the drawing, he installs connector plugs or sockets at various locations.
When the layout matches each item specified in the drawing, Jamel groups the wires into a bundle and secures it with plastic cable ties at specified distances along the bundle. When complete, the layout of the wiring bundle is measured by an inspector, who compares it to the drawing and the specification.

Then it is tested by another inspector, using an electrical source and a meter to confirm continuity in the wires and successful installation of connectors. It is then ready for installation, at a later date, into the fuselage; that process requires two or three more electricians, along with Jamel, to handle the large bundle and to make the necessary connections to other wires or electrical apparatus.

But, since he works alone at the layout and bundling table, Jamel takes the opportunity to install two extra wires, of his own choice. One of these comes from spools of Kapton wire which have been discontinued for use by AIRBUS, but never discarded; they had simply been stored in a shelf location separate from the spools in regular use. The second looks exactly like the first extra wire, but it is a bit larger in diameter and comes from a roll of wire that Jamel has been able to smuggle into the plant in his backpack, along with his lunch.

Jamel worked in this same job in 2005, when the Kapton wire was discontinued, so he knew the reason why: it was determined to be a very dangerous wire type. Kapton is a brand name for a type of plastic introduced in 1966 by Dupont Chemical Co. When used as insulation over a metal wire it is very thin, at 8.4 microns.

Wire insulated only by Kapton was discontinued because it 'explodes' and burns fiercely at flash-over during an 'arc tracking' event, severely damaging adjacent wires and igniting the surrounding structure (i.e. it behaves like a detonator fuse.) One of the reports published on the subject of dangerous wire types described 'arc tracking':

Arc tracking is the process by which electrical conductance can occur through and along the insulating coating, rather than just the wire conductor. This is made possible by the formation of carbon along cracks within the insulation material and because carbon is an electrical conductor, once formed the carbon track tends to grow associated with the localized heat that is generated along the track by the electricity leaking through it. The heat generated by the current flow leakage causes a chemical breakdown of the insulating material adjacent to the carbon track, forming more carbon along the track.
In other words, once initiated the formation of a carbon track becomes self propagating and therefore continues to grow with the passage of time. Once started, arc tracking is capable of self propagation through the virtual instant creation of its own combustion-induced carbon char leading to a massive leakage of electrical current through the carbon track so formed and the damage of adjacent wires in the same wire-bundle. This process is called 'flash-over'.
The initiator of arc tracking can be a flaw in the insulation caused by imprint labeling, radial cracking, chafing between wires or contact between a wire conductor and the airframe, hygroscopic absorption of water, salt and other contaminants or an electrical short circuit.

Jamel realized that 'arc tracking' could also be initiated by small man-made slices through the insulation layer. So when he lays out a length of the Kapton wire on his work table he uses a small knife with a very thin, sharp blade to make short slices at random along the wire. Then he carefully places that wire, alongside his own thicker wire, in the center of the bundle. When he has completed the assembly of the bundle, the two wires are not visible to the layout inspector and the ends of these wires do not extend outside the bundle, so they are not tested by the electrical inspector. Their presence is known only to Jamel.

The thicker wire has been made for Jamel by explosives experts at a workshop located somewhere in North Africa, he thinks. The exterior insulation layer is made of the same material, Kapton, but rather than a wire, the interior material is a plastic explosive which has been formulated with a binder material, and is flexible at normal room temperature. The explosive material was selected for its brisance.

In addition to strength or explosive power, explosives display a second characteristic, which is their shattering effect or *brisance* (from the French meaning to "break"), which is separate from their total work capacity. The rapidity with which an explosive reaches its peak pressure is a measure of its brisance. This characteristic is of practical importance in determining the effectiveness of an explosion in fragmenting shells, bomb casings, or, for Jamel's purposes, the skin of an aircraft fuselage.

The rain continued through the night and into the next day as Piet set off to the southeast from Arnhem, traveling upriver on the Neder-Rijn (lower Rhine). Just as he started out of the haven a huge river cruise ship came out of the rain, headed east from Rotterdam or Amsterdam for a cruise up the Rhine. It seemed that he waited five minutes as the very long ship passed, then he fell in behind it. Visibility was poor but he could easily see the stern of the ship and so didn't worry too much about other traffic, other than keeping a watch for any boats coming from the left at the IJssel intersection.

Piet followed this branch of the Rhine to its junction with the Waal river, just 1.5 km from the German border. There he made a sharp turn back to the right onto the Waal, headed downstream. He left the shelter of the cruise ship as it continued into Germany and quickly caught a ride from the river, a big change from three days of going against the current. He throttled back and cruised along easily at 12 km/hr, on the limestone-laden gray waters of the Rhine main stream, toward the sea. There was a constant flow of barges coming toward him, sometimes two abreast as one barge passed others. The river is wide and the rain had eased, so visibility was adequate and he had no trouble staying clear of traffic.

Margriet had now become an extension of Piet's mind, through his hands. He knew the proper tone of the engine, with just a glance at the tachometer to set the throttle at the most efficient revolutions per minute. He knew that the boat will pull to starboard when in reverse, bringing the stern toward the dock, or to the wall of a lock; then a brief burst of power forward, with the rudder hard to starboard, will bring the bow alongside also. He had no need of the modern tools, such as bow and stern thrusters, which utilize a small propellor installed transversely for the purpose of moving the bow or stern to the right or left.

At Nijmegen he passed under the bridge that was captured by the US 82nd Airborne Division during Operation Market Garden, watching carefully for the entrance to the Maas-Waalkanaal, the path south to the river Maas. It required another sharp turn back, this time to the left, across river traffic. Piet used the recommended procedure for such crossings, to go on beyond the turn and then circle back, leaving plenty of space to pick the best time for entering the other lane of traffic.

One kilometer down the canal is the huge Sluis Weurt complex, two locks side-by-side with an island between. These are huge locks, 16 meters wide and 266 meters long; that's three USA football fields (or 2.5 European football pitches) in length. Piet was monitoring the lock's VHF channel and called to identify himself to the lockkeeper. She told him to wait for a barge coming from behind, then follow it in.

The bridges on this 13 km canal are all 10 meters high and the second lock stays open, so there were no delays as he completed the passage in a little less than two hours. And as he started upstream again, now on the Maas river, southbound to Belgium and France, the rain stopped and a bright sun broke through in the southwest. He entered the province of Limburg, watching the east side of the river for the Mookerplas, a lake formed from an abandoned gravel quarry.

Mookerplas is the only overnight mooring on the Maas river in the near-south of Nijmegen. There are riverfront quays at Mook and Cuijk but both of these prohibit overnight mooring. Piet thought, if they prohibit mooring on the river overnight, it's probably not a good idea anyway. Better to go a short way off the river onto a lake.

He easily found some low mooring posts on the north shore of the lake, about 1 km in from the river. On this night there were no other boats in sight, as well as no dock, pontoon or other facilities, just a bank covered with high grass and a few trees, with a narrow paved road beyond. It looked perfect, since he just wanted to tie up, take a long walk down the road, enjoy a quiet dinner aboard and have a restful evening alone and in silence.

It was his tenth day away from Rotterdam and his need for a woman was getting strong. For the past six years Piet's choice for 'companionship' was Denise, tall, blonde, well-built and the rarest of Dutch *hoertjes* (whores, prostitutes), an American. They usually are from Eastern Europe, Asia, Africa, South or Central America, in fact almost anywhere around the world except from North America. Whenever Piet asked her about how she got to Rotterdam, all he could ever get out of her was "It's a long story." But she did tell him that she wanted to work where her trade was legal, giving her the right to health benefits and a pension, as well as the right to refuse a customer and be protected by the police.

An ad in the *Algemeen Dagblad* (Rotterdam daily newspaper) is how Piet first met her: *lange blonde Amerikaanse biedt gezelschap privé...* (tall blonde American offers companionship in private...) He wrote down the telephone number and after a few weeks of thinking about her, he called and made an appointment.

Prostitution is an official occupation in Holland; Amsterdam's red light district draws millions of visitors every year to its cinemas, live sex shows, and sex stores. In Rotterdam there is no window prostitution like at *De Wallen* in Amsterdam, where the whores are on display in a window on the street, dressed only in lingerie. Denise's *privéhuis* was in a normal four-story brick apartment building, like all the others in the block.

Piet was nervous on his first visit. As he went into her room she stopped him just inside the door and looked him straight in the face for what seemed like several minutes. Then she undressed him very slowly and got down on her knees. After that she laid him down on the bed and performed a striptease. Then she sat over him and used her hips to pull him up into her... What a woman! Nothing in his life had prepared him for this, even a couple of youthful experiences before Matje.

At least once a week Piet went to visit her at 's Gravendijkwal 89A, across the boulevard from the strip clubs near Nieuwe Binnenweg, in the southwest of Rotterdam, halfway between the bus lines that he used to go to and from his work at the Seaport Police or the civic center of Rotterdam. It was just a 15 minute walk from the police district office at Parkhaven.

Her price was 150 euros for a one-hour visit; more than most of the girls charged, but well worth it, even on a policeman's salary. Piet didn't have a car, he used his bicycle and buses to get around, so he figured that was a savings that he could use to get the pleasures that a man needs.

He liked the privacy of dealing directly with Denise; after calling her phone to see if she was available, he could enter from the street, walk up the stairs and knock on her door. She insisted on punctuality, so that she would be alone and her other clients wouldn't be disturbed. Piet didn't have to feel like a customer, but as a friend.

He liked to visit Denise because her tiny room was decorated simply and painted brightly, not at all like the usual idea of a bordello. The four walls were each a different light pastel color; the closet was covered by a plastic shower curtain printed with the geometric color blocks of his namesake, Piet Mondriaan. The single window, with a sheer lace curtain (and no lamp in the window) looked out on the two parallel rows of trees that lined the center of the boulevard, on each side of the sunken highway through-route.

There was a narrow bed, but most often they used a big soft chair, which reclined so that Piet could lay back. Denise would settle him down into the chair and disrobe herself above him, then loosen his pants and pull them down. She had full, soft lips that did a perfect job on him - she didn't ask him to wear a condom and could use those great lips to full advantage.

When he began to raise a second erection, she would get a condom from the basket on a table beside the chair, slide it on gently the full length and then stand above him, lowering herself onto him. She rode him with her thighs tight around him - the motion of her hips was so strong that it sometimes felt like she was penetrating him, as she drew him inside her.

Although he often invited her to join him, she never went with him across the street for an after-sex coffee at the *Cafe Nemo* or the occasional dinner at the *Alibaba eetcafe* restaurant. Although the block included the nightclub *Lido*, labeled as 'the place to be', Piet never went in. He felt sorry for the poor saps that did go there, spending a lot more money for a lot less enjoyment than he had just had.

He thought now about looking for a hoertje in a couple of days when he would be in Maastricht, his last chance for a legal encounter with a prostitute, but decided she could never be as good for him as Denise was. He would rather go without paid sex for now and just see what comes along.

Piet left the Mookerplas and turned south on the Maas through Limburg province, the long narrow strip of land along both sides of the river, the southeastern 'finger' of the Netherlands, squeezed in between the hillsides of Belgium and Germany. The province stretches along the river, with towns named Horst aan de Maas, Peel en Maas, Maasgouw and Maastricht.

The flow in the river has been tamed by locks, so southbound boats are facing a current of 3 to 5 km/hr, usually less than encountered on the IJssel or Waal rivers. His first planned stop was at the city of Venlo, about seven hours travel time. The *WV De Maas* boat club marina at Venlo was recommended, so he selected that as the day's destination. For one thing, he needed a pumpout of his wastewater tank, which they offer.

Navigating on the Maas is very easy; the river is a uniform width and the curves are gentle. There is a constant flow of commercial barges and a few leisure boats, but cruising is much more peaceful than the Waal. The surroundings are peaceful as well; the river is lined by trees and flood plains, and just a few towns front directly on the river. Venlo is one of those, in fact the river splits the cities of Venlo and Blerick. Even there, the grass fields of the floodplain are the view from the river, with the towns set back behind concrete levees.

The only lock of the day came at Sambeek, a double lock alongside a weir. It is the same width as the Weurt lock at Nijmegen, much shorter (at 142 meters, still very long) and about the same rise. He joined into a line of three leisure boats on the starboard side; a long barge took up most of the port side. The barge skipper allowed the small boats to leave first, in somewhat of a charge forward, so much so that the ferry one kilometer downstream waited for all of this group to pass before crossing.

The *Jachthaven WSV De Maas* is located about 3 km north of the city, on the same inlet from the river as a large area of industrial wharves. The haven is isolated by the flood plain on the east side and a high wooded hill on the west side. (Yes, there are hills in Holland, especially in Limburg.) The yacht club is run by volunteers, all friendly and helpful. Piet rode his bike into Venlo for a beer at a small bar, then returned for an evening aboard and an 'okay' meat and fish dinner in the *Brasserie De Admiraal* at the marina.

In the morning a passing tanker barge caused him to wait at the exit of the haven. Then he joined the morning river traffic, a busy flow of barges and small boats in both directions. As on the previous day it wasn't hectic, simply two lanes of orderly traffic.

There are very few bridges over the Maas, in fact the last one he passed was the Zuiderbrug at Venlo, kilometer 106. So the rail bridge at kilometer 85.5 was a clear signal that he was watching for, to move to the east side of the river, through a lock and into Roermond, the destination for that day. There are marinas scattered around the nearby lakes but he entered the *Haven La Bonne Aventure* right in front of the town center and docked at the *Jachthaven RWV Nautilus*, a marina with the full set of services and a central location, including a great view out over the lakes on the west. The haven is behind a dike of the namesake for the town, the river Roer; the banks of the Roer made a good path for his sightseeing walk through town.

Piet's last day of travel in the Netherlands was to the city of Maastricht on the Julianakanaal. For four hours he followed the straight cut of the canal, passing through three locks. The good feature of this canal is that the waterway is not enclosed within high dikes that block the view; for much of the distance the water level is the same as the surrounding land, or in some places even well above the valley. The view encompasses nearby towns, sand quarries and farm fields, back to the hillsides in Belgium and Germany. As he traveled south the valley (and the Belgian/German borders) closed in on the river. The chart shows no mooring quays or jachthavens along the entire Julianakanaal; even a concrete quay at the town of Berg, which looked to be a possible short-term stop, was walled off by a steel railing, with no gate.

By early afternoon he was in Maastricht, docked in the *Oude Bassin*. He took a slip on the south side of the rectangular harbor, toward the river end, so as to be near the restaurants and bars, which have tables on the quay, but not directly in front of one. He wanted to enjoy the night life to some extent, but also be able to have some privacy.

He walked one long block south to the central *Markt Square*; he was not too late for the Friday market, which includes fish vendors among hundreds of stalls with a great variety of products: vegetables, cheese, textiles, flowers, clothes, perfumes, jewelry, greeting cards, zippers, leather bags, underwear, lingerie. Piet was mainly interested in the vegetables, cheese, and fish and went away with a good supply of each. And he did select new underwear, in a style and color that was a little more adventurous than his standard white jockey shorts. "Why not, it's a new life, I need new shorts," he thought, "let's see how I look in leopard skin."

After storing the provisions on the boat, Piet returned, going past the market square into the center of the city. He was on the lookout for the *Selexyz* bookstore, highly recommended by the Englishman he had chatted with in Zwolle. He found it easily enough, one block west on Grote Gracht from the Markt square, then south on Helmstraat to the Vrijhof square, down a short alley; there was the plaza of the Dominican church with the outdoor cafe *Grandcafe Amadeus*. Stepping inside the church entrance, Piet was amazed to find long rows of books under the tall arches and stained glass windows of the nave.

Piet had decided that he wanted more books onboard, especially any of the *Maigret* series that he hadn't already read. He located the Mysteries section and browsed through the Georges Simenon shelf. There he saw a booklet by Christian Libens entitled *Sur les traces de Simenon à Liège*. He bought that as well, thinking that the next day he would be in Liège and might spend the afternoon following that trail.

Piet picked a small table at the cafe and had coffee and pastry for a late afternoon snack, avidly reading through the Simenon booklet. Along with his interest in the author, the fact that the booklet was in French helped to get his brain back in gear with that language. He had been very good at both reading and speaking French in school, in fact that was in his favor when he applied at the Rotterdam Seaport Police, but it had faded over the years to just the jargon used by French-speaking mariners on the ships coming into the port of Rotterdam.

He returned to the boat via the west bank of the Maas. He walked quickly north along the river, noting the *Nautica Jansen* fuel dock. Just a minute later he was back at Sluis 20, the entrance to the haven. He followed a small park down to the bassin, one level below the streets. After a couple hours rest stretched out on one of the side benches in Margriet's cockpit, Piet walked over to *Le Bon Bassin* for beer and a dozen oysters.

Although he had decided not to search out a hoertje, later he did walk the narrow streets of the city center just in case he might bump into a woman who also needed a friend. He saw a few nice looking ladies but none of them took notice of him. He passed by the marijuana cafes with little interest; as an earnest young student at the university, he had been too busy studying and cycling to do much more than try a few puffs and never got started. He had a pleasant enough time just walking around but ended up in bed alone.

Early the next morning he left the haven and stopped at the fuel dock for a top-up of his diesel fuel tank: 100 liters, consumption calculated at just about 1.5 liters per hour of engine time. Just as he had hoped, this verified the expected low cost of traveling on Margriet. Leaving Maastricht, he headed up the Maas (soon to be the Meuse). In less than an hour he was in Belgium, and out of his native Holland for the first time.

The A380 is a huge aircraft. Its two full-length decks total 6,000 square feet, 50 percent more than the original jumbo jet, the Boeing 747. Its wingspan barely fits inside a football field. Its four engines take this 560-ton airplane to a cruising altitude of 39,000 feet in less than 15 minutes, a surprisingly smooth ascent for such a bulky plane. Passengers love it because it's quiet and more reminiscent of a cruise ship than an airplane.

Jamel is a part of the A380 electrical wiring team which installs the bundles of wires that he has previously made into the fuselage of the aircraft, making up several hundred kilometers of electrical cables in all. Some of these bundles extend in a full circle vertically around the inside of the skin of the aircraft, rings of wire used to connect other wiring which stretch horizontally from the nose of the aircraft to its tail.

He has built his own two wires into the bundle intended for installation at a point ahead of the wings, near one of the large cargo doors. The team brings this bundle, on a large spool, into the fuselage and they pull it through the interior structure, attaching it at various points to the structure around the ring of the fuselage. Each member of the team works to connect the plugs and sockets to other wiring and electrical apparatus in their zone of workspace. Jamel always manages to situate himself near the cargo door; while connecting to the sensors and equipment which operate the door, he also does a quick bit of work of his own.

Selecting a point on the wire bundle near the forward upper corner of the cargo door, he uses a tool he has brought along, a simple plastic crocheting hook, to reach inside the bundle and locate the Kapton wire. He pulls a short section of it into view, then cuts the wire, trims back the insulation on each cut end and twists onto those bare ends a stainless-steel wire just a few centimeters long. Pushing these connections back into the bundle, he leaves the bare ends of the wire tucked into the outside of the bundle, noticeable only if one knows where to look.

Jamel has done this on each of the A380 aircraft which have been built. If no one ever finds those bare ends of wire, then nothing will happen; the Kapton wire will have no electricity connected to it, thus it will not create arc tracks and will not act as a detonator for the plastic explosive. But if Jamel, or someone who has been instructed by him, locates those bare ends and attaches them, after the aircraft is in service, to a small box containing a battery, a circuit board and an altitude sensor, then the Kapton wire can be electrified; the wire will immediately arc and detonate the explosive wire. The resulting explosion will cut off the nose of the plane in flight.

───────────────

Just before noon Piet docked at the Port des Yachts in the city which the Dutch call Luik but is better known by its French name, Liège. Stopping in the middle of the day, as at Maastricht, Piet had decided to follow the Georges Simenon trail, just a short walk back down the river to Rue Léopold and then more across the river in the Outremeuse district.

As a teenager Piet had read many of Simenon's Inspector Maigret novels and later watched the English-language television films, with Michael Chambon as Maigret. He had also read a lengthy biographical magazine article about Simenon and became fascinated with the stories of his nightlife: prostitutes, drunkenness and carousing with anarchists, bohemian artists and murderers. Much of this took place in Liège.

Piet first became aware of the French canals, and their attractions compared to the Dutch canals, from Simenon's biography. In 1929 Simenon had a boat built, the *Ostrogoth*, on which Simenon, his wife Tigy, their cook and house-keeper Henriette Liberge, and their dog Olaf lived on board and traveled the French canal system. More interesting yet, to Piet, was the story of Simenon's long-lasting sexual affair with Henriette (known as *Boule* because of her pudgy shape) despite remaining married to Tigy.

Piet set off along the Quai sur Meuse, following the promenade on the river's west bank. He didn't expect much of seeing the birthplace house, just a building after all, but he did feel the attraction and had the opportunity. They had told him at the port office to walk past the La Passerelle footbridge, then take the street just before the west end of the arched street bridge, to get up to the higher level of Rue Léopold. There he watched for the street numbers, arriving quickly at #24, the Simenon birthplace.

In just a couple of minutes he spotted the historical plaque on the wall of the building: *The house where Georges Simenon was born. The writer was born on Friday, 13 February 1903, in a second floor apartment "without water or gas". Fearing this date might augur ill omen for her son's future, his mother decided to change the date of birth to 12 February in the official documents.*

He crossed the street, to the open plaza named Place Maigret, where he could turn around and get a full view of the building. The ground level is now occupied by a 'salon de coiffure' and a 'boutique'. On the facade above those storefront windows is a long sign stretching across both #24 and #26, on the left 'Georges' in large letters, *y est né* in smaller letters and on the right in similar style 'Joséphine' and *y trouve son bonheur*. Piet assumed that this meant "here he was born" and "he found happiness". The sign shows the name of the salon and boutique, with a twist in homage to Simenon; Josephine Baker had been one of his many liaisons.

Looking up at the full five stories, Piet saw a narrow, handsome building of white brick, with black trim around tall windows and black wrought-iron false balconies. It's a nice place to be born, he thought. As he turned to leave a large mural on the wall of a tavern caught his eye; he recognized it as Simenon in his twenties, with a black fedora hat and a cigarette dangling from his lips. Piet said to himself, "They do honor him here, don't they?"

He walked over the bridge to the Outremeuse district to follow the trail of the various buildings where Simenon grew up. It wasn't hard, as the Tourist Office has helpfully provided brass markers in the pavement. With his guide book and the historical markers on walls Piet was able to get a good feel of what life had been like for Simenon during the first decades of the 20th century. Along the way he found postcards of the Maigret trail at a small shop and bought a few, writing a note to Jan on one, to be mailed from the port.

That Saturday evening, Piet thought "When in Rome…" so he decided to try to experience some of Simenon's lifestyle. Liège is renowned for its significant nightlife; the city blocks known locally as *Le Carré* has many lively pubs which remain open until the last customer leaves. Piet didn't think he would last that long, but a man can try, can't he?

The Simenon booklet mentioned Rue Pot d'Or, which Piet found to be the southeastern border of Le Carré. The *Gai Moulin* nightclub was located on this street in *Maigret at the Gai Moulin*, so it was a good place to start the pub crawl. That was not the actual name of a nightclub, even at the time the book was written. But that didn't matter, there were plenty of substitutes. Three pedestrian-only street cross Rue Pot d'Or: Rue d'Amay, Rue Saint-Adalbert and Rue Tête de Boeuf. They are lined with bars and clubs. Even early in the evening the clubs were filled with people partying. Most were college-age, but that didn't stop Piet from joining in. No one in Liegé knew him, so he couldn't be embarrassed.

His first stop was classy, *Le Cuba'r*, but it didn't have the rough feel that he wanted, so he moved on through *L'Escalier, L'Aller Simple, L'A-fond Liégeois* and eventually a half-dozen others. He kept an eye out for suitable women that he might carouse with, but didn't find one. As the night wore on, the women ranged from "too glamourous and aloof" to "too young" to "too ugly". And by that time any woman that might want him was not the kind of woman he was looking for.

Sometime in the early morning hours he found himself looking up at the cathedral, thinking that it looked familiar from his walk to the quarter many hours ago. He knew that he should go around the cathedral to get back to the port, but he had no idea whether to go to the right or left to get past the building. A passing police car saw him and stopped; the two officers gave a quick check and decided that he was 'publicly intoxicated' but they are lenient with stragglers from Le Carré. And when he was asked for identification they saw his seaport police ID card, now expired but good enough to get him a ride in the back of their Renault, right to the dock near his boat. One of the officers thought it prudent to help him walk to his boat and get him aboard. Piet was not sober enough to thank him for the effort.

The native people of Liège are known as 'Walloons' (the city is in the province of Wallonie/Wallonia). After his night of joining in with the local partying, Piet felt that he qualified as a Walloon. However, Walloon is also a slang term for "fool"; he felt that he qualified in that regard as well. He also thought of the French terms, *couillon*, a bloody fool, or *con*, an asshole.

That's enough fun, time to make some distance. Piet didn't get an early start on Sunday but when he did leave Liège he was able to put in nine hours of straight running through the industrial valley of Belgium, docking at Namur shortly after 5PM. Along the way he had a good view of the ancient citadels at Huy and Namur from the river, so he didn't need to spend time there as a tourist.

The dock at Namur is located across the river at the town of Jambes, which had a full range of shops nearby. Piet made a shopping list and provisioned the boat so that he could be self-sufficient for the next four or five days as he traveled the twists of the Meuse river through the Ardennes forest. Not that there aren't towns scattered along that route where he could get supplies, but he wasn't sure what he could find without wasting a lot of time.

After a 7AM departure Piet cruised steadily up the Meuse, generally headed south but following the curves of the river, five of them connected in a series which added half-again to the distance between Dinant and Hastière. It was easy to enjoy the time, as the rock cliffs are spectacular, some rising over 100 meters straight up from the water. He realized just how high they are when he spotted a lone climber, looking like an mouse rather than a grown man.

He tied up for the night just a few hundred meters north of the French border; he knew that as soon as he crossed to the first lock in France he would have to register his boat and pay the fee for use of the French canals. He decided to put that off until the next morning and stretched his legs with a ten-kilometer bicycle ride back to the north on the towpath before another quiet evening alone.

In the morning Piet walked the short distance to the first lock in France, *les 4 Cheminées*, and was ready to register his boat when the lockkeeper arrived at 7AM. He paid the fee for the remainder of the calendar year, €253 for a boat the size of his; that will give him access to all of the canals and rivers throughout the country. He applied the *vignette* to the side window of Margriet and proceeded into the lock, which was open and ready for him.

Within an hour he was in a canal tunnel, a little more than half a kilometer long, near the small town of Ham. That was a first for him, so steering the boat carefully between the narrow walls took full concentration. His relatively small boat, with a comfortably low wheelhouse, took away much of his concern that he had when he had first seen the stone arch of the tunnel; small deviations from the centerline didn't cause a "crunching" sound. After the tunnel it was another day of 50 kilometers and 11 locks. The locks on this river are operated by a hand-held remote control; with traffic very light, Piet made good time by having control of opening each lock himself.

Although the tunnel cut off a long loop of the river, there were many more such *boucles* as the river twisted its way through the Ardennes mountains. At Fumay he watched the compass rotate through a full circle; as he approached the heading was due south but on the other side of the town it showed due north, before soon turning south again. It would have been the same at Revin except for the tunnel which cut through the narrow neck of a loop.

Piet cleared the last lock of the day just as it closed and tied up at the town mooring in Laifour. It was a pleasant *halte*, as they are called in France. A concrete quay and a grass park with picnic tables, but no toilet or shower facilities. Electricity and water connections are provided but are in service only during the summer. That probably means that no one will be around to collect the mooring fee, Piet thought; I will just have a quiet night alone here. He immediately changed into his cycling suit and lifted his bike off the boat; it had been unused since Venlo, five days earlier.

The mooring was at the end of a street leading into the center of town but he could see that where he wanted to ride would be across the river, on a high wooded ridge overlooking the town. As he looked on the waterway chart for the nearest bridge, another cyclist rode up and called out "Hallo Rabobank". Piet was startled but quickly realized that he was wearing his cycling team shirt, bright orange and featuring the name of the well-known sponsor, Rabobank.

"Bonjour", Piet replied, not sure if it was proper to switch to *bonsoir* in the early evening, while it was still daylight.

"I'm Michel Lambert, riding for Festina", he said, laughing at himself and their common, rather silly-looking outfits. "I see you are Dutch, should I speak English?"

"I do speak some French," Piet said, "but I need a lot more practice."

"Bon, je vais parler en français," Michel replied. "Voulez-vous monter avec moi sur un circuit 10k?" He pointed to the top of the ridge. Piet nodded yes and swung his leg over the bike as they set out together. Michel led the way through town, where Piet noticed only a single shop, a *tabac/épicerie*; he thought that he could get some minimal supplies there in the morning. They rode up a long grade past drab brick and stone houses, then turned to the north toward a bridge, high over the Meuse. Michel stopped on the bridge to point out the route: they will cross the bridge then circle left down a narrow lane and back under the bridge to the paved towpath along the eastern river bank.

As they passed under a railroad viaduct that Piet had noted just as he found the mooring, Michel pointed up to the rugged stone outcropping on his left and called back to Piet: "*Les Roches de Laifour*". Piet looked up, but he also couldn't resist a look across at Margriet, looking very handsome in this bucolic setting.

They passed by a weir and lock, then a few homes in a small riverfront village, then turned left on a dirt road to go straight up the ridge and through some of the densest forest Piet had yet seen. He dropped back a bit on the climb, the steepest of his entire cycling experience. Michel slowed to wait for him, but as the road began to level out he didn't stop, leading on for another twenty minutes to a viewpoint outlook.

"Nous allons nous reposer ici", Michel said. Piet happily obliged, needing to catch his breath. Piet was confused for a moment, then he realized that they had cut across a loop in the river and he was looking down on the last lock that he had passed an hour ago, and at the village of Anchamps, not Laifour. "C'est la plus belle vue de mon voyage", Piet said.

Michel switched to English to say "We will ride another two kilometers along the ridge then down to the highway and return to Laifour. May I invite you for dinner with me at *Chez Gillen*, the little brasserie that we passed near the bridge?"

"I would enjoy that", Piet replied. "I haven't had a substantial conversation with anyone since I started my trip," thinking back to his evening with Jan at Groningen.

Over steak-frites and *1664* beer, Michel asked Piet about his cycling. Piet was happy to talk about it, his work and his cycling had been the two centers of his life. Piet told Michel that he had always cycled, even more seriously than the average Dutch boy. He rode 13 kilometers one-way every school day, to his high school in Eindhoven. Then back again to Eindhoven, or in the other direction to Tilburg, on the weekends to find adventure in the cities. Often he rode the 100 km round trip along the towpath of the Wilhelminakanaal to the Amer river. The barges and the industrial wharves along that route piqued his interest in commercial water transport, leading to his selection of Erasmus University in Rotterdam for his college work, and then to his job on the Rotterdam Seaport Police. Early every Sunday morning the cycling team of Seaport Police officers met at Parkhaven, at least a dozen riders and sometimes 18 or 20. Piet described their three routes, each approximately 100 kilometers:

South across the Erasmusbrug, then west through the suburbs south of the Nieuwe Maas and then across open fields to the seacoast and the Haringvliet-
dam, returning over the Haringvlietbrug 30 kilometers to the east. This was the most difficult route because of the winds coming in from the sea.

Or west on Maassluisdijk to Hoek van Holland, then north along the coast through Den Haag, returning through Delft. On these days Piet joined the riders near his home in Schiedam and then dropped off late in the day, turning towards home as they passed the Rotterdam airport.

Or northeast along the west bank of the Hollandse IJssel river to Gouda and then on to Montfoort, returning first to Schoonhoven then west along the river Lek.

Piet told how he and his friends on the team had last year watched the Tour de France prologue race through the streets of Rotterdam from a prime viewing spot at the Erasmus bridge, then the next day they cycled to the coast to watch Stage 1 from Rotterdam to Brussels. They had their fun by racing alongside the Tour cyclists in another roadway lane at the Brouwersdam.

"I'm sure you must miss your team," said Michel. "I ride with a few friends here, along the river and in the forest, but we don't have a team or a regular schedule."

"Yes," Piet said, "I am already missing the usual Sunday rides. But I have been doing that for a long time, and I'm ready to see what I have been missing of life."

"Bon chance," said Michel. "I hope we might meet again if you return this way. You'll see my home, I will stop there on our way back into town. Just come and knock at my door when you are here again."

"I'll do that, but I have no idea when it might be," said Piet.

South from Laifour, another day of twisting along the river past endless forested ridges brought him to Charleville-Mézières, a small city at the northern edge of the agricultural plain of northeastern France, which stretches to Paris and to Burgundy. The next six days, cruising as almost the only boat on the Canal de la Meuse, were pleasant enough but each day was repetitive, an uneventful cruise along the gently curving river, with some canalized sections and locks at regular intervals. The view was the same each day, of brush and trees along the waterway just leafing out in springtime, with plowed fields beyond and, in the distance, low wooded hills.

Piet was happy to find a section of locks with a lockkeeper on duty, giving him brief contacts with human beings; some were friendly, some not. That's okay, he didn't want friends anyway, just needed to use his voice once in a while. When the locks were closed for the lunch break he usually took the opportunity to have his own lunch, and sometimes to top off his fresh-water tank at the lock.

The route passed by villages, towns and even a couple of small cities. On some days he simply stopped at an isolated place and tied up to the bank.

He stopped briefly at Sedan for milk and bread and had decided to spend a bit of time at Verdun, as it offered plenty of shops to restock his supplies and was of interest because of its history during World War I.

Other than that afternoon and evening visit to Verdun, he kept traveling as long as possible each day. The river Meuse eventually became just a small stream as he neared the headwaters; a canal then connected through a tunnel to another river valley at Toul, that of the river Moselle. The port at Toul was busier than most, as it is the junction of canal or river routes leading north, east, south and west across France.

He docked at Toul on a short finger pier; just as he completed tying on to the cleats, he heard a voice behind him: "It'd be better if you took the line the other way around that cleat."

Irritated, Piet stood up and was confronted by a short, wiry man of about 70, with curly white hair and beard.

"Hello there, Waldo Quarry. From Western Australia. That's my 24-meter Luxemotor, Le Roy, over there."

Taken aback briefly by such a strong greeting after all those days pretty much alone, and by the unwanted advice, Piet could only say "Where…?"

"Tied along the lock pier, over there… say, this is the smallest Dutch barge I've ever seen. It is Dutch, right?"

"Well, yes…It's a Wadden sleepbote," Piet said, trying to cut this conversation short.

"C'mon over, have a look around my barge, I'll show you my photos of the last barge gathering in Paris and you can meet the little woman."

"Uh, I need to go into town to get some supplies, maybe later…"

Piet stepped back inside the wheelhouse to finish the shutdown, then quickly went below. Piet ignored this strange man until he finally went away. After he was sure that the coast was clear, Piet took his backpack and set off briskly on foot into the town of Toul, thinking "Christ, now how am I going to avoid this pain-in-the-ass? I've been lucky so far, it's still off-season, so there's been almost no one around to bother me."

He decided to have a walk around the town. He wasn't really in as much of a rush as he had told Waldo (Waldo Quarry? he thought - what a strange name). After leaving the docks he wandered toward the town on Avenue Victor Hugo; at the end of the block long grass banks stretched back to the edge of the canal, the ramparts of the ancient fortifications. These were the defenses of the town, a walled oval protected by seven arrows of land and stone walls pointing outward. It reminded Piet of a star fort that he biked to as a teenager, at Heusden. As here at Toul, that town has preserved most of the ramparts, as well as the stone walls and entrances.

He climbed to the top of the grass bank and walked until he came to a fence with a sign *propriété privé*. He slipped around the end of the fence and down into a parking lot at the edge of the canal, then walked on until he found another long section of preserved ramparts. From there he had a good view of the very tall, impressive cathedral and, to the east, the river Moselle. Tomorrow he will travel there, on another of the major rivers of France.

Piet laid low in the morning, as he saw Waldo bustling about the deck of the barge; looks like he is getting ready to leave. Sure enough, a half hour later Le Roy left the port and turned westbound. Good news, as Piet will be headed the other way.

After finishing the fuel and provisioning tasks he left the port and immediately passed under a massive, and very impressive, stone footbridge which was part of the original fortifications; windows in the stone wall were probably defense ports in earlier days, he thought. In a short while he was southbound, upstream on the Moselle river.

―――――――――――――

Jamel woke up early on Wednesday, an unusual day off in midweek. That's what he wanted, a time when there would fewer people out for a day in the mountains. After a quick breakfast of coffee and juice he carefully placed a roll of cable made of his two special wires, Kapton and explosive, in a backpack, along with a trigger box. A brief stop to pick up a baguette for snacks along the way, then he was off to the southwest of Toulouse, bound for the Pyrénées.

He rode to a familiar place, the Spanish border between Fos, France and Les, Spain. But then he continued south on that highway into the mountains along the Aran valley, intending to find a spot above the tree line and away from other people. As he passed through the town of Bossost he could see bare mountaintops ahead. "That's what I'm looking for," he said to himself, "if I can find a road that I can ride up on the moto."

He found it twenty kilometers later, just before the Vielha tunnel. A single-lane road, paved some long time ago and cut by a series of cattle-guard steel grids and open-top concrete drainage channels. Not really suitable for street motorcycles like his Yamaha but manageable at low speed. He rode past a few isolated farms and into a dense forest, then out of the trees and into a small field among the mountain peaks, the end of the road.

Zigzag trails made by cattle or sheep led along and up the hillsides. Driving the motorcycle out of sight behind a small outcropping of boulders, he set off up the trails on foot toward a peak with a southern slope, where the snow had already melted for the season. He was somewhere above the tunnel which cuts through some of the highest mountains of the Pyrénées.

He climbed until he came to a flat area, out of sight from the field below. There was a stretch of smooth stone about 100 meters in diameter, perfect for his plan. He laid out a oval of the two wires, bound together by tape and plastic ties, in the same shape and size as the oval fuselage of an A380.

Nearby there was a large rock that he could use as shelter; he ran wires from the cable to the trigger box and crouched behind the rock. Taking a deep breath, he pressed the button on the trigger box. There was a loud blast, then tiny pieces of stone rained down. He walked to the blast spot and examined the result: a circle cut into the rock about 2 centimeters deep. A successful test.

Piet spent a day on the broad Moselle, traveling 30 kilometers upstream amid green surroundings, the tree-covered low ridges which line both sides of the river. The pleasant solitude of those woodlands convinced Piet to pass up a potential public mooring quay near the town of Richardménil and continue for another three hours after leaving the natural river for the Canal des Vosges, which parallels the non-navigable upper Moselle.

He continued on until he was well away from towns and any sign of people. The canal crossed over two channels of the Moselle on a *pont canal*; Piet noticed on the chart a weir, a short distance upstream from the bridge, which he wanted to see up close. A brief bike ride from his canal-side mooring took him there, along with a bottle of Heineken. He sat mesmerized by the rushing flow of water over the weir until it was almost dark, then he was ready for a night in the peace and quiet of the countryside.

Two days on the northern section of the Canal des Vosges, from Neuves-Maisons to Épinal, were similar to the previous week. The canal followed alongside the curves of the Moselle river, through an agricultural area. Trees and brush lined the canal but opened up at times to views of low ridges to the east, and occasionally a glimpse of the much higher Vosges mountains behind those ridges. Piet thought about Alsace behind those mountains, and Germany just beyond; places to go someday.

Épinal was a different town than he had ever visited, one set right in the mountains (they weren't the Alps, but to a Dutchman they were certainly mountains.) He arrived there on Friday night and planned to spend Saturday on a full-day bicycle ride in those densely-wooded hills. He was able to find the Tourist Office before it closed; they suggested a route to the tiny hamlet of Préfoisse, where he could enter a maze of lanes throughout an unbroken 20-square-kilometer area of the forest. There were no maps, so he would be on his own to find a way back out, although they did suggest that he travel generally south, to end up on the east bank of the Moselle above the city. That would give him an easy-to-follow route along the river back into the center of town and directly to the port.

It was a great day; Piet got an early start and had packed a lunch, planning to spend a long day in the forest. As promised, narrow dirt roads went in all directions through the forest. At forks or tees, he made a quick decision which way to go, based on nothing special, except an occasional sight of the tall red and white communications tower at the southeastern corner of Épinal. He only had his sense of direction to keep him from going in circles.

He came across an ancient fort, sections of the moat and stone walls remaining. Nearby he came to a fountain, a natural spring made into a small pond by stone rims. A tiny stream leading from the fountain into a small meadow made this an excellent spot for lunch and a half-hour nap.

A woman's voice woke him from his nap: "Bonjour, vous allez bien?"

He looked up at a classic French beauty. Her chestnut-brown hair was pulled tightly back into a bun, accentuating her pure white oval face. Dark brown eyes peered down at him past long black eyelashes. She was dressed in elegant riding clothes, but there was no horse; she had laid her bicycle down near his.

"Bonjour, oui, c'est bien, je m'appelle Piet."

"Ah, a Dutchman, I think," she said. "We have a Dutch family staying at our hotel right now. My name is Delphine."

"Is your hotel near here?" asked Piet, as he rose.

"Yes, not far, in the middle of this forest, the *Forêt Communale d'Épinal*. We have a small hotel and restaurant for people who enjoy the forest, and sometimes for conferences."

"I am enjoying the forest, as you can see," said Piet. "I'm traveling on my boat, it's moored at the port."

"I see, so you didn't ride all the way here from Holland on your bicycle," she said, with a grin.

"No, I travel all day on the boat, I've been on it for four weeks now, so I am taking a day off for some exercise. I'm used to a long ride every Sunday with my cycling club."

"That's what I do every day, after serving the breakfast and cleaning up, I ride the roads of the forest," she said as she walked over to sit on a broad flat stone at the fountain, waving to him to join her.

"Where are you going," she asked.

"I've just retired and I have decided to restart my life; just like on a computer, I have clicked 'Restart' to wipe out all open files and start again with a clean desktop. I'm headed for the south of France, but I don't know just where I will end up."

43

"Well, I am glad that you stopped here in my woods and that I found you, you are a very handsome man," she said, as he blushed but returned her look, directly into her eyes. "Why don't we ride together for a while, I will show you some of the best places."

This is like a fairy tale, thought Piet. I fall asleep in the forest and am awakened by a beautiful woman; what will happen next?

As they got on their bikes, Piet asked "Do you always wear horse-riding clothes when you bike?"

"Yes," she replied, "I don't have a horse but I like to wear these clothes, and the high boots are good for protection from the bike chain. Also they're good for walking in the forest, they protect my legs from burrs and scratches. What about you, why do you wear that garish Rabobank uniform?"

Piet laughed; "All the cycling clubs wear uniforms like these; we need bright clothes so that we can be seen on the road, and it does make us feel like our cycling heroes, I suppose."

"This is the best time to see the forest," she said, as they rode along one of the dirt lanes; "The spring flowers of the Vosges are just beginning to blossom, out in the forest. The daffodils around our hotel were very beautiful, but they are starting to die off for this year."

After riding for a while, she stopped and told Piet "Let's leave the bikes here and walk in here a few hundred meters, this is the best place for flowers right now."

Soon after they left the road Piet exclaimed "Look at this sea of purple spears, they are everywhere in this field of green."

"Yes, they are *Digitales rose*, the pink variety. Some groups are a little darker, the *Digitales poupre*. And over here are the *Violettes des bois*; they are very low, don't step on them."

"No, I'll be careful," said Piet. "It's wonderful to see these blossoms here in the forest. Holland is of course famous for flowers, this time of year the fields are spread with rows of tulips, every color you can imagine, and most homes have flowers in the yard and in window boxes. But this is more beautiful, to see the natural flowers under the trees."

Twice more they rode to her favorite places in the forest, where she led him to orchids in bloom: *Orchis bouffon* and an especially elegant and unusual blossom, the *Ophrys bourdon*.

 Late in the afternoon they rode past a small lake and into the tiny settlement of Uzéfaing, just six or eight houses and the hotel, grouped in a clearing. Each of the houses had large gardens, mixed with flowers and vegetables, and rows of blueberry bushes. There were a variety of crude outbuildings, for gardening and for firewood storage, he thought. "A mountain settlement," Piet said to himself, "not very fancy but cosy and inviting."

The hotel was Alpine style, log siding and a steeply-pitched roof, two stories high, each with a row of six rooms. "Come down to the end, my cottage is there," Delphine said, "We can have an aperitif and I will serve you a Vosgien dinner, *les tofailles*. It's a typical dish made of potatoes, bacon, onions, butter and Alsatian white wine, and this time of year with leeks from the forest."

"I think I should ask," Piet said, "before we go much further, do you have a husband?"

"Yes, Jacques. He is twenty years older than me... some time ago he lost most of his interest in me, and the hotel. Now he spends as much time as he can fishing; right now he is with his friends on the southern coast of Brittany, fishing in the sea. So we are alone, and I will enjoy making dinner for you."

"Well, I guess, 'Why not?', I'm in no rush, no one is waiting for me at my boat," Piet said, settling into a very comfortable-looking overstuffed chair. "But I'll need to ride back before dark, I don't have a light fitted on my bike."

"Oh, don't worry about that, you can just stay here tonight," said Delphine.

Piet was a little taken aback by that offer, but he thought again, 'Why not?'

She brought a glass of white wine for each of them. "What about you, do you have a wife?"

"I suppose I do still have a wife, she's in her apartment back in Schiedam, near Rotterdam. We have lived together but apart for many years, since our baby died. I finally decided that there wasn't much reason for me to keep on living with her, especially now that I won't be going off to work most days. I certainly didn't want to be 'hanging around' the apartment."

"That's mostly what I do here," Delphine said, "I hang around the hotel. But there are guests just about all of the time year-round and I enjoy talking with them. Of course I enjoy my time in the forest. I do have a staff to care for the rooms and operate the restaurant. Because of the staff I don't have much money left over, but I have enough for a good life. And now I have a handsome man to spend the night with me, what more could I want?"

She served him a delicious meal, put the dishes in the sink and "slipped into something more comfortable". She invited him to leave his big chair and join her on the couch, well-lit by a bright moon. Piet thanked her for the great dinner and continued to chat a bit, until she said "Enough of that," rolled her leg over him and kissed him on the lips. He kissed back and slipped the nightgown off over her head, exposing a pair of just-right breasts with erect nipples. He could see that the bike-riding had been good for her, her body was trim and she moved with grace.

Piet pulled her to him so that he could suck each nipple and feel the soft curves of her breasts. Before he knew it she slid her hips down over his. Perfect, Piet thought, as he relaxed everywhere except where he pushed up into her. He was totally satisfied, at least for the time being. She rolled over alongside him and just let him lay there to savor the time after. They laid there for a long time and fell asleep with arms and legs wrapped together.

On Sunday morning, after coffee, juice and a croissant, Delphine pointed him toward the shortest route back to the port, a paved road leading straight to the river. There he joined the Route d'Archettes, which followed every curve of the river and brought him to the port, past what he thought was probably the best views of the town.

He was soon again southbound, first ascending through a staircase of fourteen locks in 3 kilometers. That took the entire morning, but it was good news because after that it was all downhill. This is the *Partage des eaux*, the point where the higher lands separate the north-flowing waters, those which lead to the North Sea and the English Channel, from the waters flowing south down the Saône/Rhône river corridor, leading to the Mediterranean Sea.

Until today his entire trip, with the exception of a 10 km section at Toul, had been against the current and ascending through locks. Although Piet had become proficient at handling these locks alone, it had been more difficult and more time-consuming than it will be when descending through locks. And now the current will be added to his speed over the ground, rather than subtracting from it. He was three days short of a month from the start in Groningen but he expected to reach the Med in just ten more days.

After crossing the summit plateau through twenty kilometers of man-made canal, the Canal des Vosges joined the river Coney. Dammed by weirs and mills as it follows alongside the canal, the Coney is a sparkling mountain stream that winds through the pine forests, with the canal alongside or sometimes right in the bed of the river. It was an uneventful but very pleasant three days later that the canal ended at the town of Corre, where the the Coney joins with the southbound Petite Saône river.

The Petite Saône is much larger than the Coney, so the navigable route was now primarily in the river itself, with a few canal cuts to bypass weirs or to shortcut long boucles. At the end of the first day on the Petite Saône, Piet missed the turnoff into a narrow canal cut and found himself approaching a weir across the river at Scey-sur-Saône. It was not a problem, as the town provides a wooden dock just above the weir. It was without any facilities, but that didn't matter to Piet, as it was a very quiet little town and there was no charge for overnight mooring.

The second day on the Petite Saône river included two tunnels, each less than one kilometer long, which presented no problem. He stopped for the night just after the second tunnel, at Savoyeux. This time he passed by the port and left the designated channel on purpose, to follow a loop for several kilometers back upstream on the natural river to tie up on the river bank across from the town. The shallow draft of his boat was essential for this excursion; he enjoyed not being one of the "marinas only" crowd.

On the third day the current in the river had increased substantially, due to rains in the Vosges and on the plain to the west. So he covered a distance half-again as much as the previous day, and about twice his daily average for the trip. He was forced to stop at Auxonne at 19:00, as the next lock downstream would be closed for the day. The town docks are right on the open river, but he tied-on securely and slept soundly despite some knocking about by the river flow.

Early the next day there was an obvious widening of the river and the name now changed to Basse Saône. He stopped briefly early in the day to take advantage of a convenient fuel dock on the river at the junction with the Canal de Bourgogne; 100 liters almost filled the tank. At 16:00 he turned east into the mouth of the river Doubs, to moor in the town of Verdun-sur-le-Doubs. Shops were located right nearby, so he restored his stock of onboard provisions, before continuing on to an overnight at a pontoon on the river near the village of Gergy and dinner alone at the *Hotel du Cheval Blanc*.

Piet spent the next night in Beaujolais wine country, at Mâcon. The port is a short distance north of the city, so he brought out his bicycle, unused for over a week, for a ride down the river and through the center of the city.

On the next day, with clear sailing (just one lock) and a strong current pushing them along, Piet and Margriet traveled 80 kilometers to the city of Lyon, arriving in early afternoon. He fueled the boat at a commercial barge fuel station, then moored on the east bank of the Saône at Quai Maréchal Joffre, right in the heart of the vibrant city.

Piet was feeling vibrant himself, ready for a good walk after so many days spent sitting in his helm chair. But first he stopped for a draft beer in a bar near his mooring and asked for advice about seeing Lyon. The bartender said he would have been better off moored at the new marina in the Confluence district, in the midst of some fantastic new architecture. "You have to see them," he said, "especially the one that looks like a block of Gouda cheese with a bite out of it. Just walk down this side of the river." Piet had noticed the building when he was turning to tie up at the fuel barge and knew that he wanted a better look at it.

He walked south along the Saône to the fuel barge and over a footbridge at the entrance to the new marina, constructed by digging a lagoon into the land of the city. He stopped to look it over from the bridge and did agree that it looked to be a good marina, with full facilities, but he only planned to stay overnight and needed no services.

The bright orange "block of cheese" building stood out ahead, with simulated air bubbles in the walls just like in Gouda cheese and a large piece of the corner of the building built to look like a bite taken out of it. Very realistic, and fun, Piet thought, except Gouda cheese is yellow, not orange. Other nearby buildings were of more workmanlike modern architecture, but still very handsome. Piet continued to walk through the ultramodern residential, office and shops development on its south side. Quite a good job, he thought, something like the modern buildings in Rotterdam but refreshingly new and interesting.

He walked east, across the six-block-wide peninsula that is the central part of Lyon, to Cours Charlemagne, then south for few blocks, then east again to the right bank of the Rhône, at Quai Perrache. He passed by some African young ladies waiting on the street for seemingly no purpose, who would make eye-contact and smile; then "je t'aimerez chez moi." He didn't, these girls were very young; he didn't want to feel like a pedophile! But they were also very attractive, especially the one wearing a white halter top and white short-shorts; her skin was smooth ebony. Piet thought that her color was just like his favorite 90% cocoa Lindt bar. He stopped to think "Well maybe…" but then kept going.

On Quai Perrache he found a line of white vans parked under the row of plane trees alongside the Rhône. Most of them weren't inviting, too dirty and shabby, he didn't bother to look inside the few open doors. But then he saw a very clean dark-green Mercedes van, with the side door open. The light inside was a dim orange glow, but bright enough to see that the rear of the van was separated off by a large green and red flag with a shield in the center; he knew from his seaport work that it was the flag of Portugal. A pair of bare legs, pulled up so that shiny knees were prominent, made him stop at the door. At the doorsill were ten bright-red toenails; as his eyes became used to the dim light, he saw that the legs were attached to a white woman, close to forty, in a short pink nightgown, laying back against scattered pillows on a red mattress. "My name is Paulette," she said "Come on in."

Very attractive, Piet thought, but he resisted a quite strong urge. "No thanks," he said to Paulette, thinking that sex in a van, on a city street, was not for him. Not after his years with Denise, and not right after his experience with Delphine back in the forest. Who knows what may come in the time ahead?

The street had been dark at Quai Perrache, separated from the riverbank by the traffic on the Autoroute du Soleil, the A7 from Paris to Marseille. But as he walked north under the ramps of the autoroute and out to the quay of the river, he could see the lighted spans of the University, Guillotière and Wilson bridges. He found bars, terraces and restaurants on gaily-painted boats and barges moored to the quayside. Music was playing and people were having fun everywhere. The river's beautiful bridges and the majestic buildings on either side of them have been illuminated in what must be one of the most tastefully lightscaped scenes in all of Europe.

Eventually he turned west, the street didn't matter because he knew that he could just walk across the peninsula to the Saône to get back to his boat. The streets felt perfectly safe. He happened to be on Rue Grenette, which was probably very busy in the daytime but almost empty at night; it led straight across and brought him out a few blocks north of Margriet's mooring.

Settled inside the boat for the night, Piet thought, "This is a nice city, but too much like Rotterdam. I'm looking for something different. Let's see what it's like near the Med."

Margriet sped south the next morning on the Rhône river, and for three long days, to reach the Med. Piet stopped twice at small docks right on the river and cooked dinners onboard. Now he just wanted to "get there", to get this long trip done. Enough sightseeing until the Med.

Just north of Arles he turned to the west, branching off the main river onto Le Petit Rhône. Piet wondered, why is it Le Petit Rhône (male) when it is La Petite Saône (female)? Who decides these things, anyway?

Although the scenery had been pleasant enough, Piet was glad to leave behind the large, and often extremely deep, locks on the broad Rhône; the Bollène lock is a 23 meter descent, leaving Margriet at the bottom of a narrow concrete box with walls higher than a seven-story building. The "little" Rhone seems more friendly as it twists through the flat, sandy Camargue. The scenery can be described as stark, desolate, monotonous or beautiful; a combination of all of these best describes it. On the river, thick belts of trees and reeds line the banks and for some of the distance there are high levees; little can be seen of the surrounding landscape.

But at one spot there was an open view over grassland; there a dozen or so of the famous Camargue black bulls grazed the field. One of them, close to the river bank, looked directly at Piet as he slowed and steered close to the bank; he thought that the curving horns looked exactly like a pair of parentheses marks, picturing the word (bull) between them.

Before he got back up to speed he realized that he was almost at the Bac du Sauvage, a cable-operated car ferry. The ferry was just leaving the east bank, so he backed off the throttle again. There were a few cars on the ferry and two bicyclists; that made him realize that this would be a good place for a bike ride, there must be roads that serve the farms that he could see from the water. And the roads will be dead-flat, just like home.

Le Petit Rhône reached the sea at the small fishing village of Les Saintes-Maries-de-la-Mer. He went straight past the docks and out into the Med a few hundred meters before turning a circle back into Port Gardian, to moor at a concrete quay. Now he could truly say that he had traveled from the far north of the Netherlands to the Mediterranean Sea.

Piet had no previous knowledge of Stes-Maries-de-la-Mer, in fact he thought it a strange name: a plural version of Saint Mary? The first thing that he saw as he walked in on the quay was a bullring. He didn't immediately recognize what it was, just a sign over the gate stating "ARENES", then he noticed the bullfight posters on both sides of the gate. When he thought about the Camargue bulls he realized the connection. He knew of the bullring in the city of Arles but he was surprised to see this bullring, built right on the beach.

As he walked past he arena he was even more surprised to see that the building also housed the *Bibliotheque Municipale*, the town library! Then he saw what he was really looking for, a bar, *Brasserie La Chamade*, whose awning sign offered *Kronenbourg* beer as *pression*. He sat at a table right on the street, Avenue Van Gogh, enjoying the fresh, cold draft beer. Then he thought about the name of the bar but couldn't translate it; he tried it in the translate program on his iPod and found "pounding", so it must relate to the bullfights across the street. Then the street name, Avenue Van Gogh, jogged his memory and he recalled a visit to the Van Gogh Museum in

Amsterdam. He had taken special notice of one painting, the title was something like "Fishing boats on the beach..." He realized that the rest of the title was probably "...at Saintes-Maries-de-la-Mer". This town would have been an easy trip from Arles, even in Van Gogh's time there.
As Piet sat at the bar he reflected on his trip, and realized that he had been forgetful about writing to Jan. He thought this would be an appropriate place to let him know that he had made it all the way to the Med, and probably to end the postcards. He bought a card showing both the bullring and the marina; he wrote to Jan that Margriet was now moored next to this scene, in the waters of the Mediterranean Sea.

He stayed at the town for a few days, relaxing on the beach and enjoying the camaraderie of drinking and meals at the coarse bars and restaurants of the seaside village. He particularly liked La Chamade, a down-to-earth pizza bar. There he attracted one of the local women, Sara, the one that he thought of as a "wench" from a pirate boat; petite, deeply tanned, with shiny, long black hair, and even a red scarf tied around her neck. She was short and stood with a straight back, which helped to amplify her large breasts. It wasn't long before she was on his lap, sharing beer from the bottle and later sharing the night with him on the pull-out dinette bench on Margriet. They needed the extra space overhead, the front deck over his bunk was too low to allow Sara to sit up straight on top of him, where he could easily cup both breasts in his hands. He thought, now I know what they mean by a 'handfull'.

On the *naturiste* beach the next day he could see how she got her all-over tan; not even a bikini mark to be seen. Later he learned that her name wasn't really Sara, she just took that up herself after she arrived a few years earlier. The town is a pilgrimage destination for the Roma, who gather yearly for a religious festival in honor of Saint Sara. Dark-skinned Saint Sara is said to have possibly been the Egyptian servant of the three saints Mary Magdalene, Mary Salomé and Mary Jacobi. After the crucifixion of Jesus they set sail from Alexandria, Egypt. According to a longstanding French legend, they arrived at the French coast, at the location which later became Les Saintes-Maries-de-la-Mer.

The annual pilgrimage was just winding down as he arrived, although there were still plenty of people that he took to be Roma. He wasn't sure if Sara was Roma, or just a wannabe. It didn't matter, she looked the part and he was having great fun.

Sara told him about the events of the few days just before he arrived. Gypsies come from all over Europe and even from other continents to worship their saint, the Black Sara. They settle in the squares and at the seaside. For a week or more, they feel at home. The pilgrimage is also the opportunity to meet up again and most of the new children are baptized in the rustic stone church of the Saintes Maries.

On May 24 the shrine is taken down and Sara's statue is carried by the gypsies to the sea, to symbolize the welcoming of the Saintes Maries by Sara, patroness of the gypsies. Then they parade back to the church with the accompaniment of cheers, musical instruments and the peal of church bells. Black Sara's statue is returned to the crypt of the church, at the right of the altar; she wears a multicolored dress and jewels.

After a day on the beach and two nights on the boat with Sara, Piet spent the next day alone, on a long bike ride. He first rode east along the edge of the beach, where the strong wind off the sea reminded him of his many bike rides along the North Sea. But this was different, the sea here was green rather than the gray sea off of Holland.

Then the narrow road turned away from the sea and passed through a series of *étangs*, lakes shallow enough that large flocks of flamingoes were standing in water well below their knees. There must have been a thousand birds in each of the small lakes. Some were in flight, a strange sight, with their long necks stretched out in front and long legs trailing behind, their wingspan much wider than he thought when he saw them standing.

The road circled to the north and then back to the west, passing many salt ponds and eventually the large Étang de Vaccarès, wide enough that the far shore was obscured in the hazy spray from the sea. Here a huge flock of flamingoes were standing with their heads raised high and their pink and black wings raised from their white bodies. It was a beautiful sight, Piet stayed quite a while enjoying his first sightings of these magnificent creatures.

On the north and west of the lake were farmlands and, standing out above the flatlands, the bullring of the *Clubs Taurins Paul Ricard* at Domaine de Méjanes. This was not a concrete structure as at the town of Saintes Maries, it was a circle of open bleacher rows, so it was not as startling as a large white ring would be in this setting. *Les gardians*, the cowboys on sturdy white horses, were herding a group of black bulls across the parking lot and into a corral and barn. A flapping banner tied to the railing of the bleachers welcomed the Ferrari Team to an event to be held here on the coming weekend.

Returning from his ride, Piet stopped at the tourist office and picked up a brochure listing the pilgrimages and events that stretch throughout the year; he thought that he might return later to witness some of them, but he knew it was not a place where he could stay for very long. His brief stop at Lyon had convinced him that, after more than thirty years in Rotterdam, he was a big-city person. So he planned to go west to the city of Toulouse, perhaps that might be his destination in the south of France.

Piet was ready get moving again; maybe he would come back, who knows? Sara didn't mind, it was just a brief interlude for her as well. Lots of fun, but there are other guys around too.

————————————

Jamel had become very familiar with the resources of his local library and spent much of his days off poring through books and using their computer to search magazine and newspaper files, and the internet. He had asked for advice from one of his friends at Airbus who was known as a 'flight freak', someone who spends hours online following the track of airplanes in flight. The recommended websites were 'flightaware.com' and 'flightstats.com'.

He found these websites to be fascinating and spent hours researching the flights and their schedules. He eventually settled on one particular flight that would meet his needs: Air France 990 from Paris to Johannesburg. The aircraft used on the flight is always an Airbus A380-800. Departure time is 11:30PM every day.

Jamel found that he could zoom in on the websites' maps and view the actual flight path in detail. The first thing that he noticed was the obvious, that the direction of takeoff is determined by the wind. It seemed that the most common wind was from the west, coming in off the Atlantic Ocean over Normandy. That was good news, because the flight track with a west wind meant that a flight headed for Johannesburg would arc to the south soon after takeoff and fly almost directly over Paris. On days when the wind comes from the east, takeoff would be toward the east and the flight path would be too far away from Paris.

When Jamel spoke to his friend Jacques about his success at finding what he wanted, Jacques invited him to be at his house when the flight was scheduled to depart so that they could watch it together on the screen. Jamel showed up at 11:20PM and Jacques logged-in on the website www.flightradar24.com. Jamel watched in amazement as the flight took off, making notes of the plane's path, altitude and time over certain locations. Exactly what he needed to know, with just one problem: the plane took off to the east and did not fly over Paris at all. They agreed that Jamel would return the next night and try again.

The second try was successful. The flight pushed back from the gate at 23:40 and started the takeoff run at 24:01. Four minutes later it crossed over the Boulevard Périphérique at an altitude of 4,775 feet, climbing at a rate of 1,400 feet per minute. "Five thousand feet will be just right," Jamel said aloud.

Jacques looked at him and asked, "Just right for what?"

"Oh... never mind," Jamel replied.

———————————

It took two days for Piet to go back up the Petit Rhône a short distance and then follow the Canal du Rhône à Sète west to the Étang de Thau, and then cross that large lagoon to reach the eastern end of the famous Canal du Midi.

The Canal du Midi links the Atlantic and the Mediterranean. Connecting from the Atlantic by means of the Garonne river and Canal latéral à la Garonne, the Canal du Midi descends eastward from Toulouse to the coastal plain of the Med through the beautiful hills of the Languedoc region, between the Pyrenees & Black Mountains. The creation of the Midi opened a route that is sometimes called the *Canaux des Deux Mers*, used by boaters to travel from the Atlantic to the Med without the long open-sea route around Portugal and Spain.

The Midi is the most popular waterway in France for holiday cruising. In July and August it will be crowded with hotel barges, privately-owned pleasure boats and hundreds of rental boats. Many of those rental boats will be operated by first-timers or fun-lovers who don't care to learn the rules and techniques. There will be delays at locks; travel would be too slow in those months for Piet, who just wanted to go straight through.

But this was still the first week of June and traffic was relatively light. Piet did no sightseeing, other than what could be seen from the canal as he passed by. The locks are open for nine hours each day (they are closed for lunch from 12:30 to 13:30.) By constantly pressing on, Piet was able to complete the Midi, 240 kilometers and 89 locks, to Port St Saveur, in the center of Toulouse, in six days.

"This is about far enough" Piet said to himself, after 2,070 kilometers and 48 days from Groningen. He had come to a familiar city, the size of the one that he left behind, Rotterdam. But now he was in the south of France, in an entirely different culture.

Part II

A Dutchman in Toulouse

Piet tied-up on the quay at Port St Saveur and made arrangements with Sylvianne at the *capitainerie* for an indefinite stay: €127 per month for the slip, with full services - water and electricity connections for the boat; showers, toilets, washer and dryer in the capitainerie building. A locked security fence surrounds the docks and facilities. The other boats moored there include everything from short, white motorboats to *vedettes hollandaise* (Dutch motorboats) and handsome converted barges, most of them two or three times as big as Margriet.

It was still early in the afternoon, so Piet set off on foot toward the center of Toulouse. The *Éditions du Breil* waterway chartbook that he had used on the Midi canal included a tourist map for the *Ville Rose*, so Piet decided to follow the suggested route as a first look at the city. Starting back to the south along the canal for a few blocks, the walk under the shade of the broad-leafed *platane* trees was pleasant after the hot sun on the boat at the dock.

It didn't take long to realize that the Ville Rose is not the 'City of Roses' but that it is named for the pink bricks of the homes and buildings. His first stop, right alongside the canal, was the *Georges Labit Museum*. A moorish villa, it is a tall cube of white bricks, with rows of pink bricks and some sea-blue trim: "I could live there, like King Tut" Piet thought, with a laugh. But that wasn't true, Piet could never live in such elegance.

Turning right on rue des Martyrs de la Libération, Piet thought that this wasn't too different from his home streets in Schiedam: brick row houses mixed with four-story apartment blocks, a strong middle-class neighborhood. At the end of the street he found a large park and what he assumed would be the site of local *boules* games, although on this day there was just one white-haired, bronze-skinned Frenchman on a bench, watching over the empty gray dirt.

A tall stone arch and iron gates for the *Jardin des Plantes* looked inviting as a pleasant route into the city center. He took the narrow path along the west side of the garden, enjoying the greenery and the row of pink and white brick houses beyond the fence. Skipping two of the art museums shown on the map, at least for now, he zig-zagged west to the river Garonne, at a spot where he could watch the mesmerizing flow of water over a barrage. At this time of year the stone weir was littered with stumps and trunks of trees, yet to be removed after the high flows of spring. He walked along the quay of the river, watching the swirls of the current.

A magnificent seven-arch stone bridge across the Garonne turned out to be the Pont Neuf; as usual in France the 'new bridge' turned out to be the old bridge, 450 years old - of course, it was new when it was built and the name remains. The *Brasserie des Beaux Arts*, at the eastern end of the bridge, reminded Piet that it was time for an afternoon beer, but it was too early for dinner and the place too fancy for just a beer - nearby he found a small *SPAR* market with a cold beer locker. A large *Heineken* was just the thing he needed, he took that back to a bench on the river. Finishing the bottle, he walked on and soon came to the tour-boat dock. No need for that, he had been on the water for seven weeks.

But he did like the change of the path, from a walled quay high above the water to a narrow concrete strip right at the water's edge, with the city up and behind a tall brick rampart. The path continued right under the next bridge, Pont St Pierre, to the lock which connects the river, via the Canal de Brienne, back to the Canal du Midi. On another day he will walk that longer route, a semicircle around the northern edge of the city.

But today Piet returned to the tour-guide map; a few steps back along the river and up into Place St Pierre, then along the narrow sidewalks and single-lane traffic of rue Pargaminères. Piet thought "This street is not very nice, too closed-in; the slight curves make me feel I'm inside a hose, with cars and trucks zipping by alongside. Lots of small shops and restaurants, most of them dark and dreary, and some not even open."

Just when he had enough of rue Pargaminères, suddenly the bright open sky of Le Capitole appeared. This enormous, beautiful plaza is the very heart of the city, according to the guide. A 'square' in the truest sense, with four nearly-equal sides, nothing but flat pavement within. No fountains or statues, just a business-like central meeting place for the citizens. *Terasse* cafés line the west side; the broad pink and white brick building Le Capitole forms the east side. Quite a handsome building, nice to see after the long line of dirty gray, seemingly endless, storefronts that he had just passed. Not much happening on the square this afternoon, it must fill-up on market mornings. Everything happens here, according to the tourist guide; the Capitole building houses the town hall and the opera house.

Piet watched the people walking past, all in a rush to get somewhere, just like in Rotterdam. They mostly seemed to be walking north on a pedestrians-only shopping street, Rue d'Alsace-Lorraine. As he window-shopped past the Virgin Megastore, he especially watched the women, with not much interest. "They're all dressed in jeans," he thought, "that's okay if they've got the ass for it, most of them don't. Baggy jeans don't work on women, makes them look sloppy.

"Now there's a real woman," Piet said to himself, noticing a shapely woman in a short white dress with a blue print, the hem pulled in right under her nice round, high ass. The back of her strapless dress rises only a few inches above her waistline; her upper back and shoulders are bare, and her legs show from the middle of her thighs down. She doesn't look "tanned", she's already a nice buckskin color all over. Simple red sandals, a low heel and a single strap. A silver soft-leather bag slung on her left shoulder. Lots of black curly hair, down to her shoulders. "Not skinny, just the right amount of meat on her bones." He followed her for a block or so out of his way, taking it all in and enjoying it. When she glanced back at him, he quickly turned the corner onto rue Lafayette and went back into the square.

Piet strolled past the umbrellas and tables of the cafes to rue Saint-Rome, at the southwest corner of the square, and found another narrow passage of shops and restaurants but more inviting, paved with stone blocks and intended for pedestrians only, except for the delivery vans scattered along the way. No traffic rushing past. The storefronts here are wide glass windows rather than a steel rollup door, and the restaurants look bright and inviting.

Piet stayed on the same street as it went through a series of other names and crossed the broad boulevard coming east from Pont Neuf; on the section named rue des Filatiers he found beautiful tall, 400 year-old residences, their face of pink, white or beige brick with very detailed windows and colorful shutters, on a very narrow section of the street. He wished that he could step back to see the buildings better.

At the large circular multi-story parking garage of Carmes he turned toward Port St Saveur, choosing streets at random to go in the general direction of the port. Crossing Place Perchepinte, he noticed a menu board at a tiny salon de thé: *Norvégien* food. Pickled herring and a draft beer, at a tall sidewalk table, was just what he needed to end the walk.

Halfway through his second beer, she walked past: the woman from Le Capitole! She breezed past him and stopped at the door of a restaurant two doors down. It must be still closed for the afternoon break, as the door was locked. She took a key from her purse and let herself in.

An omen - Piet had thought that he would probably never see her again, in such a large city, then she was right there. She must work there; that might be a good choice for dinner tomorrow night. A sign above the door showed *Le Toubkal* as the name of the restaurant, offering Moroccan food.

Leaving reluctantly, he took a short, narrow, curving street which brought him to the greenery of the *Jardin Royal* and the *Grand Rond*, concentric circles of paved walks and tall trees surrounding a grand fountain. Just one block east under another row of trees on rue de Tivoli took him to the port. Piet settled in for an early nap, and maybe a dream about a woman.

Piet did return to Le Toubkal, the very next evening. It is in the classic French restaurant style: a half-timbered brick building, with shutters on the windows of the upper stories; at street level, multiple-paned glass in the doors and windows, framed in wood painted dark green. Some of the window panes are covered with lengthy descriptions of the dishes offered inside. A short awning over the entrance doors reads *Restaurant Marocain*.

Inside, rough brick walls arch overhead. Moroccan-style arches separate the rooms and hallways. Paintings on the walls, chandeliers of stained glass and the patterned fabric on the banquettes give a feel of faded elegance. The atmosphere achieves the intent of seeming to be in Morocco.

Piet arrived at the door promptly at 7:30 PM, the opening time for the evening service. Being that early, and on a Tuesday, there were no other diners yet seated. When he stepped into the entry foyer he came face-to-face with the woman that he had seen in great detail, albeit from the back only. A pretty face, closely framed by black hair in bangs that covered her eyebrows and dropped to curls on her shoulders. Dark brown eyes with long curving eyelashes. Full cheeks under her eyes but her lower cheeks and jaws draw in to a narrow chin. Smile marks like parentheses at the ends of her full and well-shaped lips, with a soft shade of shimmering magenta lipstick which went perfectly with her skin color. "She has an extremely attractive face," Piet thought, "just like the view from the back." She was wearing long silver earrings but no necklace; there was no need for jewelry to draw his eyes to her neck, the smooth shape and prominent collarbone made him want to reach over the desk and kiss her softly on the side of her neck.

"Bonsoir m'sieu, êtes-vous seul?" When she spoke he was stopped for an instant by the sight of her perfect, pure white teeth. He replied that "Oui, il n'y a que moi." She led him past a long table, perhaps a dozen chairs on each side, to a table for two by the wall. She removed the extra setting and handed him a very large menu, waited a moment and asked, in a pretty good Dutch accent, ""Wat wil je drinken?"

He was taken aback but managed "Ik zal een Heineken, neem dan." She laughed and said, in English, "We speak six languages at this restaurant, our clientele is international. I heard the Dutch inflection in your French, and you do look like a Dutchman." A pause, and then "My name is Zakia. I will bring you a Heineken."

"I am Piet Roefs, from Rotterdam." As she walked away he took the opportunity for another good look at her backside; conclusion: not bad! She felt his eyes, just as if he had put his hand on her buttocks.

Piet had eaten in Oriental restaurants many times in the Netherlands but he wasn't familiar with North African dishes. The menu featured the house specialty: *Pastilla aux pigeons (pâte feuilletée sucrée salée garnie d'amandes concassées et de pigeons)* 18.50 € That one was out of the question anyway: *Commande minimum 2 personnes et 48h à l'avance.*

Being basically a meat-and-potatoes man, Piet's eye went quickly to the list of various meats with couscous and settled on *Couscous au poulet* at 17.00 €. He wasn't really certain what couscous are, but figured he could deal with it. Then the waiter asked him to select a side dish, *Légumes* seemed like a safe choice over *Raisins confits* or *Pois chiches.*

He felt a bit foolish sitting there alone while he waited for the food to be served, but in a while the long table next to him was filled by what seemed to be three generations of two families; they spoke in French but appeared to be North African. Their cheerful but noisy conversation gave him cover for his solitary feeling.

The meal was served on a single large round platter: a thick layer of couscous covered with carrots, onions and peppers, with a half of a roast chicken and a broth of spicy stew over all. Piet had no trouble finishing most of the plate, he found it delicious.

Zakia came to take his plate and asked if he had enjoyed the meal. "Very much" he answered truthfully. She lingered a moment, asking "Are you here on business?"

"No," Piet replied. "I have just retired from the Rotterdam Seaport Police and I decided to see if I would like living in the south of France. I came here on my boat, I am docked at Port St Saveur."

"Ah, that is where I live, my apartment is across the canal, at the other end of the *passerelle*."

"You should be able to see my boat, it's a small Dutch barge, green and white."

"Yes, I noticed that boat yesterday, at the end of the pier. I often stop on the passerelle and look at the boats; they change frequently. You must have just arrived."

"Well, I think mine will be there for a while. I have paid for one month, then I will decide if I want to stay longer."

"This is a nice city, I think you will." She laughed and said "Of course, what do I know? This is where I have lived my whole life, within a few blocks of this restaurant… Would you like to see the dessert cart?"

"No thank you, I'm too full for dessert." He finished with an espresso, in no rush to leave. Eventually he asked for the check and paid the waiter.

At the foyer, Zakia said to him "J'espère que tu reviendrez". Piet was slightly startled by her use of the familiar 'tu', expecting the usual 'vous', but he did appreciate it, it made him feel more welcome, in fact a bit intimate. After a moment's thought he responded simply "Je vais revenir bientôt - bonsoir." He thought to himself, I will definitely be back soon, to see you!

The next few days he explored Toulouse, on foot and on his bicycle. The canal map showed that the Canal du Midi makes almost a half-circle around the east and north sides of the old city and connects with the Garonne river on the west side of the city. These were Piet's primary routes on the bicycle because he could use the *chemin de halage* (towpath along the canal) or designated pedestrian/bicycle paths free of car traffic.

He still needed to cross major boulevards and sometimes ride in the street, but he was used to big-city biking from his years in Rotterdam. He was spoiled, though, by the bicycle-only paths in Holland, some of which do not allow even pedestrian traffic. And he now more fully appreciated the traffic lights back home which included a separate sequence for the bike lane, halting all other traffic.

On the south side of the city the canal and the river diverge, so he needed to search out other routes, but that problem was resolved by simply setting out to the east from the river on one country road after another, knowing that eventually he would come to the canal. This gave him some pleasant rides past farms and tiny villages. One day he rode back along the canal to Negra, the place of his last overnight stop before arriving in Toulouse, a 60 km roundtrip that helped him get his biking legs back.

On the next Tuesday evening he returned to Le Toubkal; he wanted to be there on a night when Zakia would be the least busy, so that he might talk with her again. He arrived later this time, at 8:30, so that he could stay until closing time.

"I'm glad to see you again, Zakia, I enjoyed my dinner here last week... You said you have lived near here all of your life; have you worked here long?"

She laughed: "Forever! It was my father's restaurant, when he died five years ago it was left to me. My mother lives not far away, here in the old city, but she never comes here since my father died… Would you like your usual table?"

Piet laughed and said that would be fine.

This time Piet ordered the *Couscous à l'agneau* and, in no hurry to leave, a lemon sorbet for dessert.

When Piet ordered an espresso, it was delivered by Zakia, who had brought one for herself. "May I join you?"

"Please do, I would like that."

"Are you enjoying Toulouse after another week here?"

"I am, it seems much like Rotterdam, except of course there is no seaport here, and in Rotterdam there are almost no historical buildings, like there are here, since nearly everything was destroyed by German bombs in 1940, except the city hall and the *Witte Huis*, one of the first skyscrapers in the world."

"I saw your city on television when the Tour de France started there last year. That bridge that they raced across is very beautiful, with all of those cables stretching from just a single two-legged tower."

"That's the *Erasmusbrug*, in Rotterdam they call it the 'white swan'."
"Yes, I can see that, it does look like a swan."

"You have your own very beautiful bridge here in Toulouse, the Pont Neuf. I saw it lit at night, the red lights under the stone arches were reflected in the water, it made a spectacular row of red ovals. What are there, seven arches? I like that they aren't identical, they get smaller toward each end of the bridge."

"The restaurant is closed on Sunday and Monday," Zakia replied, "usually on one of those days I walk through the Grand Rond and then take the boulevard out to the river. I go to the island and then onto the Pont de Halage. I stop in the middle to watch the Garonne flow over the dam, the water is so smooth and it glistens. Then I walk along the river and find a bench as it gets dark and the lights come on at the bridges, the red lights on the Pont Neuf and the green lights under the Pont St Michel are so beautiful."

"The Grand Rond and the boulevard, the Allée Jules Guesde with the grass in the middle, are something that we don't have in Rotterdam, all of those trees on a straight line cutting right through the city."

"Yes, it's been my favorite walk since I was a little girl... We'll be closing soon, why don't you wait while I finish up and then walk me home?"

"I'd like that - don't you have to stay while the kitchen is closed up?"

"No, the chef worked for my father, the kitchen has been entirely his for over twenty years, so I leave him alone. His staff will clean up and they will leave through the back."

Soon she was ready, locking the entry door behind her. They walked down Rue Perchepinte, then Piet turned onto Rue Vélane, the narrow alley that he had already become accustomed to using. Zakia stopped him and said:

"Wait, come with me to *La Coupole* for a brandy. I've been going there a long time - my father took me there when I was 17." Of course Piet agreed and they continued on to Place Sainte Scarbes.

"You should use this next alley, Rue Neuve, instead of Vélane, it's a bit shorter, it's much more pleasant than those tall, narrow walls and there are never any cars." As they passed the entrance to Rue Neuve, Piet looked down it and said "Oh, I see what you mean. I'll go that way next time." They continued on past the cathedral St-Étienne and toward the canal; at Place Dupuy she led him into La Coupole. The sidewalk tables were empty but inside the brasserie was busy; they found two stools open at the end of the curved bar.

The bartender said "Bonsoir Zaki" as he poured her an Armagnac brandy, then looked at Piet "m'sieu?" "Calvados, s'Il vous plait."

"Ah, good, the working man's cognac" said Zakia. "I don't know about that" said Piet, "I just like it."

"Well, I drink Armagnac because I think it is better for me than Cognac, they tell me that it helps to keep me from getting fat! Nothing wrong with my favorite digestif being good for me too. And it's almost local here, it's produced just to the west of the Garonne, in Gascony."

"It doesn't look to me that you have to worry about getting fat," Piet said. She smiled, and they sat there for some time without saying any more. The bartender knew that Zakia would drink just one brandy and Piet declined his offer to pour another Calvados. They left and she pointed the way to Pont Montaudran, a bridge over the Canal du Midi. They walked south along the canal and in just two hundred meters Piet could see Margriet, moored at Port St Saveur.

The concrete footbridge arcs over the canal just past the docks. At its eastern end, on Boulevard Griffoul Dorval, Zakia led him to her building and used the code panel to open the main door. They took an elevator to the fourth floor of the seven-story building. When they entered the apartment Piet was drawn to the window, where he could look down on the boats moored along with his.

She stood next to him at the window and said "I love it here, it is so wonderful to see the canal and the boats that come and go."
Piet didn't say anything, but put his arm on her shoulder as they enjoyed they view. She turned slightly toward him so he did the same; she lifted her face and he carefully put his lips directly on hers. They kissed for a long moment; he thought that she had the best lips that his had ever touched. He thought "This is it, a woman who truly wants me."

And she did; Zakia was feeling the same emotion. Piet moved his lips along her cheek and down into the curve of her neck. It was smooth and warm, with a slight hint of perfume. He kept his lips there for a while, then nibbled on her short, tender earlobe, pushing away the dangling earring with his nose. "Wait" she said "I'm wearing my working clothes, I'll be back in a minute."

Piet settled into the soft couch, looking absently over the port to the older apartment buildings that ringed the west side of the docks. He wondered who Griffoul Dorval was; the French certainly like to name their streets after someone: generals, writers, artists, resistance fighters. Piet thought he would ask Zakia if she knew that name, but sometime later, not right now!

She returned in a long white negligé; "just like in the movies" flashed through Piet's mind. But why not, this whole evening felt like a movie to him. She sat beside him, joining him in a silent view of the city; she knew it well, often sitting here like this when she came home from the restaurant, to wind down from the busy, boisterous time at work.

Piet put his head on her shoulder, thinking of when he had first seen it as he followed her on the street. He kissed her shoulder, and her neck, and opened the negligé to slide his face down between her breasts. She pulled the lapels open, exposing them to him. "Luscious" he said quietly, as he cupped each breast in his hands and gently kissed the nipple. "This is heaven."

He started to unbutton his shirt, then realized that she already had it undone down to his belt buckle. He stood up, dropped his pants and took off his shirt, and laid beside her on the sofa. She pulled his shoulder, ready to have him on top. She used her hand to help him find the right place, then he was well inside her.

It seemed to him that they made love for an hour, even though he knew it was just a few minutes. He knew how to bring her along slowly, building up her passion to a long, loud orgasm. He had learned this from Denise, although he always suspected that she faked it; if she did, it was always a pretty good act.
He collapsed on top of her and they stayed like that for a very long time, until he realized that he should roll off so she could breathe. Then they didn't move; the next thing he knew was the sun reflecting off a white building across the way.

Piet arose quietly, leaving Zakia asleep, and went to the kitchen to see if he could make coffee. The coffeemaker was new to him, he was still trying to figure it out when she came in.

"Here, I'll do it, you have to read the instructions. I did that and I can work it, but now I don't know what I did with the booklet."

When the coffee was ready they went out on the balcony, overlooking the canal and the rows of plane trees on each side. Below them stretched a line of permanently-moored barges, several of them private homes, more than one a restaurant *péniche* with dining on a large open top deck or in the dining room below, with plentiful windows on the canal and even a floating bed & breakfast. "A nice place for the tourists, but not my style," Piet said.

"Your barge is so much smaller than those, I guess you want it that way, if it's just for yourself. "

"Yes, it's just right for me, but two people would be just as comfortable. It's small because it wasn't a barge that hauled freight, it was a tugboat. In Dutch it's called a *sleepboot*. That sounds like a boat that you sleep on, but really it means a tugboat."

"I'd like to see it, can I visit you onboard?"

"Sure, why don't you stop on your way to the restaurant this morning. I'll get a baguette and make some coffee, I do know how to do it."

"See you in an hour or so, after I get dressed for work."

Piet stopped at the Casino market for butter and at the boulangerie nearby, both right off the passerelle, then straightened up the cabin of the boat before starting the coffee.

Soon he heard Zakia call from the security gate; he unlocked the gate and led her onto the dock. "It's a handsome boat," she said, "It looks like it has a purpose, right now its purpose is to transport you. It's your style, I can see that."
"Come inside. This is the wheelhouse, not very big, just a stool for me at the helm and a bench for a couple of guests. And this little refrigerator, there isn't enough room for it in the main cabin. Fifty years ago when they built this boat they usually didn't have a refrigerator onboard."

"The stool looks comfortable enough, I guess you've spent lots of time there."

"I have, although only on the trip to here. I bought Margriet just for this purpose, I never owned a boat before this one."

"I thought you were a seaport policeman, and you didn't have a boat?"

He laughed, "No, the *Politie* had plenty of boats, I spent thirty years on their boats. On my time off I liked to ride with a cycling club, not get back on a boat. We rode every weekend for long distances and if I had a day off during the week I often rode alone. Holland is flat and the riding is easy, except for winds coming in off the North Sea. I'm doing a lot of riding here, and soon I hope to ride up into the Pyrénées."

"That's a long way, 100 kilometers at least just to get into the foothills. Do you ride that far?"

"Yes, although I don't think I can ride out there and back in the same day, I will stay overnight in the mountains."

"If you get too tired I could come and get you, except I don't have a car."

"Maybe you could rent one," he joked. She replied "Well I would if I had to. Sometimes I go on driving trips, I rent a car for that."

"Where do you go on those trips?"

"I like to go to Italy. My favorite place is the Italian lakes, I go to the one that is the closest, but most people don't know about it. Lago d'Orta is a quiet, beautiful place, I close the restaurant in August and rent a small apartment in the town of Orta San Giulio. I cruise around the lake in the tourist boats, sometimes I am the only passenger and I feel like the princess of the lake."

"Don't you go there with friends?"

"No, I like to be alone. On some days when I am at Orta I drive into the mountains, the lake is close to the Swiss alps. I have even found roads that lead to the Italian side of the Matterhorn. After working here in the city all year and walking these narrow streets, it feels really good to be alone on a small road high up in the mountains, where I can see forever."

"I know what you mean, I like my solitary bike rides also. There aren't any mountains in Holland but I can ride into the wetlands where I am totally alone, looking over a panoramic sweep of tall grass and lakes… Here we are talking on and I haven't offered you a coffee, it's all ready. Come down into the cabin, watch your step; the top stair had to be cut back so that the door to the toilet closet could swing open."

Piet poured the coffee and they shared the baguette. "Did you buy this at the boulangerie next to the Casino store? It's okay but I can show you a better place, up the hill just a bit," Zakia said.

"It's nice in here" she went on. "I like the blue-on-blue stripes on the cushions. The varnished wood is great, and the white ceiling makes it feel bigger. The kitchen's a little basic, though, isn't it."

"This isn't a restaurant," Piet said defensively "I'm only cooking for me and maybe a guest sometime."

Zakia laughed "I didn't mean to hurt your feelings, I'm just not used to boats."

"Some boats can have a fancy kitchen, but this is all I need. Take a look at my bedroom."

Poking just her head through the doorway, Zakia said "That is really small, and a low ceiling. Can two people sleep in that bed?"

"They can if they are really friendly" Piet joked. "If not, these two benches both can open up into bunks."

"We'll have to try it, won't we. Can I come by tonight after work?"

"That's a good idea. Shall I meet you at La Coupole."

"Sure, I'll be there about half-past ten... You know, on the day that you first came to my restaurant I saw you following me at Le Capitole. And then I saw you again, sitting at the salon de thé, drinking a beer. I liked your looks, that's why I was so glad to see you come in for dinner. I am so happy that you did!"

Piet blushed, "Sorry, I shouldn't look at women on the street. But when I saw you, you looked so different than all the rest. And it was just a coincidence that I sat down next to Le Toubkal, I had no idea that you would show up there!"

"Well, it was meant to be, wasn't it? See you tonight, unless you find some other woman to follow!"

"I don't think that's likely, I'll be there," said Piet.

Zakia left and walked to the restaurant, while Piet sat at the back end of the boat, watching her leave and then looking up at the balcony of her apartment. He thought that he was a pretty lucky guy, things have gone well in Toulouse so far.

He spent the rest of the day on the boat, catching up on some needed maintenance and giving the interior a more thorough cleaning, now that it looks like he will have some frequent company. Neighboring boaters had told him that he needed to visit Place Saint Georges, a very nice plaza with several good bars and restaurants, as well as lots of shops. They told him how to find it, it's on the most direct route from the port to Place du Capitole and the main shopping streets. Piet thought, "Okay, I'll go there this evening. I haven't done much of the basic tourist thing, and I can easily walk back to La Coupole later."

Most of the way there was along the Allée Forain Francois Verdier, a wide swath of trees and grass with traffic lanes on both sides, a grand boulevard lined with elegant old apartment buildings. He took his time there, stopping several times on benches to just enjoy the pleasant space in the middle of the city, watching people pass by.

As his port neighbor had suggested, he turned left on Rue de Metz and then found the narrow Rue d'Astorg. A slight shiver ran through him as he passed the shop *Oxford - meubles de style Anglais*, filled with just the sort of frilly, silly things that Matje loved, exactly what he was getting away from.

The narrow lane opened into what he had been told, a park with many trees and numerous sidewalk cafes. They were right about the shops, he thought, there are lots of places to spend money at the plaza and on the nearby streets. He circled the plaza and settled at a small table in front of *Le Wallace* bar, ordering *un pression*.

Piet noticed with interest an attractive woman, about his age, at a nearby table; leaning against the low stone wall of a planted area was a tall red plastic case, in the shape of a bass violin; shoulder straps allow her to carry it like a backpack. He wanted to strike up a conversation but she was engrossed in what looked to be a serious hardback book, he couldn't read the title and decided not to disturb her. Anyway, he had an appointment later with another very attractive lady.

He decided to walk on to Place du Capitole and then return to this plaza for dinner at *Créperie St Georges*. As he wandered around he noticed for the first time the Spanish influence here, close to the Pyrénées, in the street signs. One plaque read Rue de la Pomme and another below it read Carriéra de la Poma d'Aur.

Piet thought that he liked Toulouse very much. A historic city with much beautiful traditional architecture, it hasn't been tarnished too much by modern buildings, at least in the old city. The circular parking garage that he saw on his first day was one of the few truly ugly sights, but he considered that a necessary evil in these times. There were certainly plenty of high-class shops and not very many stores selling a cheap line of goods, at least on the streets that he had walked; the old city seemed well-preserved and the shops upscale.

Except that his wandering brought him to the huge Centre St Georges. Piet realized that he had seen one end of it, a seven-story block of apartments, when he was on Rue d'Astorg earlier. That view had been startling, a high wall of long rows of modern apartment windows towered above the tiny street. Now he was at the main entrance to the commercial part of the development, with a Lacoste shop on his left and the Hotel Mercure at right. He was familiar with such large modern structures in Rotterdam, which had to be totally rebuilt after the German bombing in World War II. But there most of the city is structures like this, here in Toulouse it stands out like a sore thumb. He briefly toured the galleries inside, then left quickly, disgusted with the whole thing. Outside, he turned south and quickly found a pedestrian lane which led directly back into Place St Georges.

After a simple but very good dinner at the créperie, Piet walked to La Coupole and waited for Zakia at an outside table, entertained by a steady stream of cars, buses and scooters headed into the center of the city. When she arrived they went in for a perfunctory drink, then hurried off to the boat, at Port St Saveur.

Piet didn't have to hurry things along, it was Zakia who unbuttoned her dress and slipped out of it as soon as she went into the cabin. She had evidently prepared for this before leaving the restaurant, when the dress fell to the floor she was standing there wearing only her shoes and her earrings. Facing him, as if to say, here I am, you're welcome to me.

Since she was shamelessly displaying herself, Piet just stood there, taking it all in. He started at her smooth neck and graceful collarbones, which he had appreciated when he first saw her in the restaurant. Then her breasts: full, smooth, standing straight and round on her chest, prominent nipples with a small, soft circle of pink around each one. She's not skinny, he thought, and certainly not flabby, good solid meat throughout.

Then his eyes went down to her hips and pelvis. There she proudly displayed a true beaver, a thick bush of black hair, terrific!

The prostitute that he had used was always shaved clean. Denise had told him that the young guys demand it, but that old guys like him always wanted a beaver. Now he looked approvingly at Zakia's dark fur, like a mink muff. What's that American expression, a 'muff-diver', that's for me, thought Piet.

He held her as they stood together for a moment, for a kiss that Piet felt through his whole body. He guided her up the step and onto his bed, then disrobed as she laid back and watched. He laid next to her, erect and ready, eager to feel her body against him. Then he slid down and put his face in the beaver, searching with his tongue for the right spot. It was easy to tell when he found it, her pelvis pushed back against him and she caught her breath.

They made love for a long time before he put his lips on hers to try to muffle her during their 'come together' orgasm.

"Are you afraid the neighbors will hear me?" she laughed.

"Yes, they are all retired couples, probably asleep by now. They seem a bit prudish. I haven't been very friendly with them, being a single guy."

"You're not single right now, are you?"

"No, not until you go off to your apartment."

"I don't think I will, if you don't mind, at least not very soon. Why don't you fold out one of those dinette benches so we can be more comfortable?" He did that and they laid down again, under a light blanket, for their second night together. "I could get used to this," Piet thought.

They woke up early, when a barge at the next dock started its engine and soon headed off to the east on the canal. Piet made coffee and they sat side by side on the bench.

"If you like, I'll show you where to get a really good traditional baguette," Zakia said.

"Sure, if you have enough time."

She went to her apartment alone, to shower and dress for the new day's work. When she was ready she stepped out on her balcony and waved to Piet, who met her at the front door of her building. She led him north along the canal, then east on Ave Jean Rieux; about a ten minute walk up a long slope.

Zakia told him as they walked "This is the Côte Pavée district, the 'paved hillside'. It's not much of a hill, but it does rise steadily up the slope from the canal. Quite a bit different than the old city, isn't it? The old part was there in the middle ages, but the part outside the Canal du Midi was only built-up after the revolution, in the 19th century. This is the section where most of the Jewish and Muslim people live. Here we are…"

The shop was busy with morning sales of baguettes. Zakia told Piet that you can't just ask for a baguette, they have several styles. "The best is their version of a traditional baguette, here they call it a *Toulousiane*." When Piet asked for it, the baker looked puzzled so Zakia stepped up: "Bonjour Jean-Pierre, une Toulousiane s'il vous plait."

"Bonjour Zaki, ça va?"

"Tres bien, this is my friend Piet"

"Bonjour Piet, are you visiting our city?"

"Yes, I am on a boat at Port St Saveur. But I intend to stay a while."

"Bon, please come back for your baguettes."

"I will, the lady at the boulangerie near the port is not very friendly."

As they walked back down to the port Zakia said "I'm glad that you will be staying. You should meet some of the people here, not just the boaters. Why don't you come to the restaurant on Saturday night? There is a group of guys that ride motorcycles every Saturday, usually tearing up the roads in the Pyrénées, then they have dinner with me. I'll introduce you."

"Okay, I'll be there" Piet replied, although he wasn't too sure that he wanted friends, so far he was doing okay by himself. But why not, I don't have to follow up, he thought.

Piet did show up for dinner at Le Toubkal on Saturday night. He had noticed that the triangular traffic island in the street was filled with motorcycles, so he wasn't surprised that the long table was filled by six men, in their 40s and 50s, wearing motorcycle gear. As she led Piet to his usual table she introduced the men: Edine, Toumi, Moussa, Ahmed, Abdou and Jamel. All had dark skin and black hair, from their names and their looks obviously North African. Piet greeted each one but continued to his own table, where he sat almost shoulder-to-shoulder with Jamel. When they ordered he heard Jamel say simply 'kefta'. The waiter obviously expected to hear it.

For his previous dinners Piet had ordered from the words on the menu that he knew: poulet, agneau. But he had wondered about kefta, so he asked Jamel "Jamel, would you please tell me, what is kefta?"

"Oh, it's croquettes, or meatballs, made from ground veal with spices and onions. I like it better than just a plain piece of meat. And it's okay for Muslims, all of the dishes here are *halal*. The meat dinners come from cows or sheep, grass-eaters. There is no pork on the menu."

"Are all of you Muslim?" asked Piet, gesturing around the table.

"Yes, we met at the mosque. We all ride motorcycles, so we became friends."

Piet laughed "I ride a bicycle, not a motorcycle, and I'm not a Muslim, but I'll try to be friendly anyway."

"Where are you from?"

"Rotterdam, in the Netherlands. I grew up in a small town in southeastern Holland."

"My aunt tells me that she thinks I have relatives in Rotterdam, cousins, but I've never been there," Jamel said.

"Yes, there are a lot of North Africans in Rotterdam, in fact the guy who's the mayor right now is Moroccan."

"I'm not Moroccan, my father was Algerian. But I grew up here, raised by my aunt and uncle, they are French. My father died before I was born. I'm one of what are called the *Beurs*, the children of Maghreb immigrants, those who came to France from Morocco, Algeria or Tunisia... but you're Dutch, are you here on holiday?"
"On permanent holiday. I have just retired and I came here on my boat, it's docked at Port St Saveur. I was a seaport policeman in Rotterdam for the past thirty years."

"I can give you a ride to the port on my moto, if you are ready to go when we are finished. I cross the Pont Montaudran, it's on my way."

"So you live in the Côte Pavée? Zakia just took me up there, to the boulangerie on Ave Jean Rieux."

"That's probably the same one I use, I live around the corner on Rue Julien Cassange."

"I would like a ride, you know I have never been on a motorcycle. I can show you my boat, if you like."

Piet did order the kefta and found that he liked it a lot. During the evening he talked with some of the other men but found himself most interested in Jamel, whose soft and well-spoken voice didn't match his strong build and rugged, handsome looks. Piet wanted to get to know him a bit.

As they all left the restaurant and said goodbye to Zakia, she gave Piet a what-about-me? look; he smiled and asked "Will I see you tomorrow, Zaki?" "I hope so" she replied.

On the street Jamel asked "Do you see Zakia outside the restaurant?"

"Yes, we have been spending time together. She lives right near the port, and she has been showing me some of the places in the neighborhood," such as her own apartment, he thought.
As Jamel pulled on his helmet he told Piet "You won't need a helmet, it's only a short ride and I'll be careful."

"I hope so," Piet joked as he slid a leg over the back of the seat.

Jamel gave Piet quite a thrill, and probably upset some of the neighbors, as he blasted off down the narrow Rue Vélane, its high walls magnifying the high-pitched sound of the exhaust. Ahead Piet could see the concrete wall approaching at the end of the street and wished that he did have a helmet. Jamel braked hard for the abrupt left turn, accelerating again for a brief burst of speed before turning right to the wide boulevard that circles the Grand Rond, where he slowed and calmly rode with the traffic. In another two minutes he stopped at the gate of the port.

Piet got off the moto and asked "Why did you drive slowly on the wide streets, after scaring the shit out of me on those narrow alleys?"

Jamel laughed. "Because there aren't any police in the alleys, but they like to hang out along the Grand Rond. Besides, it's fun. That's why I ride a moto instead of a Renault sedan."

"I'm afraid my boat is not nearly as exciting, it will only do 10 or 12 kilometers per hour, at top speed. But it got me here from the north of Holland, even if it did take seven weeks. When I traveled all day, seven or eight hours, I only averaged less than 50 kilometers…Come on aboard."

Piet asked, as he took a bottle of Calvados from a shelf "Would you like a drink, a digestif? I saw you drinking wine tonight, but I thought you are a Muslim? Is alcohol allowed?"

"I would like a drink, thanks. I'm not a practicing Muslim, I was raised as a Catholic. And my friends that you met tonight, they are Muslims but they don't practice the religion rigidly. I didn't know anything about Islam until just a few years ago, when my neighbor, Hassan, began telling me about it. He was very intense, he felt that he was *mujahideen*. But he didn't get many others to join him here in Toulouse. He tried to get me involved but he was killed too soon, I didn't really get to know him."

"How was he killed?"

"I'll tell you, it's quite a story. His name was Hassan Jandoubi, he lived in the same small apartment building as I do now; there are three floors, with only five apartments. My apartment is on the top floor and his was just below me, so we got to be friends. We had the same birthday, although I was four years older.

"On the morning of September 21, 2001, you'll notice the date, it was ten days after the World Trade Center attacks in the United States, a huge explosion destroyed the AZF chemical factory just about four kilometers south of here, on the west side of the river. The explosion killed 29 people and destroyed about 600 homes in the Le Mirail district.

"I knew that area well, I worked for my uncle as an electrician, we had wired many of the houses built there in the 1980s and 90s. Hassan was hired to unload ammonium nitrate at the plant only five days before the explosion. On the day of the blast, he was working in a hangar just 30 yards from hangar 221, the one that blew up.

"I was questioned by police after the explosion, when they searched Hassan's apartment. They went after him because some of the guys at the factory told police that on the day before the blast, they saw him arguing angrily with a truck driver who had decorated his cabin with a miniature Stars and Stripes out of sympathy with the victims of the September 11 attacks. He had been happy about those attacks, he thought it was justified revenge.

"The police thought it was suspicious that his body was found wearing two pairs of trousers and four pairs of underpants, the way some Islamic militants go on suicide missions. When they searched the apartment a few days later, it had been cleaned out of his clothes, personal effects and photos. His girlfriend living in the apartment said she had destroyed his belongings to overcome her loss.

"The official decision was that ammonium nitrate had exploded following improper handling, or perhaps an electrical surge, but a lot of police and the media suspected Hassan."

Piet had been listening intently. "You're right, that's quite a story. I remember that explosion, vaguely. It was big news even in Rotterdam, because we have lots of storage of hazardous products scattered around the seaport and some of us talked about the possibility of a terrorist attack. The Muslims in Rotterdam have always been under suspicion, more so after 9/11."

"Hassan could have done it, for sure, but he never talked to me about it" Jamel said. "I think the police had me under surveillance after that, sometimes I saw the same car, with someone sitting in it, near the mosque in Le Mirail and also here on my street. Then in 2004 there was a terrorist group in France that operated under the name AZF, probably named for the explosion. They tried to extort money from the French government, by threatening to place bombs along the rail lines. Once, to demonstrate their power, they led French railway workers to a bomb, then neutralized it. A week or so later another bomb was found on the TGV train tracks, but it wasn't live and wasn't the same as the one found earlier. The police again came and questioned me at that time, but I had nothing at all to tell them."

"But that hasn't stopped you from going to the mosque and making friends who might be terrorists?" Piet asked.

"No, I go there all the time, and those guys are my friends. The police can't stop me from that."

"Your friends seem to be pretty calm guys, but they could be terrorists if they thought it necessary, I guess."

"They could, and so could I," Jamel said as he stood up to leave. "Thanks for the drink. I like your boat, it's comfortable. I'll go on home now, and I hope to see you again."

"Same here. Please drop by whenever you want."

Jamel drove off up the quay with his usual quick burst of speed, then crossed the bridge quietly and disappeared up the hill into the Côte Pavée. Piet thought "What a story, I like Jamel but am I getting myself into something by making friends with him? Maybe."

It wasn't Jamel who "dropped by" to visit Piet on Sunday morning, it was Zakia. He was sitting on the stern rail of Margriet with his first coffee when she hailed him from the gate. When he opened the gate for her, she immediately reached over to kiss him on the cheek. "I missed you last night," she said.

"Me too, but I had a good visit with Jamel. Want some coffee?"

"Oui, s'il vous plait. What did you talk about?"

"He told me a little bit about himself, about his friendship with Hassan Jandoubi and the AZF explosion."

"Oh, that was a terrible time. It was our own version of the 9/11 attacks and questions about whether it was an accident or terrorism went on for years."

"Well, that's ten years ago now, let's think about today. That's what I'm doing, on April 18, just two months ago, I started a new life… You said that you enjoy your holidays at lake Orta, how did you find it?"

"We serve Moroccan and French wines at Le Toubkal, but when I took over I wanted to also have some Italian wines. I like the wines of the Piedmont; Barbera, Barolo, Barbaresco, Dolcetto, Nebbiolo, Asti Spumante. I decided that I should visit some of the vineyards, so that I would know what I am doing. I got a map of the Piedmont vineyards from a bookstore, rented a car and drove first to Savona, on the Mediterranean coast. Then I went inland to Asti and stayed in a hotel there for a few nights. I drove north from there, vineyard to vineyard. Eventually I got to Borgomanero, late in the day. I asked a winemaker where I might find a place to stay overnight and he directed me to Orta San Giulio. I loved it and stayed for a week, and have been going back ever since."

"August is coming soon, are you going there then?" Piet asked.

"I was planning to, but now I'm not so sure I want to; I would miss you."

"I've never been to Italy," Piet said, "in fact I've never been anywhere outside of Holland. I usually just spend my holiday riding my bicycle around the low country. Have you finished your coffee? Let's go inside," Piet suggested.

He didn't have to ask twice, she was the first one down the steps into the cabin. She turned and kissed him, this time straight on the lips, then reached down to fold out the dinette bench. Piet laid down beside her and soon found that the very pretty flowered dress was all she had on. It didn't take long before she didn't have that on either.

In the afternoon they went for a long walk, circling the old city. Zakia had asked him, "Have you figured out our word Allée? I know that in English it would mean a very narrow street, like Rue Vélane, but in French it means a tree-lined avenue. We can start right here at the port, on Allée des Soupirs, the avenue of sighs, to the Grand Rond and then all the way around to the river, under the trees the whole way."

"That sounds good, I'm sure we can find places to rest where they serve food and drink."
"I know some nice places, just let me know when you're dying of thirst."

Piet told her that he had been on the Allée Forain Francois Verdier a few days ago, and that he had enjoyed a slow walk for those few blocks. This time she pointed out the large war memorial, like the Arc de Triomphe in Paris except smaller, and lots of columns instead of an arch.

Where Piet had earlier turned off to go to Place St Georges, they continued north, following the line of tall trees. The name of the avenue changed every few blocks but they just stayed under the trees, passing many very beautiful old apartment buildings, each four to seven stories high, with tall windows behind shallow balconies and wrought-iron railings. Some modern apartments and office buildings intruded, nearly all of them were of uninspired architecture, best to try and ignore them.

But he couldn't ignore a very tall, slender box of stacked apartments, with a strange space-ship type entrance structure. Then he saw the sign "Espace St Georges" and he realized that this was the other end of the commercial development that he had so disliked a few days earlier. In another block Zakia pointed out the Theatre de la Cité, a new, modern building but in a design that paid homage to the Ville Rose, with red and white bricks. She said that she liked to go to plays there.

These allées were obviously the place for a choice of bars and restaurants, sidewalk tables were to be found in every block. He would have to let her show him the best places.

After an hour or so of window-shopping and sightseeing, Piet said "I'm ready for a beer." Zakia pointed across the street to La Rotonde, a café with sidewalk tables. Piet had his usual pression while Zakia ordered a gin-and-tonic. "Do you know why they call this place La Rotonde?" Piet asked. "Take a look around the corner," Zakia replied.

Omigod, Piet said to himself, another big round parking garage, in all its harsh concrete glory, attached to a block-long building with three horizontal rows of balconies, each balcony set at 45 degrees to the side of the building, so that the rows looked like the teeth of a saw. "What is that?" he asked Zakia.

"That's the Marché Victor Hugo. The ground floor has stalls displaying some of the most gorgeous food of the region. Bakeries, butchers offering Toulouse sausage as well as horse meat, cheese, seafood, every kind of food shop that you could think of. The next floor has restaurants; the view of the old buildings of the neighborhood from those restaurants is just great, a lot better than looking into the building, it's too stark. All of the restaurants look the same, but they have different menus. And the top floors are parking, it's a huge parking garage. There is a spiral ramp at each end of the building. The streets on the west side are a good shopping district, from here to Le Capitole, so people drive in from all around the area."

"Why do all those little balconies stick out from the roof like a row of teeth?"

"They are rows of parking stalls, angled along the outside of the building. Each of those balconies can hold the front end of a car."

"What won't they think of next?"

"Shopping the food stalls is great, lots to look at and to find any kind of food that you want. If you like fish especially, fresh fish is brought in every morning. It's best to get there between 6 and 9AM to have the best choice. They're open every day but Monday."

"I'll try it some day this week," Piet said.

They continued on around the curve of the allées, after another hour arriving at the Canal de Brienne. "I know where we are now," said Piet, "I came here on my bicycle when I followed the Canal du Midi to its end. This canal connects the Midi to the Garonne river. We can follow it down to the St Pierre lock, and the bridge. I walked down the river to this bridge on my first day here," Piet said when they came to the bridge. "Let's follow the river back. Do you know a place where we can get dinner?"

"Of course, but you know that a lot of the good restaurants, like mine, are not open on Sunday."

"That's okay, just a croque-monsieur or something like that would be good."

"Right near the Pont Neuf there's a place called *Beaucoup*, I know that will be open."

It was open, and they had a simple meal at a table on what is a very busy street during the week but on Sunday there were few cars and no trucks, just people strolling to and from the bridge. Afterward they followed the river and another allée back to the port.

They spent that night together in Zakia's apartment ("It's more comfortable," she said) and stayed together again on Monday, Zakia showing Piet more of her city. Late in the day he told her "I'm going to ride to the Pyrénées tomorrow."

"But I have to open the restaurant, what if you need me to come and get you?"

Piet laughed and said "I'll be fine, I've ridden on long trips before. If I get tired I'll find a hotel and rest."

"All right, but I'll miss you!"

"Me too. I'll be back soon enough."

Stretching the width of southwestern France, from the Atlantic to the Mediterranean, the Pyrénées form a magnificent backdrop of shark's-tooth mountains 100 kilometers south of Toulouse; they act as the natural frontier between France and Spain.

Piet was looking forward to a good long-distance ride on his bicycle and had always wanted to ride in the Pyrénées. He bought a Michelin road map and plotted his route: south along the east bank of the Garonne river on the *départmental* highway D4, passing through St Sulpice sur Lèze, and then west on smaller roads to Cazères, where the route includes small climbs over the rolling countryside and the view ahead shows the foothills to come. Then a twisting route through the foothills themselves, following one back road after another; these were particularly enjoyable, lined by rows of plane trees and occasional sights of well-kept farms and tiny villages, with almost no traffic. Yellow fields of rape grain stood out brightly from the relentless green in every direction.

Piet stopped for a long rest at Aspet, a market town which marked the 100 kilometer point of the day's ride. From a table at *Cafe Francais* in the town square he looked up along the long main street to a view of the sharply-pointed peak of Cagire, standing above a layer of fog which formed the boundary between the wooded slope and the bare rock above.
His legs weren't ready for the tough climb on the high road which skirts the peak, so he took the valley roads to the west, past Cazaunous, then up and

over a forested ridge. The one switchback climb that was required was just long enough to give him a feel for mountain climbing without taking him to his limit. And the 4 km slope down from that climb was pure joy, as he descended again to the valley of the Haute Garonne at Fronsac.

 He followed a straight highway along that valley and finally a long, steady climb, not very steep or difficult, across the Spanish border between the towns of Fos, France and Les, Spain. As he crossed the border he stopped and looked ahead at the mountains; the slopes formed a nearly perfect V, each slope stretching above him more than a thousand feet, with only enough width across the narrow valley for the river and the road alongside. Certainly foreign territory for Piet the Dutchman.

There he checked into the *Ostau Dera Nheu* restaurant/pension for dinner and an overnight stay. It was a spectacular day, better than any ride that he had experienced in the flat country of Holland. Although he wasn't really comfortable riding on the busy roads near Toulouse, the cars did give him enough room. When he got into the Pyrénées on the narrow lanes, the rare traffic was familiar with cyclists and were very courteous.

In the restaurant he was surprised to see Jamel in this place; he was dining with a short dark man with a tiny face, mostly covered by a droop of black hair and bushy black eyebrows. It was not someone that he recognized from Le Toubkal. Piet didn't intrude on their intense conversation and took a table alone, with a small wave to Jamel when he looked up, giving a nod in return. The pair left together shortly after.

When Piet came in for breakfast the next morning Jamel was alone at a table; he signaled to Piet to join him.

"Bonjour Piet, ça va? I'm on holiday this week, I came up here for a night alone. But I'm surprised to see you, how did you find this place? And how did you get here, do you have a car?"

"Bonjour Jamel, je suis très bien. I rode my bicycle. Even before I left Holland I decided that one thing I wanted to do for sure would be to ride in the Pyrénées. I've always been a fan of the Tour de France so I know some of the routes through these hills and mountains, from watching on television. So I got a map and laid out a route to get here. It looked best to simply use the Garonne river as a guide, and let that decide where I should start out for my first ride in the Pyrénées. And here I am, that's the

Garonne river right across the road, although I see they call it the Garona here in Spain."

"Yes, that's right. You met my biker friends, they brought me up here when I began to ride with them. This is our destination just about every Saturday, we always stop here for lunch before turning back to Toulouse."

"Well, I couldn't make it here and back in one day. I planned to ride into the mountains until I found an auberge or hostel, then stay overnight and ride back the next day. I'll be using the same route back as soon as I finish breakfast."

"Oh, don't just go back from here, you'll miss the best part. We always go on to the next town, Bossost, and go up over the Col de Portillon."

"I remember that name, but I don't think it's one of the big climbs on the Tour. Maybe It's one that I can handle."

"I'm sure you can, it's not too steep or long. Most of it is on the French side of the summit, and that's all downhill. The roadway is wide and smooth, and most of it is in the forest but there are a few open places with a low concrete guardrail. There are a few switchbacks going up, but it's only eight kilometers from Bossost to the summit. That's the border of France, the road is called the *Carretera de Bossost enta França*. Going down is great fun, there are tight turns and sweepers. You'll more than make up for the energy you use to get up there. You end up in Luchon; the valley goes right back to the N125, you probably came in on that."

"I'll check it out on my map, but sounds good."

"I'm heading back soon on my Yamaha, maybe I should give you a tow up to the col?"

"No, I think I can handle it. You'll be back in Toulouse a lot quicker than me, but I'll see you at Le Toubkal sometime. Thanks for the tip."

They shook hands, with a mutual "bonne journée". As he walked away, Piet thought, if you came up here to be alone, who was that man that you had dinner with? From his room Piet could hear the motorcycle start up and head to the south; a short while later, he took the same road. He had no trouble finding it, as it seems that the Spanish do a good job with highway signs. Piet doesn't speak or read the language but the signs were easy enough to interpret.

Part way up the mountain he wanted to say to Jamel "That's easy for you to say, you're on a motorcycle!" When he came to an open place with a view far below he gulped and thought "That low wall isn't a guardrail, it's a curb; I could tip right over it very easily."

Piet never liked to stop on an upslope so he pedaled at a steady rate and made the summit in just under an hour. He stopped there for a brief rest then set off downhill. Jamel was right about this part, the long fast run through the turns was fabulous, not at all like his homeland. There you pedal out from the start, often against the wind, and then sometimes you pedal back against the wind. No hills to go up, that's the good news, but also no hills to go down, that's the bad news.

At the bottom of the hill a sign welcomed him to *Luchon - Reine des Pyrénées*. He rode through a long line of modern suburban homes, then on a street of dull gray, tightly closed buildings, common in small French towns, before turning onto the main street where he found the large, impressive white multi-columned buildings of the hot baths at Bagnères-de-Luchon. Next time I'll make this my destination and try out the baths, Piet thought.

He bypassed the rest of the town on the D125 and continued north down the valley, still a long way back to Toulouse. When he came to the road through the foothills that he had used the day before, he decided to stay in the valley and follow it out to the plain. There he sat down with his map and plotted a route that was slightly more direct than following the Garonne, which bows to the east before turning north. It was an assemblage of a bunch of the 'D' highways, shown in yellow on the map, that would take him across new country and looked to be a bit shorter.

As he rode out from the mountains and foothills of the Pyrénées he understood what he had begun to notice on his ride in: the houses in the towns and villages are in two quite different zones of style. In the foothills they resemble those out on the plain, white-walled buildings with red clay rounded-tile roofs, grouped more or less within a circle around the central plaza. In the valleys and on the slopes of the mountains, the houses and businesses are lined along the road, often forced to be this way by the walls of rock cliffs narrowing the flat strip of land. Even more noticeable was the drab, gray similarity of the buildings, with somber gray walls and roof tiles of flat stone, in various shades of gray. He preferred the more cheerful style of the foothills towns, but realized that the mountain style was a result of the topography and the harsh winters.

The route was shorter and flatter than the day before; he returned in two hours less than he had done on the way out, of course that had quite a few uphill sections while the return route was almost dead-flat across the plain. Piet was well satisfied with his ride, although he was still wondering why Jamel was up there, and who was the little man?

On the evening of Piet's return from the Pyrénées ride, he rested for a few hours and then walked to Le Toubkal. Zakia was alone at the desk in the entry foyer; she immediately came out from the desk to give him a tight hug and kiss on the cheek. "I'm so glad to see you're back safely," she said.

"I'm glad to see you too, I missed you last night when I stayed in Spain."

"Spain? You rode all the way into Spain?"

"Yes, but just barely. I stayed at the town of Les, a few kilometers past the border. Then this morning I came back into France at Bagnères-de-Luchon, and straight back to here from there."

"Well, I hope you had a good time, but don't go away overnight again without me, okay? Are you having dinner?"

"Yes, my usual table please, madame."

She seated him and brought his beer right away; "You look like you needed this," she said.

"I do, just like I needed you." She paused and looked at him, then said "I'll come directly to the boat after I close."

Piet ordered his meal. Shortly after it was served, Jamel came to the table. "Zakia said you were here; I went to your boat, then I thought that I might find you here. I need to talk to you, but privately."

"Sure, but not tonight. Are you still on holiday tomorrow? Come to my boat anytime, but not too early."

"I'm on holiday all week. I'll come by at 9 o'clock. I'll bring a baguette from Jean-Pierre."

"Good, we can talk privately on the boat."

Jamel left quickly, then just as quickly Zakia came to ask Piet "He acted strangely, is everything okay?"

"I don't know, he's coming to talk to me tomorrow morning, on the boat."

"I hope he's all right. I've known him a few years, since he's been coming here with those 'moto muslims' as I call them. I think they have been telling him a lot of things that he didn't know before."

"It sounds like he wants to open up to me, I'll try to be a good listener."

"I'm sure you will be, you are interested in other people, not just yourself."

In the morning Piet made coffee early for Zakia and himself, then made another batch after Zakia left for her apartment. He had seen Jamel drinking espresso, so Piet guessed that he would drink morning coffee.

Jamel arrived promptly at 9. They shared the baguette and coffee, while Jamel asked about Piet's ride back to Toulouse. Then Piet said, "Go ahead, I have no plans for today, especially not to get back on my bike."

"I'm sure," said Jamel "I don't know how you did it, that's an easy trip on a moto but not on a bike."

As Jamel began to talk, Piet looked at him closely. Tall, well-built from his daily workouts at a gym, Piet thought "he's handsome, he must easily attract women, but as far as I know he lives alone, and I wonder why." His skin color is caramel; his hair is cropped short and his beard is kept as stubble. His nose is broad and his lips are full; the earring in his left ear is a shiny silver ball.

"My full name is Jamel Hammad. I was born on March 1, 1962 in Toulouse. I'm telling you that not because I want a birthday card, but because the date is important to my story.

"My mother, Doriane, grew up in Toulouse and went to Paris right after high school. She couldn't find a career job and ended up as a chambermaid at the Hotel du Nord. She met my father there, he worked in maintenance of the building; they were married in 1960. But he was killed in 1961 and my mother came back here to live with her sister, Marie-Christine, and her husband Silvain Pouget. Doriane died three years after I was born; I never knew why, but my aunt told me she thought it was from a broken heart and from fears of whatever had happened there.

"I was raised, as French and Catholic, by my aunt and uncle. When they thought I was old enough, they told me that my father, Majid Hammad, had left Algiers in 1957 at the age of 19 and came to the Paris suburb of Bobigny, where a group of Algerians helped him settle into a new life. My mother lived not far away in the 19th arrondissement. They both used the same Metro line to go to work, probably.

"But Marie-Christine and Silvain told me nothing about Algeria, they knew only bits and pieces of the Algerian War."

Piet interrupted to say "I know that there was an Algerian revolution, but that was before I was born and we Dutch had our own problems, when I was growing up there were refugees from Indonesia that lived in a camp near my town. Even in Rotterdam, we have a lot of immigrants there from North Africa, but I didn't pay much attention to their issues."

Jamel continued, "I never thought much about being Algerian, or half Algerian. l guess I look Algerian; most of the foreign population of Toulouse are North African, and more than half of those are from Algeria, so it was no problem when I was growing up. We lived in the Côte Pavée quarter, where much of the ethnic people live.

"I went to Catholic schools and after high school I worked with my uncle, Silvain, to learn the trade of an electrician. I eventually became a Master Electrician. Together we wired hundreds of the new homes and apartment buildings going up at Le Mirail, in the southwest of Toulouse.

"After Silvain died in 1999 the Airbus plant at Blagnac was starting to grow, and I got a well-paying job there as a wiring installer on the A320 assembly line; later I moved to work on the giant A380, which is what I do now.

"I never knew anything at all about the Algerian revolution, I don't think my aunt and uncle knew much about it, they were just teenagers and it didn't affect them. But when I got to know Hassan Jandoubi, he told me something about it, and he gave me a video tape of the 1966 movie *La Bataille d'Alger*, 'The Battle of Algiers'. I have watched it many times. It's about the years between 1954 and 1957 in the city of Algiers, when the FLN freedom fighters expanded in the casbah, only to face violence and torture by the French paratroopers sent there to wipe them out."
Piet asked "FLN?"

"It stands for *Front de Libération Nationale*, it started as a small group of Algerian muslims who wanted independence from France. Algeria had been occupied as a colony by the French for 130 years. The FLN call themselves Mujahideen - 'strugglers' or 'people doing jihad', muslims who believe they struggle in the path of God.

"I don't know what Algiers is like now, but then there were two parts of the city: the Cité Européen, where there were the businesses and the residences of the French colonists and the loyalists, Algerians who worked and lived with the French. And there was the Casbah, the ghetto of old buildings and narrow alleys rambling up the hillsides, the home of native Algerians.

"The movie begins in 1954 with the guillotine execution of a man that could have been my grandfather. But before the execution the movie introduces the main character, Ali La Pointe. I don't think he was an actual person, it's probably a composite of lower-level FLN members, the lieutenants that organize sections of the Casbah and do the killings ordered by the leaders. Ali is the hero of the movie. I think he looks like me, he was about my size and build, same hair, except the actor had a more narrow face, and intense, sinister eyes; he was a perfect choice for this movie.

"Ali La Pointe had a long history of convictions for juvenile delinquency. As the movie starts he is chased and arrested while running a gambling operation on the street. He is in jail for that when an FLN leader is dragged through the cell blocks and out to the guillotine block, yelling 'Allah akbar, vive l'Agerie' - 'God is great, long live Algeria'.

"Ali was then was recruited by the FLN. He was ordered to kill, by shooting in the back, a French police officer who comes every afternoon to the cafe of Merabi, who is an informer. Ali meets a girl on the street, fully covered in white except her eyes, carrying a basket. They follow the policeman, Ali takes a gun from her basket and confronts the policeman face-to-face. Ali pulls the trigger several times but the gun is empty; he gives the gun back to the girl and runs away, after pushing the policeman to the ground. Later he asks the FLN leader El-Hadi Jaffar "What was that about?" Jaffar explains in detail that it was a test of his loyalty, which he passed.

"The violence starts in 1956 - French policemen are randomly shot on the street. In the first French bombing in retaliation, on rue Thèbes, the wrong house is destroyed; Ali La Pointe was there, distraught, picking up bodies of women and children from the wreckage.

"The French army sets up checkpoints and fences in the Casbah. Guards at the checkpoints learn not to touch the women, so they are used to carry weapons which they give to the men outside the Casbah. Later the women, their style changed to look French, carry and place bombs - at the Air France lobby, a disco and a luncheonette.

"France sends tough paratroopers commanded by Colonel Mathieu, that's his movie name, I found out later that his real name was Colonel Bigeard, to control the violence, using any means necessary. This is successful, the FLN leaders are captured or killed and the organization is decimated. They rebuild and in 1957 set off a bomb among the spectators at a horse racetrack.

"In one very dramatic scene, Ali is seen driving a French ambulance that he had stolen, very fast, down a main shopping street filled with pedestrians. First we see the body of a doctor, who has been stabbed, thrown from the back of the ambulance. Then a man in the ambulance shoots dozens of people on the sidewalks, creating havoc. In an effort to run down a group of French soldiers, the ambulance crashes into the front of a building.

"At the end of the movie, Ali and three others are found in a hiding place, behind a false tile wall in the bathroom of an apartment at 3 rue des Abderames; all are killed. FLN activities are stopped until December 1960, when there is a general uprising throughout the Casbah, more than the police can handle. Independence came on July 2, 1962.

"So when I watch this movie I think that there is a good chance that my grandfather was the one executed in 1954 and that my father might have been in a group doing violence, until he left for France in 1957. And that has me very upset!"

Piet thought about all of this for a minute, then said "You sure remember a lot of that movie."

Jamel laughed, "I should, I must have watched it fifty times. The tape is almost worn out. Want to watch it sometime?"

"Sure," Piet said. "Whenever it's good for you, my plans are open."

"Why don't you come up to my apartment tomorrow afternoon?" Jamel said. "Just walk up Avenue Jean Rieux and take the second left after Jean-Pierre's boulangerie. It's the street right after the Moroccan consulate. I'm at 33 rue Julien Cassange. You'll see my name, ring the buzzer."

"Okay, I'll be there at about two, that all right?" Piet asked.

"See you then, thanks for the coffee, and for listening to me" Jamel said.

After he left, Piet asked himself "Am I getting into something I shouldn't? Maybe, but it's interesting, and I like this guy a lot, he's intelligent and he does his research. We'll see. Anyway, I'm retired, what else do I have to do?"

Piet showed up at Jamel's apartment right at two o'clock. When he pushed the top button on the panel by the door he heard the buzz of the lock opening. Inside he found a narrow hallway leading back through the building and alongside it a set of steep, narrow stairs. Both were very clean and well-polished, not what Piet expected after seeing the drab gray exterior. He wound his way up the stairs, past six landings, to the top, the *deuxième étage*. There were two apartments, Jamel's at the rear, away from the street. Jamel had the door open.

"Come in, thanks for coming"

As he walked into a surprisingly bright room, Piet looked to his left through a row of tall windows and was shocked to see that he was looking down on a grove of trees and beyond to a large plain of grass.

Jamel said "That's an internal private park, completely surrounded by the buildings on four sides of the block. Most of it belongs to that modern apartment building over there, but all of us can use it, we just walk out our back door. This building has a patio in back that we all share. We can go down there after the movie."

"Good, I'd like to see it, it's certainly a welcome sight here in the city," said Piet. "I don't want to say disparage your neighborhood, but the streets of the Côte Pavée are not like, say, the Allée Verdier with all those beautiful trees."

"No, this side of the canal is a lot different than the old city, I agree. But the rent is a lot less! … Want something to drink?" Jamel asked.

"No thanks, maybe later. Let's see this movie."

Jamel pulled drapes over the windows and beckoned Piet to sit in one of the two identical black-leather IKEA chairs, facing a large flat-screen television and a rack of various electronics and speakers. Jamel took the other chair and started the tape.

"Very dramatic music," Piet said.

"Yes, the whole movie is a bit overly dramatic, but I think you'll see that it's also very realistic" said Jamel. "Let's just watch, we can go outside and talk about it later."

Not a word passed between them through the entire two-hour movie. When the tape finished Piet said "Wow. I see what you mean. What a powerful movie, and it didn't seem like there were any actors, just real people. I can see why it has affected you so, and became so personal. Ali La Pointe is a haunting character."

"Let's go outside," Jamel said. "I'll get a couple of beers. Heineken, right?"

"Right, that's my usual," said Piet.

They went out on the patio of the back of the house, picked up white plastic chairs and sat down under some very large trees; at least they looked large to Piet, in that setting.

"Now I want to tell you the rest of the story, if you still have time," Jamel said.

"I'm in no rush, and I'd like to hear it," replied Piet.

"It's about the death of my father, in 1961, in Paris," said Jamel. "But before I get into that, as I told you yesterday, I think that there is a good chance that my grandfather was the one in the movie who was executed in 1954. After that my father was probably involved in the violence, and tortured for it by the French. The aim of torture was not just to make people talk and get intelligence about possible bombings, but to break the the FLN teams and the civilian population's morale."

"How do you know about this, beyond the movie?" asked Piet.

"You're right," Jamel said, "I grew up as a French boy in Toulouse, knowing nothing about Algeria. But in the past ten years I've been going regularly to the mosque and talking with some of the old men there, who were in Algiers at that time. They remember many of the most well-known activists."

"Where is the mosque, I haven't seen it yet," asked Piet.

"No, you won't see it, because there is no mosque building here in Toulouse. There are dozens of mosques in France, mostly in Paris and the *banlieue* around Paris, and there are some down here in the Midi. But they don't all look like what you would expect, most don't have the traditional domes and minarets. The word mosque doesn't mean a building, it means a place of worship, and that's what we have here, just a meeting room in the Le Mirail district. And, as I told you the other day, I don't worship regularly. I'm mainly interested in finding out more about Algeria."

"Okay, sorry to interrupt," said Piet, "I was thinking of the mosque in Rotterdam, near where I lived. I rode my bicycle by it often, it's very beautiful. I think it is unusual because it has two minarets, one on each side of the dome. Go ahead, tell me what you have learned from these elders."

Jamel went on "I have often spoken with Abdenour Essad, a man now in his eighties, who was there in the Casbah during the revolution. He knew a very young man named Majid who was an active member of the ALN, the *Armée de Libération Nationale*. Majid was the son of Yacef, who was executed by guillotine. These men may have been my father and grandfather, I don't know for sure because they went only by the single name and tried to keep their families unknown.

"Abdenour Essad told me that he knew that Majid had been tortured, more than once. The French used the worst techniques; first, the officer questions the prisoner in the 'traditional' manner, hitting him with fists and kicking him. Then they go to torture: hanging a man from his bound hands, simulated drowning, touching his bare body with electric wires or burning it with cigarettes. Between sessions, the men were locked in cells without food. Some of the cells were too small to lay down. They tortured very young teenagers and others, old men of 75, 80 years or more, and sometimes women as well.

"They even went beyond torture, to what were called 'Death Flights'. They began by throwing people into the sea at the port, then they took to dropping them further out to sea from helicopters. These were known as *crevettes Bigeard* (Bigeard's shrimps).

"My god," Piet interrupted again, "I thought the French were civilized people, I had no idea they did such things."

"There was a lot of controversy about it, both at the time and for years afterward. It was defended by the saying 'Exceptional circumstances call for exceptional measures'. I have learned a lot more about this by reading newspaper and magazine articles at the library, there's one just a little bit further out Avenue Jean Rieux, the *Bilbliothèque Côte Pavée*. I go there often to use their computers to search for information on the internet.

"I found an article in Le Monde from June 2000 about Louisette Ighilahriz, an ALN activist. At the age of twenty she had been captured, in September 1957 during the Battle of Algiers, and raped and tortured for three months. She blamed General Massu, the man in charge of all French forces in Algeria and Colonel Bigeard's commanding officer. Massu was quoted as saying 'When I look back on Algeria, it saddens me... One could have done things differently.' But Bigeard called her statement in Le Monde a 'tissue of lies'.

"Anyway," Jamel said "I think there came a time when Majid decided that he didn't want to become one of the crevettes. So he probably was able to get on a boat to Marseille and then make his way to Paris, with the help of Algerians already living in France. But he stayed committed to freedom for Algeria and he was part of protests, and probably some of the bombings, in Paris.

"The FLN started bombing attacks against the police in Paris during August 1961; from the end of August to the beginning of October, eleven policemen were killed. The bombings did what the FLN expected, they spread fear in the police, but they also made the police hate Algerians even more. Just for looking Algerian, men were arrested at work or in the streets, then beaten or killed in jail.

"In October, during the funeral of a policeman killed by the FLN, the police prefect Maurice Papon said to his men: 'For one hit taken we shall give back ten!' Just like the Nazis! That was an okay to kill Algerians. He told the policemen 'You will be covered, I give you my word on that.' I read that Papon was the same person who had organized the deportation of French Jews for the Nazis in World War II.

"Papon ordered a curfew for Paris and the surroundings, only for Algerians. This was totally racist, and the FLN called for a huge demonstration. On October 17, 1961, 40,000 men and women came out onto the streets; about a quarter of them were arrested and held in sports stadiums and expo halls. Some were shot or beaten to death there and in the courtyard of police headquarters. Men were thrown into the Seine with their hands tied in order to drown them. The Saint Michel bridge over the Seine is right there next to police headquarters; dozens of bodies were later recovered downstream from there.

"I think that my father died there. I'm sure that he would have taken part in the demonstration and, as far as I know, he wasn't seen again after that day. My mother went to Toulouse in late October, just a few days after those events. She went there alone, by train, and told her sister that Majid had not come home and that she knew he must be dead.

"So I grew up without a father. Silvain was very good to me, but I knew that I didn't look like him. I always wondered why, until my aunt told me when I was about twelve that my father was Algerian, like many of the men we see on the streets here. It took me a long time, but now I feel that I am a true Algerian."

"It's hard for me to understand your situation," said Piet, "my childhood was so normal that it was boring, the things that I might tell you were so mundane that I would feel silly telling you about them. But what you have told me is very interesting, they are things that I never would have thought would happen to someone that I know. Now I want to know a lot more about them."

Jamel replied "I can tell you a lot more, or you can read about it at the library. The Algerian war, and the Paris massacre in particular, are still a controversy in France even now." Jamel paused and then concluded, "The torture, the massacre were an official French operation and coverup. I want revenge on official France, and on the Paris police."

Piet didn't know how to reply to that, and suggested "Why don't we take a walk around this very nice backyard that you have here?"

As they walked Piet thought about how he might help Jamel, at least by listening to his stories and his emotions. But he didn't talk about it, instead he looked around at some of the buildings which surround the park.

Piet said, "This is amazing, it's big enough here for a small golf course."

Jamel laughed, "Well not quite, but I have seen men out here hitting practice balls. That big building there is an old people's home and hospital. We might see some of the folks out for a walk, or in a wheelchair. The rest of the buildings are homes or offices or apartments. There are a few places where you could walk in from the street, but all of them have locked gates. So it's really private back here."

Piet asked, "I didn't see your moto out front or in here, do you have someplace to keep it off the street?

"Yes, there's a garage right across the street that is attached to the school building but actually it belongs to the owner of my building, so he lets all of us use it for storage. For me, that means storing my moto off the street, which makes me sleep much better."

As they completed the circuit inside the block, Piet said, "I think I'll go now. I'll give a lot of thought to what you have told me. I'm sure I'll see you at Le Toubkal, or stop by at the port if you want."

"Thanks for listening," Jamel said. "You are the first person I could talk to about this except for my friends at the mosque, it helps to talk to someone who's not muslim."

Piet walked down to his boat and made a quick dinner, then decided to go to the restaurant to see Zakia before she opened for the evening.

It was still an hour before opening so Piet knocked at the locked door. Zakia could see it was Piet and opened the door, happy to see him.

"Sorry to bother you, do you have a few minutes before you open?" asked Piet.

"Piet, you don't get it, I always have time for you," Zakia said as she put both arms around his waist and looked him directly in the face.

"Well, this is not about me, it's about Jamel," Piet replied. "If you have time, let's sit outside at the teahouse."

"Sure, I'll just tell the headwaiter that I'll be away for a while."

They sat on the stools at the tall table two doors from the entrance to Zakia's restaurant. Piet ordered tea for both of them, then began "I've told you that Jamel talked to me about the AZF explosion. Now I have watched his movie, the one that he talks about, La Bataille d'Alger, and he told me about the Paris massacre of Algerians in 1961. Do you know about all of this?"

"Not much," Zakia replied. "I only have known him since he started coming in with the 'moto muslims'. But I have noticed that he doesn't really seem like them, he's quiet and usually doesn't talk as much as the rest of them."

Piet asked, "I guess he doesn't have a girlfriend? He's such a good-looking guy, I wouldn't think he would have any trouble attracting girls."

"You're right," Zakia laughed, "He sure attracted me. But he doesn't seem to show much interest, he looks like his thoughts are elsewhere most of the time."

"I'm worried," Piet said, "because he told me that he wants revenge against France, and especially Paris, for the death of his father. I'm not sure what he has in mind."

"I don't know either," said Zakia, "but it would be good if you could help him. I can see that he likes you and respects you."

"I guess I'll see what I can do. First I'll do some research of my own into what he's been telling me," said Piet. "I'll start on it tomorrow morning."

"Good. Coming in for dinner?"

"No, but I'll meet you at closing, if you want."

"I do! And then I'll take your mind off of Jamel, at least for a while."

Piet and Zakia had coffee on the back deck of Margriet, enjoying the early sun. It had moved far enough north that it was no longer blocked by the huge apartment building straight across from the port. It now rose over the low two-story duplex residence which Piet had often noticed, and thought that it would be a good place to live, especially if you liked looking at boats.

After a while Piet said, "Jamel told me that there is a library not too far up Avenue Jean Rieux, I'm going up there today to see what I can find out."

Zakia said, "Yes, I know that one. If you'll walk me across the passerelle I'll show you a shortcut."

"Okay, I'll get a backpack, with my notebook, and then we can go."

Piet locked the boat and they walked over the bridge, stopping as usual at the top of the arc to look both ways on the canal. "It's starting to get busy with holiday boaters," Piet said, "I'm glad that I got here early enough to get a good space on the dock."

Zakia replied "Yes, but just wait until August, it's a zoo in the port, and in the old city. It's full of French tourists who come down from Paris and the northern regions, along with all of the foreigners who come on rental boats, or their own boat as you did. That's why I get out of town and go to Orta… Why don't you come with me?"

"I thought you went there to be alone," said Piet.
"I do, but that was before I met you. I don't want to go away and be without you."

"Well, let's think about it. It's a few weeks yet," said Piet. "Now show me how to find the library."

"Take that street on the left of my building," said Zakia, pointing, "you'll come to a footbridge over the railroad tracks, cross over and then jog a bit to the left, then just keep going on Rue Raspail. When you get to Avenue Jean Rieux, turn right and the library is about a block further, on the left."

"Thanks, I always like to see new neighborhoods when I can. See you tonight?"

"I'll leave early to go to the restaurant, I'll stop to see you. Bye."
Piet followed her directions; the first blocks from the canal were all apartment buildings, new ones near the port and older buildings near the rail lines. On the east side of the rail lines he found small homes and two-story apartment buildings, some with trees and shrubbery in the front yard. Trumpet vines hanging from balconies and crawling over a garage roof added orange and crimson colors to the pleasant scene. He passed a small park surrounded by oak trees, with a *terrain de pétanque*, according to a sign; at this early hour no old men had yet gathered to pursue their favorite pastime. Piet liked this narrow, simple street, with its greenery and its neighborhood feel.

When he came to Avenue Jean Rieux it was all new to him, beyond where he had turned off to visit Jamel; he thought that he should return that way when he was finished, to pick up some bread at Jean-Pierre's boulangerie, where he was now welcomed as a regular.

Zakia was right, he easily found the library just one block east. The librarian was a little skeptical of this obvious non-Frenchman, but he spoke the language well enough that she trusted him to be able to use their resources. She directed him to a computer and told him how to search the files of Le Monde, including how to print out any articles that he wished (at €0.30 per page, of course.)

He decided to look first at August 1961, that's when Jamel said that the bombings started in Paris. He searched for 'FLN' and 'Algerian muslims' and found numerous mentions. In one article he saw, in addition to his search terms, the letters 'FPA' and a reference to the Christian magazine *Témoignage Chrétien*; he followed that link and read the article. He learned something that Jamel had not told him about, and perhaps didn't know.

Piet made notes from the article:
Auxiliary Police Force (FPA-Force de police auxiliaire) created in Paris 1959.
A special force under the control of the police prefect, Maurice Papon.
Composed entirely of Algerian Muslims, recruited either in Algeria or in France.
By autumn 1960, the FPA had 600 members.
Operated from requisitioned hotels in Paris.
By the summer of 1961, FPA was also active in the suburbs.
Torture is rumored to have been used, along with disappearances.
Quote from article: "It is not possible to stay mute when, in our Paris, men are resurrecting the methods of the Gestapo".

Piet printed the article, thinking that he would ask Jamel if he knew of this use of Algerians against Algerians, yet another provocation.

He continued on through Le Monde for August, finding the first notices of *les attentats* (terrorist attacks) directed at police near the end of the month, as Jamel had said. They continued through September; Piet kept track of the number of police killed and confirmed Jamel's statement of 11 police killed by the end of September, along with 17 injured.

Another article reported that, on 2 October, during the funerals of a policeman killed by the FLN, the police prefect Maurice Papon proclaimed, in the prefecture's courtyard on Île de la Cité: "For one hit taken we shall give back ten! You will be covered, I give you my word on that." This was obviously an encouragement to kill Algerians, Piet thought.

Then he found the most important article, the trigger event: 'On 5 October 1961, police prefect Maurice Papon has ordered a curfew on all Algerians, from 8.30 p.m. to 5.30 a.m., forbidding them to leave their homes in the suburbs.'

Piet found several more articles leading to the demonstration ordered by the FLN for 17 October. The leaders of the FLN called on men, women and children to demonstrate on an illegal, but intended to be peaceful, march across the heart of Paris, along the Grands Boulevards from Place de la République to Place de l'Opéra. 30,000 to 40,000 Algerians, about one-quarter of those living in Paris and its suburbs at the time, turned out but many were blocked at metro and train stations and at the major gateway streets. 4,000 to 5,000 made it as far as Opéra, where they were blocked and driven back by police and the FPA. Shots were fired into the crowds of marchers, killing some; others were arrested.

But that is where the story stopped, as far as published reports are concerned. The police prefecture spoke only of '2 persons shot dead' in the article regarding that day. Piet continued on through the newspapers for that week and for several weeks immediately after, finding no further mention of the events of 17 October.

Piet took the articles that he had printed and showed them to the librarian, asking if she knew of further resources. "Yes," she replied, as she looked through her computer and wrote a book reference: 'La bataille de Paris: 17 octobre 1961', Jean-Luc Einaudi,1991, ISBN 2-02-013547-7. "We have that book, would you like to take it out? Please fill out this form for your library access card."

Piet did so and she handed him his card. Searching the shelves where she had directed him, Piet found the book and checked it out. "329 pages," Piet said to himself, "that will keep me busy for a while, at my rate of reading French. I don't have much else to do, though."

Piet packed his article prints and the book into his backpack, thanked the librarian profusely (might need her help again, he thought) and started to leave, then went back to the computer. He had wondered about the name of Zakia's restaurant, Le Toubkal, so he searched the name on the internet, finding: *Toubkal is a Berber word, it is the name of a mountain peak and national park in southwestern Morocco; it is the highest peak in the Atlas Mountains and in North Africa.* Okay, that's a good choice, he thought, although it doesn't exactly roll off the tongue, in French, Dutch or English.

He had noticed the *Poissonnerie Le Port Des Barques* on his way to the library, when it was closed; now it had opened and displayed a small but excellent offering of fish. He bought a filet of Merlan and asked the fishmonger if he might have Bar on another day: "Oui, le samedi." Piet replied enthusiastically "Merci, je reviendrai samedi"; his plan is to cook a fish dinner for Zakia onboard Margriet, although without an oven he wasn't sure how to do it. "Guess I'll have to fry it," he thought.

Just two doors on he stopped at *La Corbelle - Fruits - Legumes* for salad supplies and various fruits. He hadn't yet found a good source for these items near the port, especially such good quality as he found here. "This isn't very far, I should shop here often," thought Piet. As he walked on down the hill he passed more shops that looked good to him, from a pharmacy to a wine cave. Soon he came to Jamel's street, Rue Julien Cassange, and then to the boulangerie, where he stopped for a baguette. "A very successful day so far," Piet said to himself.

Zakia called to him from the passerelle in the late afternoon; he met her at the gate, taking a carton of Heineken from her hand. "I brought you a little present," she said, "and I've got even more to offer, if you're not busy." Piet took the hint and led her down into the cabin of the boat.

When he turned around she put her lips square on his and kept them there until she felt his reaction against her tummy, and his hands on her buttocks. They undressed each other, starting at the top so that she could press her breasts against his chest. Their clothes dropped to the floor and they went to Piet's bunk for a long and pleasant coupling, a quiet one because of the visiting boats tied up alongside.

After they dressed they sat outside on the boat. Zakia asked "Did you find what you need to know?"

"Well, I learned quite a bit and I printed some interesting articles that I want to talk to Jamel about, but look what else I brought back from the library," said Piet, holding up the Einaudi book. "It's a thick one, it seems to be all about the events that have Jamel so worked up, and also the decades of cover-up afterwards. I've got a lot of reading to do."

"You'd better get started," Zakia said. "I've got to be off to open the restaurant."

"I'll come by at closing time, to walk you home," Piet said.

"Good, see you then."

Piet thumbed through the book to see what it covers; looking at the dates, he could tell right away that there was a period of thirty years when the events had entered a "black hole" of memory. It will be interesting to find out why and how this was kept quiet for so long, he thought.

Le Toubkal was having a busy night when Piet arrived, so he waited outside, at the traffic island on Place Perchepinte, watching the pedestrians and the traffic pass by. He was always amazed at the number of cars and scooters that came through here, these streets are byways, not a direct route to anywhere else. But he didn't have to wait long, as Zakia came out, and locked the door behind her, almost directly behind the last group of customers.

"Whew, busy night," said Zakia. "Let's go have a drink."

"Sure," Piet replied. "At La Coupole?" He didn't need an answer, she had already started in that direction, and he had started to lag behind. "Wait, I'm coming."

"Sorry, I'm still in work mode. I'll relax when I'm sitting on the bar stool," Zakia said over her shoulder.

The atmosphere at La Coupole was calm and quiet, that's why she likes it there. It's not a place for night life, it's a place to sit at a classic, curved wooden bar, slowly enjoying a drink. Rows of glasses are suspended over the bar; soft yellow light glows through the glasses and from under the bar, at knee level. The stools are padded and have a tall back, a comfortable seat in which to linger. Their lovemaking is now mature, no need for urgency; they both know what will be waiting for them a little later.

"Did you read the book today?" Zakia asked.

Piet laughed… "A bit of it, it's slow going. Not just because it's in French, it's also very dense writing, with lots of references that I don't understand. But I've read enough so far, skipping through it, to know that it's an indictment of Maurice Papon. Do you know the history of what he did in Bordeaux during the Second World War?"

"Not much of it," Zakia said, "but I do remember that there was a trial in the late 90s. He was convicted but fled to Switzerland. He was found there, in a hotel, and brought back to serve his sentence here in France; but he was released a few years later for health reasons. I guess he's dead by now."

"Probably," said Piet "but it doesn't matter now. The damage was done in 1961, and for the thirty years afterward when it was covered up…"

"What about you," Piet asked. "How was it today at the restaurant?"

"We had a full house. That's good, I am always happy when we are busy just before we close for the August holiday. The money helps carry the restaurant through the closed weeks, and it gives me some money for my vacation. I also give a bonus to my staff on the day that we close. By the way, on the last day we refuse all reservations except from the regular families that come every week. We serve them a grand feast, *couscous royale*. Want to come?"

"Sure," said Piet. "I've grown to like your couscous dinners a lot."

"Well you'll like this dinner," said Zakia, "It's got everything - spicy lamb meatballs, lamb chops, chicken kebabs, merguez sausage, all set around couscous covered with a saffron chickpea stew. We serve it in the afternoon, under a tent in the garden at the rear of the restaurant, with music and a belly dancer. It's always quite an event!"

"I won't miss it," Piet said. "And do you leave the next day for Lago d'Orta?"

"Well," replied Zakia, "I'm not sure I want to go there this year, I would miss you. Maybe I'll just stay at home."

"Oh, you shouldn't do that." Said Piet. "You need to get away, all year you're back and forth in the apartment to restaurant neighborhood. Why don't you come with me, on the boat? Sylvianne, the capitaine at the port, is making suggestions that she would like to be able to rent my mooring to short-term visitors during August. She told me I could move to the bank of the canal south of the city, where I can tie up for free. Of course, there are no electric and water services there, but I can go for a few days without them, on the battery and the onboard water tank. We can go for walks along the canal. I can read the book during some lazy days, and I'll take my bicycle so I can go out for food."

"That's a good idea, the port is a real circus in August. I don't think you would like to be among all those holiday boaters who don't know much about what they're doing, and just want to have a good time," Zakia replied. "I will come and stay on the boat, that will be fun. So that's decided, I'll be looking forward to it, just two weeks away! Anyway, I already canceled my reservation at Orta."

"You're a clever one," said Piet, "but now I have to tell you that I am going back to the Pyrénées on my bike for a couple of days. When I was at the library I saw the newspaper *L'Équipe* with a photo on the cover of the Tour de France. I have been so busy getting to know you, and now Jamel, that I forgot about the Tour, it's happening right now. And I am near several of the daily stages, I can easily go see it. I looked up the details of the route and the time schedule online, on the computer at the library, and I was surprised that I have already ridden on part of the route that they will be using the day after tomorrow."

"Wait, you're going away from me tomorrow?"

"No, the day after, and the day after that. I'll be back on Friday," Piet said. "I'm leaving very early Wednesday morning, I made a reservation for two nights at *Ostau Dera Nheu*, the place just over the Spanish border where I stayed before, I like it there. The teams are starting from Carcassonne on Wednesday and will pass right by that hotel, but they start at two in the afternoon, if I leave early I can be there to watch them."

"Well, you sound pretty excited about this already," Zakia said.

"I am," Piet replied, "when I rode out there before I stopped to rest at the town of Aspet; they will pass by the southern end of that town and then up a climb that I just did myself. I didn't know that when I rode from Aspet out to Cazaunous and then turned to climb a ridge, I was right on the route that is part of the stage. In fact I am proud, when I climbed to the top of the Col des Ares it was a Category 3 pass. I read that the climb is only 6 km long, at about 5 percent angle, and the elevation at the top is only 800 meters. Fairly easy. Still, it's an official climb, and I did it."

"And then," Piet continued somewhat breathlessly, "last month when I rode out from the hotel to start back to Toulouse, I rode a much tougher climb, the Col de Portillon. That one is 8 km long, 7 percent, 1300 meters high, a Category 1 climb!"

"I've heard them talk about the categories but I never paid much attention," Zakia said. "I guess a Category 1 is very tough?"

"Well, it is," Piet replied, "but not the toughest. And I did it first thing in the morning, I had just a few kilometers to get warmed up but not tired. The climbs are rated from Category 4, the easiest, through 3, 2, 1 to HC, *Hors Categorie*, The organizers take into account the distance, the steepness, elevation at the top and some other characteristics. People complain about some of the ratings but overall they seem to get it right. The system is good for the fans as well as the cyclists, you can look at the map for a stage and see what kind of day it will be, and where you might like to watch.

"When I ride there on Wednesday I will stop at the hotel to check in, then I will ride up the slope of the Col de Portillon and find a good viewing spot. The expected arrival of the peleton is at about 5PM, so I should have enough time to get up there before the road is closed, if not I'll watch as they pass through the town of Bossost. Then I'll go back to the hotel for dinner. Early the next morning I will ride over to Bagnères de Luchon and up the back side of the Port de Balès, an HC climb. But I will be on the descent side, that's a 21 km ride down into Luchon. The riders will be doing as much as 100 km per hour and the peleton will stretched out across that whole distance. I've never seen cyclists go that fast, it only happens down a long grade; we don't have anything like that in Holland, to say the least!"

"Then I guess you will have to ride back to your hotel?" asked Zakia.

"Yes, I will mingle with the riders in Luchon as they get packed up to leave for their hotel, I think it's in Pau. Then I have enough daylight left to ride back up the Col de Portillon to the hotel, it's about 20 km, even though I'll get tired I can make it in two hours, still plenty of daylight. Then I'll ride home on Friday morning."

"I'm glad to hear you call this 'home'," said Zakia.

""Yes, it is my home now, isn't it? It's comfortable here, and I am so glad to have found you."

"It's a good thing you said that last part," teased Zakia. "I guess I can let you go away for a couple of days, as long as you come back to me."

Piet spent the next days just as he had planned, first watching the riders' faces as they passed by slowly and close, pedaling up the slope of the Col de Portillon, then the next day he found a good viewing spot on the descent from the Port de Balès. He knew that they would pass him in a flash, so he looked for a place where he could look down hundreds of feet down on a series of S-shaped switchback loops. Watching a line of nearly two hundred cyclists arc through those loops was something he had never seen before, and he loved it.

He moved Margriet a few days later, eight kilometers south on the Canal du Midi to beyond the port of Ramonville-St Agne. A line of live-aboard motorboats and converted commercial barges stretched from the port entrance for another kilometer along the west bank of the canal. Piet motored to the end of that line and tied temporarily to a tree. He walked back to the last barge, painted a handsome, weathered French blue but flying the Dutch flag; he hailed the man repainting the wooden wheelhouse: "Hallo, okay to moor here?", pointing to his own boat.

"Hallo, yes, are you Dutch? Come aboard."

Piet climbed the steeply-angled steel gangplank and was greeted by a strong handshake from a tall, broad man, his head covered in white hair and beard, his clothes covered in blue paint.

"I am Piet Roefs, from Schiedam. I have recently traveled here after buying my boat in Groningen."

"Henk Vos, I'm from Groningen. I recognized your boat, it was owned by my friend Ben Baartman. I have seen another Waddenzee sleepboot here in the Midi, but Ben's green and white paint scheme looked familiar. Yes, you can certainly moor there where you are tied, just drive stakes and don't tie to the trees. How long will you stay?"

"Probably about a month," Piet said. "I have been moored at Port St Saveur but Sylvianne wanted to use my space for short-term visitors."

"Ah yes, I know her, she is very friendly and helpful but also very much in charge. This is a good place to leave your boat unattended, I am usually here and I will keep an eye on it."

"I will appreciate that, thank you, but I think I will be here most of the time." Piet said. "By the way, were you a commercial bargee in Groningen?"

Henk laughed, "No, I guess I look like I could have been, but I owned an insurance company. I made enough money to retire comfortably, but instead of a villa in Provence I decided to settle here. I bought this barge in Groningen when it was to be scrapped and had it renovated by a shipyard in Franeker. My wife Liliane is here with me, she has driven into Toulouse for shopping right now. That's how I keep her happy, there are some very elegant shops in the center of Toulouse. Without them, she wouldn't be here. Every month or so we fly from Toulouse to other cities where she can show off her fancy clothes and chic handbags. What about you?"

"I live alone on my little boat," Piet replied. "I've retired after thirty years on the Rotterdam Seaport Police and I'm creating a new life. I've only been here a few weeks but I have made some close friends already and I intend to stay here for some time. In fact I'm sure you will see my lady friend visit me here on the boat."

"Good, maybe you'll want to stay moored here. It's free, but there is no water or electric service; I have water delivered by truck and I run a generator when it's needed. Wastewater is taken away by another truck. For you, you could easily motor to the port at Ramonville to get water, and charge your batteries at the same time. And there is a wastewater pumpout station there now."

"I'll keep that idea in mind. I do like being located right in the center of things at Port St Saveur, but free is nice also," Piet said. "I'll go tie up properly and then ride back into the city on my bicycle; I'll be staying at my friend's apartment until next Sunday. I'll look forward to seeing you then."

Before he had departed from Port St Saveur he had moved some of his clothes and toiletries to Zakia's apartment; after he secured the boat he rode back there on his bike. She was at work but he had his own key. He brought his bike up in the elevator, there was space enough to store it in the apartment's entry foyer. In Schiedam he would have left it outside but he wasn't comfortable doing that here in France. Actually, he realized that it wasn't so safe in Holland now either, bikes are frequently stolen or stripped of parts.

He had picked up a sandwich from *La Pause Gourmande*, a tiny *sandwicherie-restauration rapide* shop located next to his favorite boulangerie. They used Jean-Pierre's baguettes and had sources for excellent hams, sausages and cheeses. He took his sandwich and a beer out to the balcony, where he turned one of the chairs for a good view of activities at the port. He thought "I'm having a great lunch, in a great place, with a very special woman coming back later. How could I do any better?"

The closing dinner at Le Toubkal started at 4PM. Right on time, families arrived and trooped through to the back of the restaurant, occupying long tables in the small rear patio. The serving began immediately, on oval silver platters brought to the tables by Zakia and the headwaiter. First the golden mounds of buttery grains, the couscous. Then platters of tender carrots, turnips, zucchini and celery. Chickpeas and white beans in saffron-scented broth came in low, wide bowls. Plates of fiery red pepper *harissa* and caramelized onions mixed with plump golden raisins were scattered along the table, enough for everyone to reach. Silver warming dishes awaited the meats - stewed chicken and lamb, cigar-like merguez sausages, chicken nuggets on wooden skewers, grilled baby lamb chops and spicy beef meatballs. These were brought out with great fanfare, on immense platters, to much cheering. Bottles of wine were ordered by some groups, sparkling mineral water by others, but there seemed to be no difference in the excitement and joviality of the revelers.

Piet was uncomfortable at first; a lone man and a foreigner at that, he sat quietly at a table in the back. But, as Zakia had promised, the "moto muslims" arrived as a group, just back from a ride in the countryside. They joined Piet and treated him as a guest at their table. Jamel especially was glad to see him and made a point of taking the seat directly across.

The music and dancing began, on a tiny stage, as the empty platters and bowls were removed. An elderly man, with white hair and a face like worn leather boots, sat at an electronic keyboard and a lone woman with *zills* (castanets) in each hand stood front and center on the stage. Those seated with their backs to the stage turned their chairs; those at the ends of the tables crowded in; all became quiet as the first notes came from the keyboard speakers and the first pose of a beautiful woman drew all eyes. Folds of a bright blue skirt hung from a silver belt low on her hips; silver beads on dozens of blue strings flew from the belt. Her breasts were covered by the same bright blue cloth, with even more silver sequins. But the focus, as intended, was on her belly and on her right leg, which appeared frequently from a full-length slit in the skirt. The fluid movements of her abdomen, hips and leg were mesmerizing.

Piet wondered, how does a woman generate silence among a crowd of rowdy people? How does she do it without moving her feet? How does she attract the attention, the gaze, the energy toward her with each note and each movement? How does she hypnotize the place, attract everyone to her dance, wrap us up slowly giving us the movement and the music in digestible doses, creating tension until we burst into applause, all hypnotized by the magic?

After the performance most of the families left, but those at Piet's table were in no hurry. All had asked for espresso, which they nursed slowly. Jamel took this opportunity to ask Piet "Have you had a chance to look into the things that I told you about?"

"Yes," Piet replied, "I'm reading a book about the Paris massacre of Algerians and the long coverup. But it's slow going, for me to translate it from French. Zakia and I are going on holiday, I'll take it with me and read it there."

"Good," said Jamel, "I'm hoping that you will be able to give me some advice about what I can do to find out if my father really was killed in 1961."

"I'll try," said Piet. "It's all very interesting to me. I had no idea that such things could happen, in a country like France, as recently as this. And that a conspiracy to cover it up lasted until the end of the century. I promise you that I'll do what I can to help you."

"That's all I ask," said Jamel. "I trust you, and I need the help of an intelligent outsider to look at the history clearly, without the emotion that always comes up in me."

"Well, we're leaving tomorrow, so I'll be getting into it pretty soon," Piet said. "We can get together when I get back and see what the two of us can do."

"Great, I'll be waiting for you," said Jamel, as his group started to leave, to let the restaurant staff clean up and close.

Zakia sent Piet away, to her apartment, so that she could supervise the closing. Piet walked there and quickly fell asleep alone, satisfied with both food and companionship. He didn't hear Zakia come in but was very pleased to find her beside him when he woke up. "Ready for holiday?" he asked.

"I sure am," Zakia replied. "I do enjoy the restaurant, but I need my month off now. I'm glad you're here, we'll have plenty of time together."

"There's no hurry," said Piet, "but when we're ready you can take a taxi to the boat, with your bags and whatever food is here in the *frigo*. I'll ride my bike; I think we'll get there at just about the same time."

"Don't forget it's Sunday," Zakia replied, "there will many people on promenade along the canal. Don't run into anybody!"

"Don't worry," Piet laughed, "I can handle it. I'll draw a map for the taxi, and if you get there first you know my boat, just wait a few minutes."

"Okay, but first let's make good use of this nice big bed. I do know your boat, the bed isn't very wide, one of us has to be on top."

"On the boat we can fold out the dinette bunk and have plenty of room, side by side. But you're right, it's a lot more comfortable here. No rush, let's get cozy."

They soon adopted a holiday routine: lazy mornings with coffee on the boat, a few hours of reading, an occasional retreat back into the cabin for sex. In late afternoon they walked the chemin de halage.

While Zakia spent a large part of her day on a blanket that she stretched out on the grass bank of the canal, reading mystery novels, Piet sat at the stern of his boat and read more of the book about the Paris massacre, getting more interested and disturbed as he read. They spent quiet nights in the cabin of the boat, looking out from the bed through the open cabin door. The moon was high so they couldn't see it directly, but they could see the moonlight filter through the line of plane trees along the canal. This was the most romantic, rather than lustful, time that they had enjoyed so far.

Henk and Liliane visited aboard Margriet occasionally, as did Piet and Zakia go to the barge for dinner on some evenings. Zakia, on her first tour of the barge, was stunned at the interior space and the modern design of the rooms and furnishings. She said "I have seen many barges like this go past my apartment on the canal and I knew that many liveaboard barges are moored between here and Port St Saveur, but I had no idea that they could be so spacious and so beautiful! This must be more than twice as big inside as my little apartment."

"Yes, it's amazing what you can do if you spend enough money, isn't it?" laughed Henk. "As I told Piet, this is our villa in the south of France."

"Piet, why don't you provide me with a wonderful boat like this, instead of that tiny little stinkpot," Zakia scolded, with a smile.

"You seem to like it when we're tightly snuggled into our bunk," Piet replied, with a hurt look.

"I do, I'm just kidding," Zakia laughed. "And I'm glad that Margriet has its own character. But you haven't taken me anywhere in it yet. For goodness sake, I even had to come here by taxi!"

"That's a good idea, we'll go for a short cruise on the Midi," Piet replied. "But the crowds of August will make it slow going at the locks, we'll have to be patient. We won't have a destination, just go until we get tired of it then come back here. Maybe we'll go up to the summit and stay there a few days, it's a nice spot and we can get there in two or three days. I did it in a day and a half when I came here, but the canal wasn't busy then. And an Australian guy moored at Port St Saveur told me there is a nice bike path along the *rigole*, the stream that feeds the canal, it twists like a snake down from the Black Mountains. He told that I can ride about 50 kilometers, up to St Ferréol. A 100 km ride will be great."

"And what will I do while you're off on the bike? Read a book, I guess." Zakia said. "Okay, let's go the day after tomorrow. Liliane, can I borrow your car tomorrow to go for provisions?"

"Sure," Liliane replied, "I'll go along if you don't mind. I haven't made any friends in this neighborhood, if that's what you can call it out here in the fields. I could use some female companionship. There's an Intermarché not far away, but first let me take you to lunch at *Les Marins d'Eau Douce*, it's my favorite bistro, they serve terrific seafood. It's just across the canal and up a bit, but we'll have to drive a little further to get around there by car. Sometimes Henk takes me there in the dinghy."

"That sounds great," Zakia replied. "I've heard of it but I've never been there. Without a car, I tend to go to the places that I can walk to in Toulouse. There's no shortage of good restaurants."

"Like yours, I understand," Liliane replied, "I want to have your couscous when you reopen."

"Yes, you'll be my guests," Zakia said. "We'll have couscous royale."

Piet and Zakia got an early start on their cruise and easily made it through seven locks on the first day, mooring just above the last lock, in the tiny village of Negra. On the second day they had some delays at another seven locks but still reached the summit, the *Seuil de Naurouze*, the watershed between the Atlantic Ocean and the Mediterranean Sea.

Zakia was thrilled to be aboard in the oval locks, and to cross over another stream on a canal bridge. The novice holiday travelers in rental boats provided the entertainment; Piet calmly gave them lots of space and time as they jockeyed their new toy in the locks or when they attempted to dock. Zakia stifled a laugh once when a boat ahead slid along the lock wall until it left the lock, then turned sharply to the right and drove into the canal bank. No harm done, except for an embarrassed teenage girl at the wheel.

They had arrived late in the day at the summit mooring, but still with enough daylight for a walk around the park at Naurouze. Zakia found it very pleasant and said to Piet "This is a very special place. I won't mind just relaxing here while you go for your bike ride. In fact I am ready to be alone, as I always have been."

"I'm looking forward to that ride," said Piet, "and I'm glad you want to be alone, but don't worry, I'll be back for our time together at sunset."

Zakia was ready for their late-afternoon routine of Campari or wine. She had walked a few hundred meters east to the restaurant *Le Pas de Naurouze* and brought back two *Paëlla à emporter* - take-out paella. Her timing was good, Piet arrived just a few minutes after she got back to the boat. They both claimed to be happy alone, but they each realized that they were happier when together.

"I had a great day," Zakia said. "I even enjoyed seeing the Riquet Obelisk and reading the plaques about Pierre-Paul Riquet. I've seen references to him around Toulouse but never paid much attention. Now I know that he was responsible for building the Canal du Midi!"

"I'm glad he did," said Piet, "it got me to Toulouse where I found you!"

They started back to Toulouse on the morning of the second day, arriving at their mooring to be greeted by Henk and Liliane with an invitation for drinks and dinner on their barge. Piet thought to himself, "My God, what a stupid, miserable life I had in Schiedam. This is the life that I want."

All holidays must come to an end; after three weeks at the boat they went back into Toulouse by taxi. It had been decided by Zakia that Piet would move in with her, at least while Margriet was moored outside the city. At the apartment Piet stood on the balcony for a few minutes, looking down on the full house moored at Port St Saveur, happy that he wasn't in the midst of holiday revelers on their strangely-styled fiberglass rental boats, but at the same time wondering if the plans of Jamel to get revenge would be be a good idea - what am I getting myself into, he thought, yet again.

Piet and Zakia had arrived at the apartment near midnight. They slept late and, in mid-morning, Zakia went to check on the restaurant while Piet walked up the avenue to Jean-Pierre's boulangerie for a fresh supply of breads.

As he walked he saw Jamel on his motorcycle, headed downhill, and waved to him. Jamel braked to a stop, parked and came over quickly. "Bonjour Piet, I'm so glad to see you, I've missed you these weeks. I need to talk to you about my plans. Have you read the book? I've quit my job, I want to go to Paris to find out what happened to my father. Will you help me?"

"Bonjour Jamel," Piet said, "Wait a minute, slow down a little. I have read the book, I see that terrible things were done, and there has been no real justice. I will do what I can to help you. I'm going to bike down to my boat tomorrow, why don't you come there in the morning and we can talk privately."

"Good, I will. But I haven't seen your boat at the port, where is it?"

Piet gave him directions: "It's tied up on the west bank of the Canal du Midi, south of the city. Do you know the Route de Narbonne?... Follow it south and, when you pass the National Agricultural College on your left, at the next roundabout go east on Avenue de l'Agrobiopole. Stay on the paved road to the canal, then turn right on the towpath. There's a long line of barges and boats tied up, you'll see my boat, just a few hundred meters on."

"Okay, I can find it. I've ridden on the Route de Narbonne many times, I know where the college is. I'll be there at about nine."

"Bring me a baguette," Piet said, "I'll make us a pot of coffee."

A few minutes before nine Piet heard the muted rumble of Jamel's Yamaha, then he saw the cat's-head nose fairing of the motorcycle coming slowly down the dirt towpath that follows the canal. Here among the brush on the canal bank, moving slowly and cautiously, the motorcycle looked entirely different than it did on the city streets. The machinery couldn't be seen, just the narrow, slanted headlights, set at a sharp angle in the short nose fairing, resembling a cat on the prowl for field mice, albeit a cat with electric-blue fur.

The look in Jamel's eyes as he removed his helmet startled Piet for a moment, it was the same ready-to-pounce face that Piet had just seen on the moto. Jamel had said that he was ready to take action, and Piet knew that it would be serious.

Jamel made the long step from the bank to the gunwale. "Bonjour Jamel," Piet said, "You didn't forget the baguette, thanks."

"Did you have a good holiday?" Jamel asked, not waiting for a response. "Sorry to be impatient, but have you thought about the things that I told you?"

"I did as I promised," Piet said as he poured coffee, "I spent a lot of time on my holiday reading 'La bataille de Paris', I had to skip over some parts and asked Zakia for help on some of the words, but I got through it."

"And did it make you as angry as it did me?" Jamel asked.

"No, not as angry as you. I'm Dutch, not Algerian, I can't feel the same personal involvement. But we Dutch do worry about injustice and mistreatment of others, we have always tried to help out around the world. Probably we have some national guilt about exploitation when we were the world's biggest traders and colonizers."

"It's very personal for me," Jamel said, "I'm sure that the reason that I never knew my father is because he was drowned in the Seine, or maybe beaten to death and then thrown in. I need to find someone who can tell me about it. I'm sure there must still be someone in Paris who knew my father. He would be 73 now, if he were alive, so there's a good chance that men who knew him are still there in Paris. I want to go there and find them."

"Well, I agree with that, I had thought the same thing, that there are still some old men around who will remember," Piet said. "I don't have any commitments now, except Zakia, and maybe we should back off for a while. We had a great few weeks together, but I don't want to get tied up in a relationship too early in my new life, at least until I figure out what that life is going to be.

"So here's my suggestion, I thought it over while putting along the canal," Piet continued, "Let's go north in my boat, you and me, to Paris. We can live aboard and see what we can find, in the bars and cafes where old Algerian men can be found. From the research that I have done in the library and online, I think that the place to start is on the northeastern fringe of Paris, the 19th arrondissement and the suburbs just outside the city. I've looked into the ports available in Paris, there is one that is ideal, Bassin de la Villette. It is right in the middle of the area that we want, and it has good access to the metro when we want to go to the scene of the murders, on the Seine."

"Great," said Jamel "that sounds good to me. Do you think we could bring my moto on the boat?"

"No, it's too big, it would take up too much space in the cockpit. And it would be too attractive to thieves, I'd be worried about it every night and whenever we weren't on the boat," said Piet. "Anyway, we'll either be traveling or moored in the city, where we will use public transportation. I will bring my bicycle but I'll dismantle it and store it inside."

"You're right, it will be best to leave it locked away at my apartment. I'll just bring some clothes and a sleeping bag, anything else you need?"

"Not that I can think of right now. Want to leave tomorrow morning? You can sleep onboard tonight and we'll get an early start. There will probably be some boats leaving from Port St Saveur tomorrow morning, I'd like to get to the Castanets lock early and be first in line. And hope to stay that way, through as many locks as we can do in a day."

"Okay," said Jamel. "I'll go to the mosque this afternoon and tell them that I will be away for a while. I can get a moto friend to bring me down here tonight."

"Good," said Piet, "I'll go back and see Zakia, she should be back in the apartment this afternoon. She'll probably be upset, but she'll be busy reopening the restaurant and will get over it... I hope."

Piet checked over the boat for a long trip and, as his mooring neighbor Henk had suggested, motored one kilometer north on the canal to the port at Ramonville. There he filled the diesel fuel tank and pumped out the wastewater tank. He found a service mechanic and, with a bit of cajoling, convinced him of the urgent need to replace the engine oil and filter right away. All of that was completed and he returned to his mooring in just over three hours.

He hadn't seen any activity on Henk's barge as he passed by, but now he went partway up the gangplank and called out "Hallo Henk". With no response, he wrote a note on the pad in a box alongside the mailbox, telling Henk of his change of plans, and that he hoped to return in a few months.

Piet got his bike ready for the ride back to the apartment, but then he sat down on the grass bank of the canal for a few minutes. He hadn't paid much attention to the farm just across from his mooring, now he looked at it more carefully. Two low stone houses with red tile roofs, one with a swimming pool, and two small barns. A family complex, he thought, right on the water but with open fields on the other three sides. He couldn't see what crops were planted, but not a vineyard; some type of vegetables. In these days, though, maybe the fields are used by others and the people that live there commute into the city for work, only a fifteen minute drive. They have a handsome small wooden rowboat tied near a very old stone ramp into the canal, he had seen a young couple rowing it once before his holiday trip. What a great place this would be to live - quite a difference from the row-house apartment in Schiedam, which only now came into his mind. He hadn't thought about that "home" for a very long time, and he didn't think about it for long now. What he did think about was how nice it would be to have a small farm on the canal, with Margriet moored in front.

He rode his bike slowly into Toulouse. He passed three more of those small farms surrounded by fields, then the apartment blocks at Ramonville signaled the beginning of the metropolis. But the tree-lined towpath along the canal provided an avenue for bikers and walkers, a semi-private, semi-secluded path that leads right into the heart of the city. Only a few streets cross the canal path, most of them on the classic stone-arch bridges of southwestern France.

The pristine corridor is broken for a moment at the canal bridge over the wide lanes of the péripherique highway. Boats on the canal, as well as bikers and walkers, have their own viaduct over the rush of traffic below. Then the rows of trees resume, the platanes set with regular spacing one after the other, long rows of identical trees, a *parc linéaire*.

"I like this city, and this part of the country," he thought as he rode, "what a beautiful city. The markets are fantastic and the open-air cafes are to die for. Even the bars, they have such a pleasant feeling. There's no need for me to think of going back to Rotterdam. I am interested in seeing Paris, though, and we'll probably see quite a bit of it. But I do want to come back here, and moor my boat along this wonderful waterway, either out in the farmlands or maybe I can find a space among the hundreds of barges and boats moored permanently along the canal here in the city."

Even though he was glad to see her, he was startled out of these thoughts by the sight of Zakia, standing on the footbridge at the port, waving to him as he rode up. "She is a beauty," he thought, "I have been so lucky to be with her for these past weeks. Do I really want to leave her?"

"Bonjour Piet," said Zakia "I'm on my way back from the restaurant, I wondered if I would see you coming, and I did!"

"Let's sit by the canal," Piet said, "I don't want to go inside yet, it's too nice a day."

They found a bench available and sat to watch the passing boats, bikers and walkers. They were silent for many minutes, then Zakia asked "Did Jamel come to see you?"

"Yes," Piet replied, "and we made a plan. The two of us will take my boat and we will go to Paris, where I will help him try to find someone who knew his father and can tell him about the events of 1961."

"No," Zakia exclaimed. "I don't want you to go, I want you to be here with me!"

"I will be here with you" Piet said. "I have just now decided for sure, while riding along the canal, that this is where I want to be. I'll be back here as soon as I can. But I want to help Jamel, and I have become involved in this story, I want to find out more, maybe I can help publicize the wrongs that were done. Besides, I have always wanted to see Paris."

"Yes, okay, but see Paris with me," Zakia responded with emotion.

"You have a restaurant to run, maybe you can take a few days off and fly up when we are there," Piet suggested. "We've just had three very nice weeks together and alone. Now I have something I must do, but I'll be back."

Zakia was silent as she thought about this; she realized that she probably couldn't change Piet's mind. "I've had a good life here alone, before Piet, I can live without him for a while. But not forever", she thought. "Okay, but promise me that you will be back," she said to Piet.

"I will, I promise. And I already bought a new mobile yesterday, at the Orange store on Place Esquirol, so that we won't be out of touch."

"When are you leaving?" she asked. Piet replied, "I'm going to the boat tonight, we'll leave early tomorrow morning"

"Well, we don't have much time then, do we? Let's get right upstairs, where it's more private. I want to make sure that you'll remember me!"

Part III

Paris

It was almost dark when Piet set off from the apartment on his bicycle, but good enough to see the smoothly-paved path. On his back was a backpack with just minimal clothing and toiletries; he had left most of his things with Zakia, especially the wooden cigar box with his important papers: diplomas from high school and university, Seaport Police commendations, copies of his parents' wills, old photos. It made both Zakia and Piet himself feel better that his home base was now in Toulouse.

Jamel was there at the boat, waiting. He had been dropped off by a friend, like Piet carrying his things in a backpack for the brief motorcycle ride. Except that Jamel also had a shoebox, carefully taped along all sides. As they opened the cabin and went below Piet asked "What's in the box, your dress shoes?"

"No," Jamel laughed, "the ones that I'm wearing are all I have, except for my heavy motorcycle boots, and I left them behind. The box has my research on 1961. We can look at it when we get to Paris."

"Okay," said Piet, pointing, "you can store it under the right-side bench, that's where you'll sleep. Your backpack should fit there too. During the day you can put your sleeping bag in the forward cabin, on the small berth. I saw that you keep your apartment neat and tidy, I'm sure we'll get along. On a boat this small, you have to stay neat and put things away or else it gets pretty confusing."

"Yes, we will get along. I might be French-Algerian but I'm as neat as a Dutchman! I'm a pretty good cook, for routine meals, so if you want I'll take charge of the kitchen while you run the boat."

"That'll be good," said Piet, "but I'm going to show you how to run the boat too, so that we can keep going but I can still rest once in a while. There's no navigation that you need to learn, just steer the boat so that it doesn't run into the bank on either side, or other boats. You'll pick that up in the first ten minutes. On the big rivers, like the Rhone, you have to learn how to stay out of the way of the commercial barges, and particularly the big passenger boats, they go fast and think that they own the river. We're in a small and slow boat, so we'll have to be the one to stay out of the way."

"I think you drink Calvados," said Jamel. "I brought a bottle. Let's have a drink now for good luck."

"Bon, let's do that and then get to sleep. I'll wake up with the daylight and we'll be away."

Piet was the first one up, and immediately started the engine, but Jamel was ready also, looking for the coffee and getting water heating on the small gas stove. Within a few minutes they had pulled the stakes from the canal bank and were underway. So far as Piet could tell no other boats, from the two ports behind them, had passed this morning.

The first lock, Castanet, was less than three kilometers east from the mooring. They arrived within twenty minutes and, as Piet had hoped, were the only boat there. The downstream lock gates were open so Piet motored slowly into the lock chamber and steered to the right-side wall. They sat in the cockpit as Piet explained the locking:

"This is an uphill lock, and a very deep one, five meters rise. This kind gave me some trouble when I was alone, it will be good to have you helping. After we go over the summit the downhill locks will be much easier. What I want you to do is to take that line from the bow and hold it in your left hand, in loops. You see the pocket here in the lock wall, with a post inside - pass the line around the post and then take the loose end around that cleat at the stern. Pull on the line until the boat is firmly against the lock wall, you can use the line to pull either the bow or the stern, get them both against the wall. When the water starts to rise it will be turbulent, so take in the line as we rise and keep the boat straight against the wall. I'll tell you when to move the line, when we get high enough you can pass it around a bollard on top of the wall."

Now they had time to wait and drink coffee, before the lock went into service at 9AM. Piet was surprised when Jamel produced croissants, he had picked them up on his way to the boat the night before. Soon two holiday boats arrived, rented from Le Boat, Piet thought. They came in too fast; the first 'skipper' reversed the propellor and gave too much throttle but managed to stop before hitting the wall with the bow of the boat. One of the crew was able to grab the rung of the ladder built into the lock wall and pull the boat against the left-side wall. The second boat performed the same show, lightly hitting the stern of the first boat with their bow; no damage done, the rental boats are made to take this sort of abuse. "Not very elegant, but they got it done," Piet said quietly to Jamel. Jamel smiled, he had obviously learned the first lesson of locking - go in steadily but slowly, and move quickly but smoothly to secure a line.

Piet explained the next step: "There is a *borne* set back a few feet on the north wall, a post with colored buttons which operate the lock. The green button starts the cycle. I see that guy from the first boat is already up there, probably pushing the button. I expect that there will be a voice from a speaker in the post telling him to be patient, wait until 9AM. I don't like to climb the ladder like he did, the rungs are very slippery. At some places I might put you off onto the bank before we go into the lock, you can walk up to the top of the lock and I'll throw you the line. That's a lot safer, it's what they should have done, there was a good place to stop on the north bank right back there."

Right on time the lock began to operate; first the downstream gates swung slowly closed behind them, then valves opened to let water in at the upstream end. The flow started with an initial surge and soon became turbulent. Jamel did his job well, holding the boat straight against the curved wall of the lock. Not so the other two boats, both of them held their bow tight to the wall but allowed the stern to drift out. Piet had expected that and was ready with a pole to fend off if necessary. It wasn't, some scurrying around by the crew got things back under control.

"Margriet fits these locks well," said Piet to Jamel. "The locks on the Midi are the only ones that I have been through that are made this way, with curved stone walls; I think that it was done that way, centuries ago, to make them stronger. My boat is short and has a curved shape itself, it's not a straight line from the bow to the stern cleat, so we can fit against the wall nicely. Not so with those boats, they have straight sides from bow to stern, so they need separate lines at the bow and at the stern, leaving a gap to the wall in the middle of the boat. Those two have plenty of crew, so they can assign a person at the bow and stern and still have the skipper at the controls. I'd hate to try single-handing a boat like that in these locks."

When the lock had filled, the two rental boat crews rushed into a flurry of activity to get going, even before the gates opened. "Let's let them go first. Looks like they will anyway," Piet said to Jamel. "I'd rather have them in front of me than behind. It's not far to the next lock, so they shouldn't be able to leave us behind and make us miss a cycle."

The canal route curves quite a bit in this section, so Piet soon lost sight of the two boats ahead, but he was able to stay close enough that the gates were still open when the lock came in sight. The boats had each taken the front part of both walls; Piet came in behind the right-side boat and, this lock being only half as deep as the first, Jamel was able to stand atop the cabin and toss the line over a bollard at the top of the wall. "Just like an expert," Piet exclaimed, "good job."

It was a longer run to the next lock, 7.5 kilometers, more than an hour at the speed Piet preferred, a bit below the speed limit of 8 km/hr. So the other boats soon disappeared, on the high side of the speed limit, and Margriet was traveling alone. No boats had yet passed in the other direction, but on the half-kilometer straightaway before the Montgiscard lock Piet could see three rental boats coming out of the lock, headed for Toulouse. Piet increased his speed just a bit, to be there to enter the lock just after the other boats had cleared. So again they weren't delayed; as soon as Jamel had secured a line, he went to the borne and initiated the locking cycle.

Leaving the lock, Piet explained his immediate plan: "We didn't take time to get provisions before we left, so I want to do it now. When I came through here a couple of months ago, right up ahead I saw three people boarding their boat with shopping bags from a LiDL store. I watched after I passed them and I could see the store, only about 300 meters up the road from their mooring. It's on the right, just after we make that left turn that you can see ahead. I always like a LiDL store, they have good produce and the prices are good. There's one right at Port St Saveur, I went there a lot when I first arrived at the port."

"After that you had Zakia to feed you, right?" said Jamel with a laugh.

Piet blushed but took the joking, "Yeah, she's a good cook." They both laughed, and Jamel wisely decided to leave it at that.

Piet pointed to the right, and through the trees they could see the distinctive blue and red logo on a yellow background. He slowed to watch for the stopping place, not a pontoon or quay, just a sandy bank before a small bridge. Jamel was ready to jump off with a line; as Piet cut the power Jamel stepped ashore with his long stride and, taking the metal stakes and hammer from Piet, tied up the boat from bow and stern.

"I'll lock the cabin, I think the boat will be safe here. We won't be long. But that's why I didn't want to bring your Yamaha, it would be very attractive to some people, if they could figure out how to get it off the boat."

"There are people that can figure out something like that pretty quick," said Jamel. "You were right, I'd be worried about it all the time."

Barely a half-hour later they had each gathered the things that they like to eat and drink and had returned to the boat. Jamel retrieved the mooring stakes and Piet set off while Jamel stored the food below. They passed through another automated lock and then through the two chambers of the Sanglier lock, this one operated by an on-site lockkeeper. Just as they pulled away, he shut down for the lunch break, 12:30 to 13:30. That was just as Piet had hoped; they would be at the next lock, Négra, with only about 15 minutes to wait for the end of the lunch break.

Jamel asked Piet the obvious question, "Tell me, Piet, if most of these locks are automatic, why do they shut down for lunch?"

"I think it's because there are some locks, like we just passed, which have an *éclusier* on duty; being French, they are used to a full hour for their lunch. But just because the other locks are automatic doesn't mean that no one is operating them. The controls are connected to regional stations where operators keep an eye on everything, ready to send out a technician if something goes wrong with the system. Those people take a lunch break too. I will try to keep us moving as much as possible, but there will be times when we just have to sit and wait. And we will be out of the automated-lock zone after today, all the rest of the way on the Midi we will have éclusiers. You'll have to be patient, this will take a while."

"Sorry," Jamel said, "I'm used to traveling by motorcycle, at 130 km/hr when the road is open. Six km/hr is new to me, I usually walk faster than that."

"I don't know about that, I haven't seen you do much walking," Piet said.

Jamel laughed, "No, you're right about that. It's so easy to park my moto in the city that I use it to go everywhere."

"Well then, this will be good for you. I think we'll do a lot of walking in Paris," said Piet.

And so they went on across the Midi, stopping wherever they were when the locks closed at 7PM, usually alone on a quiet grass bank of the canal. On the fourth day they passed through the tourist destination city of Carcassonne during the day, finding more rental boats and thus more delays at the locks. They were lucky that evening to find an open space on the bank in the town of Trèbes, which allowed them to carouse a bit, first at two bars and then at a very crowded and noisy restaurant. The town of Homps was their next stop, conveniently tying-up right in front of a pleasant restaurant serving the local Minervois wines and, on this night, fresh seafood from the Med.

Piet stopped them a bit early on the night before descending the Fonserannes staircase of seven locks, which he wanted to do as the first boat down in the morning. This was accomplished, stopping in the afternoon in the city of Agde and leaving the Canal du Midi. More shopping for provisions, then a low-key evening on the town in this seaport city before departing at dawn for the 80 kilometer run across the open Mediterranean to the Petit Rhône, for a return visit to Saintes-Maries-de-la-Mer.

Piet had wanted to do this open-water run, it would actually be his first time out of sight of land. In his job he had been on the water most of every working day, but on a river, with a city and industrial plants on both banks. Now, as skipper of his own boat, he was free to do as he pleased. What pleased him now was to be out of the confines of the canal, on the open sea, navigating a straight-line course to the mouth of the Rhône. The shortcut would also save them a day of travel.

They were off early, down the Herault river from the center of Agde, past long rows of small boats, each tied at a private dock. Here the river itself is the harbor, rather than a man-made enclosure of marinas. Two long, parallel stone jetties conduct the river straight out into the sea. At 6AM they cleared the end of the jetties and turned southeast toward Cap d'Agde. The square box of the fort which covers that rock soon came into sight, then when it had been passed they turned to the northeast and soon were out of sight of the low shoreline. Only the hazy view of the distant Black Mountains remained.

Piet had checked the weather the day before and, as forecast, there were just low, smooth swells and almost no wind. It was just enough to unsettle Jamel. Piet advised him to not go into the cabin, where the smell of diesel fumes would only make it worse; instead he stretched out on one of the cockpit benches and tried to sleep. The slow rolling motion didn't bother Piet, he spent a happy day at the helm steering a straight line, with an occasional correction to avoid fishing boats and high-speed motorboats.

At just about the time that he had expected, Piet saw the towers of the church at Les Saintes-Maries-de-la-Mer with his binoculars. By 6PM they had found the mouth of the river and continued past it along the beach, to the marina. Jamel was relieved to be off the rolling sea but in no mood for any dinner. Piet was glad of that, he wanted to see if he could find Sara, and preferred that Jamel needn't know any of this. He walked down the beachfront promenade to La Chamade.

Sara was there, on a stool at the bar. When she saw Piet she jumped down and gave him a tight hug. "Hello, big guy!" He had forgotten how short she was, the top of her head nestled under his chin. But he hadn't forgotten her ample breasts, nor the good times that they had for a couple of days. He had no intention of repeating those days, he just wanted to see her again for a while. He ordered a beer, led her to one of the small tables, and pulled her onto his lap.

"How are you, Sara?" Piet asked. It wasn't just a greeting, he did wonder if she was doing okay in her wild lifestyle.

"I'm just the same, living life day by day and having a good time. How about you, where did you go from here?"

"I went to Toulouse " Piet replied. "I like it there a lot, I'm going back, probably for good. Right now I am on my way to Paris, with a friend, to take care of some business."

"Oh, man friend or girl friend?" Sara asked coyly.

"Man friend" laughed Piet. "My girl friend is busy in Toulouse, she owns a restaurant there."

"Too bad, I thought you were here to take me away from all this. Now you've not only got a girlfriend, but a well-off one too. Where is your man friend?"

"He's on the boat. We came across the open Med and it made him a little sick. He'll feel better tomorrow when we go up the Rhône."

"So you're going on business… business-business or monkey-business?

Piet laughed, "That's a good question. I hope it's not monkey-business. We're going to try to find some 70-year-old Algerian men who might have known my friend's father."

"Well" Sara said, "you should go to Belleville, the streets are full of cafes where the old men sit around and drink mint tea all day. Start at the Belleville metro station, it's at the heart of the *quartier*, the intersection of the four main streets: Boulevard de la Villette, Boulevard de Belleville, Rue du Faubourg du Temple and Rue de Belleville. *La Vielleuse* is a cafe right on the corner, there should be a row of old men sitting there all day. Then walk about 50 meters east on Rue de Belleville, you'll come to a pedestrian alley, Rue Dénoyez, both sides should be lined with chairs filled with people who just want to talk. Try to eat at the *Restaurant Franco-Africain* on Rue Dénoyez, if it's still open."

"That's perfect," Piet said, "We are going to moor the boat at Bassin La Villette, it must be just a few blocks away. How do you know all this?"

'I was born there," Sara said. "I lived there, on Faubourg du Temple, until I ran away, when I was fourteen. There are all kinds of immigrants there now, a lot of Vietnamese restaurants and shops, but you'll find Algerians still. I remember one old guy, he thought he was a good Muslim, but that didn't stop him from trying to get his hands on my tits. I was pretty quick though, I was used to squirming away from those guys."

"Wow, this is great to know" said Piet. "The guy I am going there with is French-Algerian, but he's never been to Paris, he doesn't know where we should start. And neither did I. But now we do, thanks."

"Maybe I should go with you, show you around", Sara said. "And I can keep you both company on the trip."

Piet laughed, "No, I don't think so. You would wear us both out and we would never get anything done. I'm hungry, want to share a pizza?"

"Sure. I don't think I really want to go back to Belleville anyway, I was so glad to get away."

Piet didn't pursue asking about her life there, even though he was curious. He thought it best to leave it alone, he wanted to just worry about his own life and now he's wrapped up in Jamel's as well, no need to take on another.

They ordered a pizza and while they waited Sara asked him about Toulouse. He told her about the wonderful cafes and markets, about the sights to be seen, but dodged her questions about his girlfriend and his life there. She let him go when the time came, but when she gave him a goodbye hug he felt a reaction to her soft, warm breasts. He thought about it for an instant, but broke free, promising to stop in on his way back to Toulouse. He wasn't sure he would do that, best to close this chapter while it was pleasant.

Jamel was ready to go early the next morning, cured of mal de mer. Piet steered into the mouth of the Petit Rhône and saw right away that he was going to have to be careful of sand bars, even with the shallow draft of Margriet. "This is good news," Piet said. "The river is very low, that means that we won't be going against a strong current on the Rhône. I was afraid that we might be going to Paris at less than walking speed. Go up on the bow and watch for shallows, point which way I should steer."

They traveled that way the entire day, Jamel leaving his station at the bow occasionally to make coffee and lunch. He liked to be at the bow even after his watching duties weren't needed. He was enjoying his view of the Camargue as the river twisted through the sometimes dense growth on the banks. Even though this was only 300 kilometers from the place where he had spent his entire life, it seemed like another planet to him. He was especially thrilled when a dozen of the white Camargue horses ran alongside, in an open field.

At dusk they moored at a tiny quay just before the junction with the Rhône; they could have gone on a bit farther before dark but Piet decided to not venture out on the 'big' river until morning, then travel to Lyon on days that would be as long as they could manage.

It took four days, staying each night on one of the pontoons located just below each lock. They arrived at Lyon's 'Confluence' marina in late afternoon, deciding to take advantage of facilities for a change, including a long, hot shower. Piet was the tour guide that evening, based on his limited experience here a few months earlier. Neither of them were looking for adventures, just seeing the sights like other tourists and stopping at a brasserie along the way.

On the Saône river they stopped overnight at riverfront quays in the cities of Mâcon and Tournus, then left the river after mid-day at Chalon-sur-Saône, for the smaller canals of Burgundy. The view approaching the first lock, 11 meters rise, was a bit daunting; the concrete-and-steel structure looming above a small entrance tunnel seemed to be a giant mechanical compactor which would grind up the boat and its passengers. But it wasn't so bad, after Jamel had secured the boat to a floating bollard; the bollard held the boat against the wall for the long ride upward. They exited the lock to find a quay near a major shopping center and decided to use this opportunity to restock provisions for another long run on the canals.

Traveling with other boats returning from summer on the Med to England, they followed the *Bourbonnais* route to Paris. It uses the Canaux du Centre, a series of four canals connected end-to-end to form a 412-kilometer waterway, joining the Saône river to the Seine while crossing over the summit which divides the watersheds of the Mediterranean Sea and the English Channel. At its southern end the route winds through the beautiful hills of the Charolais region, following the contours of the countryside, then it descends to the Loire valley. The canal parallels the Loire river as it flows slowly north to the sea, then climbs again over the low hills of the Gatinais region to join with the Seine.

It was ten days of travel from the Saône to the Seine, passing through 151 locks, then in one long day they completed the final leg, on the beautiful, winding Seine into Paris. First stop was at the Arsenal marina, the capitainerie that manages *Le Port de l'Arsenal* and *la Halte Nautique de La Villette*. Because of the late hour they stayed the first night on a visitor's mooring in front of the capitainerie, then moved on the next morning through the 2 km tunnel of the Canal St Martin and then four pairs of double locks to Bassin de la Villette, where they had arranged to dock for at least one month.

The canal exits the northern end of the tunnel through the first pair of locks, then one block north the *pont tournant* at Rue Dieu swings open to allow passage. As Margriet slowly passed through the opening, Jamel watched the crowd of pedestrians waiting to cross, early-morning commuters walking from the Belleville district into the busy Place de la République and St Denis section.

"Look, these are my people, they are North Africans," Jamel exclaimed. "I can talk to them, I know we will find someone."

The second set of locks followed soon after, at Rue Lancry. Jamel stepped up on the cabin roof to loop his line around a bollard and again reacted to what he saw: an arrow sign, pointing to his right, labeled 'Hotel du Nord'. "Piet," Jamel said, "There's the Hotel du Nord! That's where my mother worked, and met my father. This is the right place to start."

"Yes", Piet said. "Let's get moored and we'll walk back to here right away, along the canal."

From the last pair of locks they came out directly into a large rectangular basin, one block wide and six blocks long, cut into the city along a northeast-southwest line. Their assigned dock was at the far corner, on the north side, on Quai de la Seine, near the Holiday Inn Express and La Criée seafood restaurant. Piet thought it ironic that the nearest Metro station was named 'Riquet', located one block west on Rue Riquet, both presumably named for the creator of the Canal du Midi. They could also quickly walk down the north-side quay of the basin to the Stalingrad metro station, a hub for connecting lines.

Jamel was eager to get back to the Hotel du Nord, so they left as soon as the boat was tied-up securely; further settling-in could wait until later. They crossed over the middle of the basin on a passerelle, pausing at the top of the arched footbridge to get their bearings on Piet's map of Paris, then continued along the south side on Quai de la Loire. After a bit of avoiding heavy traffic while crossing Avenue Jean Jaurès, they found their way to the western side of the Canal St Martin and walked quickly south.

"Why do you think they have that sign at the lock, pointing to the hotel?" asked Piet. "I guess it's a historic place?"

"Yes," Jamel replied. "It's a national monument. There was a movie made at the hotel, an old one, black and white, I saw it in a classic movie festival a few years ago, in Toulouse. I knew that the hotel was where my parents met, so when I saw a poster for the festival, I made sure that I got there for that movie. Most of the movie takes place at the hotel, and there is a great scene of the July 14 celebration on the banks of the canal, right where we just were. The movie is about two different couples, one a pair of young lovers and the other a whore and her pimp."

"Sounds great! Well, we're almost there," Piet said. "What are we going to do, just walk up to the desk and ask if anyone remembers your mother or father? I guess that's how we should start."

But when they arrived at the tall, narrow gray-stucco building they found that it was no longer operating as a hotel, now it's a restaurant, wine bar and salon de thé. Posters on the windows advertised upcoming concerts in the library, behind the cafe. It was still early in the morning, so none of those venues were open. They could see inside through the bistro-style large glass windows and a central glass door, and motioned to a young man working behind the bar. He did his best to ignore them but eventually he came to the door and opened it slightly.

"Bonjour m'sieu, merci," Jamel said to him. "My mother and father both worked here at the hotel fifty years ago. We are looking for someone who may have known them."

"I don't think you'll have any luck," the young man replied. "Everyone that works here now is nowhere near that old." He began to close the door, but Jamel still had a hand on the edge of the door; he took advantage of his greater height and strong build to hold the door open and persist with questions.

Piet thought to ask: "Is there still an office of the hotel, where there might be some employee records?"

"I don't know," the young man said, "but come in, I'll ask Pierrette, the bookkeeper, if she can help you."

He led them up a few steps into the *bibliothèque* and asked them to wait there. Soon he returned with Pierrette, a buxom woman with curly blonde hair, dressed in a blouse and skirt both a size or two too small. Piet thought to himself "She looks like she was in the movie, in the whore part."

"Max told me what you want, but I don't know if I can help. You said fifty years ago, I'm not even that old myself."

Although his first thought was "You must be pretty close," Piet asked "Jamel's mother was a chambermaid here, and his father did maintenance. We would like to find someone who worked with them, in 1961. I'm sure there's no one that old working here now, but perhaps we could find a name and address?"

"I'm sure that we don't have employee records for the hotel, it's entirely different ownership now and I have never seen any files or boxes with old records," said Pierrette. "But I do know of someone you might ask. When I came to work here in 1999, there was an old man, an Algerian I think, who didn't work here but was the plumber on call, he had done it for a very long time. He was a nice guy, we chatted quite a bit. Actually, I had trouble getting any work done when he was here, he was kind of 'all over me'. His name is Ramon, he's retired now but I have seen him sitting around with some other old men in his workshop. It's one block down the canal, on the other quay. Use the footbridge over the canal, the shop is near the other end. The street name is Quai de Valmy, his shop is just two or three doors up from Rue Dieu."

"That's great" Jamel said. "My parents were Algerian, he was probably friends with them. Thanks Pierrette, and Max - we'll go there right away."

It was easy to find, obviously it must be the small blue storefront with no sign but with sinks, faucets, drain pipes piled haphazardly on the shelf below each of the two store-front windows. Through the hazy glass door they could see some men sitting at the back of the shop.

"What do you think, four of them?" Jamel asked. "I saw a boulangerie up the block, I'll go get some croissants."

"Good idea" Piet replied. "I'll wait at that bench and watch the boats."

When Jamel returned they knocked at the door and a short, elderly man came to the door, with a surprisingly quick step.

"Sorry, I'm not open for business" he said through the closed door.

"I know," Jamel replied, "Pierrette at the Hotel du Nord sent us to see you. We just need some information."

"Well, any friend of Pierrette's is a friend of mine. Come in. I am Ramon." He led them to the back, introducing the other men as Marcel, Hugo and Sadek.

Jamel shook the hand of the last, saying "My name is Jamel Hammad, my father was from Algiers." To all he said "This is my friend Piet, a Dutchman. May I offer you a croissant?"

There was no dissent and the bag was quickly emptied. Ramon gestured to a worktable where Jamel and Piet could sit, after clearing a space.

Jamel told his story: "Piet and I live in Toulouse. We have come here because my mother and father were married here in Paris, after they met while both worked at the Hotel du Nord. She was French, from Toulouse, and my father, as I said, was from Algiers. He had been in France less than a year when they married, but in 1961 he disappeared, during the time when many Algerian men were jailed, beaten and murdered. My mother was terrified and she returned to Toulouse, to live with her sister. I was born there, but my mother died a few years later. My aunt told me that she died of a broken heart, and of the fear that she had from the violence in Paris. I want to find someone who knew my father and can tell me what happened to him."

Ramon spoke up "Sadek and I came here together from Algiers, but it was in 1964, after independence. We have heard stories about the troubles of 1961, but we wouldn't have known your father. I don't live in this quartier, I live in the Ninth. I didn't do any work at the hotel until sometime after 1972, when I bought this shop from an old Frenchman."

"But Pierrette told us that you were friendly with the staff," Piet said. "Maybe you remember someone who worked there in 1961."

"Maybe so," Ramon said. "I got started at the hotel with the help of Lakhdar, he got me the work because he was Algerian, like me. He was a couple years older than me, he must be about 80 now. He had worked there a long time, I don't know if he was there in 1961, probably he was."

"That sounds good, we should talk to him," Piet said. "Do you know where he lives?"

"No," Ramon said, "and I don't remember his last name. I do know that he must live in Belleville, a few times over the years I have seen him walk across the turning bridge, right over there." He pointed out the window; Piet and Jamel both looked, as it had been earlier there was a small crowd of people waiting for the bridge to close so that they could cross.

"That's Belleville, right across the bridge?" Piet asked.

"Yes, it's the edge of it. Lakhdar must live in those blocks, but the center of it is along Rue du Faubourg du Temple, that street crosses the canal over the end of the tunnel, right down there, you can see the McDonald's sign."

"I know of that street," Piet said, "a friend of mine that grew up there told me to go to the intersection where it crosses the Boulevard de la Villette and ask the old men who drink tea at the cafes around there."

"That's right," Ramon said. "Belleville begins when Rue du Faubourg du Temple becomes Rue de Belleville, after it crosses the wide boulevard that is Boulevard de la Villette on the north and Boulevard de Belleville on the south. That's a good place to start. Lakhdar, L-a-k-h-d-a-r, it isn't a very common name, even among us Algerians, so you could just ask for him. Be sure to go to Rue Dénoyez, there are a lot of tables there where old people spend the day. It's a short alley, less than 100 meters east of the Boulevard de Belleville."

"What does Lakhdar look like?" asked Piet.

"He's got a lot of white hair and he wears a knitted *kufi* cap," Ramon said, "he's about my height, but much heavier. He's at least twice as big around as me. I might sit around with these guys during the day, but at night I go dancing, I stay in shape."

"I can see that," Piet said, with a laugh. "Where do you dance?"

"My wife and I drive out to Enghien-les-Bains, there's a small lake where they have a casino, theater and a dance club. We like to enjoy life!"

"Seems like a good idea to me," Piet said. "I missed out on that, my wife didn't like to enjoy life, she just wanted to relive the past and think about what might have been. I couldn't take it any more, so now here I am with this crazy Algerian."

They all laughed at that, then Piet and Jamel said their thank you and goodbye. As they went out the door Jamel turned right, ready to go looking for Lakhdar, but Piet stopped him. "Wait, we need to go back to the boat, get it cleaned up, attached to electricity and water, and make sure it's secure. We'll have lunch, you should know by now that I never miss lunch, then we'll figure out how to get to Belleville on the Metro."

"Okay," said Jamel, "you're right, I've waited a long time to do this, no need to rush things."

In mid-afternoon they walked to the Stalingrad Metro station; Piet studied the map of routes and said "Okay, the number 2 line, direction Nation, Belleville is the third stop."

Coming out of the Metro staircase they paused, confirming that they were on the northeast corner of the Belleville/Villette/Faubourg-du-Temple intersection. They looked across to the opposite corner of Rue de Belleville, where they saw the rust-red awning of La Vielleuse café. "That's where Sara told me to start," Piet thought, but didn't say it aloud to Jamel.

A row of motor scooters and bicycles chained to stanchions lined the edge of the sidewalk along Rue de Belleville. A balloon salesman stood at the corner, fighting the wind to keep his tall stack of cartoon-face balloons intact. More than a dozen tiny circular tables stretched around the corner in front of the cafe; behind them, along the wall of the cafe, a long straight row of 'Paris Cafe'-style chairs were all occupied by middle-aged and elderly men.

"That's a good place to start," said Jamel as he stepped off the curb. Piet followed, deciding that he would let Jamel do the talking; he felt like a foreigner here, the faces of nearly everyone seated at the cafe were various shades of brown to black. As Jamel walked up to speak to three men at a table, Piet hung back to look over all of the row - none of them were Lakhdar, he could see that immediately. All seemed to be middle-aged, all but one wearing blue jeans and a black or brown jacket. One stood out: a tall, rather elegant gentleman, mostly bald, wearing white pants, white polo shirt, white sneakers and a tan suede jacket, sitting alone, legs crossed, watching the crowds. Piet decided to approach him, as he had seen the man watching them as they crossed the street.

"Bonjour," said Piet, "pardon me, we are looking for a man named Lakhdar, an elderly man. Do you know him?"

"No," the man replied, "I don't know the name. What does he look like?"

"Well," Piet said, "I haven't seen him myself but he was described as a heavy man in his seventies, with white hair and a knitted cap."

" A man like that just passed," he said as he pointed around the corner of the cafe with his left hand. "But he wasn't wearing a cap and he had his long white hair pulled back into a tail. Look quickly, you'll see him."

Piet did walk to the corner and saw that man facing him, turning to descend the steps into the Metro. "Lakhdar?" he asked; the man looked up but didn't stop or reply, continuing down the steps. Doesn't look old enough, Piet decided, and returned to the cafe tables.

"Thank you," said Piet, "but I don't think that's him. I didn't think it would be that easy. We have been told to go to Rue Dénoyez, is that nearby?"

"Yes," the gentleman replied, "that's a good place, older folks sit there. It's to my right, just past the bar *Aux Folies*. Even if you don't find him, you'll enjoy the graffiti. Tourists come here to see it. But don't rush, have a seat. Your friend is still busy talking to those young men. Would you join me in a coffee?"
Piet agreed, seeing that Jamel was involved in a conversation with men that resembled his motorcycle friends. He sat with his back to the wall, so that he could watch the passers-by himself.

"You are Dutch, I think," the gentleman said.

"Yes, from Rotterdam," Piet replied. "But now I live in Toulouse." He said that with pleasure, it sounded good to him to say that he had his home there. As the coffee was served he asked "How did you know that I am Dutch?"

"I am Indonesian," the gentleman replied. "I am old enough to remember the Dutchmen who ran things there. After the end of World War II my father was involved in talks with the Dutch, he was friends with one Dutchman in particular who often came to our house for dinner. But for myself, I got into the spice trade in French Indochina, for just a couple of years, and managed to get out of there and come to Paris when the French were expelled in 1954. I have a spice importing business near here."

"This is a very cosmopolitan neighborhood," Piet said. "I see many Asian people walk by."

"Yes, as you walk to Rue Dénoyez you will pass the Tang Gourmet restaurant, and you will see many more Asian restaurants and shops in the next two blocks of Rue de Belleville, it might even be called one of the Chinatowns of Paris, although the big one is across the Seine, in the 13th. And you may know that it is the birthplace of Edith Piaf, there is a plaque for her up the hill a few blocks," waving his arm up Rue de Belleville.

"No," Piet laughed, "until now I only knew Belleville as the birthplace of my friend Sara."

Jamel came over and said excitedly to Piet "They told me that there is a mosque on Boulevard de Belleville, about three blocks down. We should go there."

"Okay," Piet replied, "We will." Turning to the Indonesian man he asked "Can we get there on Rue Dénoyez?"

"Yes, the alley is only two blocks long, turn right at the end and you will come out on the boulevard. Then turn left, I know the mosque, it's another two blocks down on the west side, right after Ben's food store, near the Couronnes metro station."

"Thank you," said Piet as he rose to go. "I am Piet and this is Jamel. I enjoyed meeting you, perhaps I will see you here again."

"Please do, I am mostly retired, I sit here every afternoon. My name is Jacob Soumokil."

They all shook hands, then Piet and Jamel set off. "So no one knew Lakhdar?" Piet asked.

"No," Jamel replied, "but they said that if he is a practicing Muslim and lives in Belleville, he would probably visit that mosque. It's a neighborhood mosque in what had been an apartment. The Grand Mosque of Paris is on the left bank, behind the Jardin des Plantes, that's pretty far away, I think."

"Yes," Piet said, "we can go there later but someone at this mosque should know Lakhdar, he's lived here for more than 50 years… Here we are, everyone has told us to look first on Rue Dénoyez."

They turned onto the narrow street, open to traffic but used as a pedestrian zone. Cafe tables and chairs lined the right side of the street, stretching down the length of the first block. As they walked Jamel studied the people, seated with their backs to the west wall. Piet was drawn to the fantastic graffiti on every surface, walls, doors, windows, everywhere, all the way up to the roofs of the two and three story buildings.

"This is amazing," Piet said, "I've never seen it like this. There is plenty of graffiti in Rotterdam, and in Toulouse, but nothing like this! There is graffiti on graffiti, in every color. Some of it is true art."

Jamel wasn't interested, he looked intently at each person that they passed. He stopped at a table with two elderly men and asked if they knew Lakhdar, but they didn't know the name. At the end of Rue Dénoyez they turned out to the boulevard and crossed to the west side, passing over the wide concrete median. They walked briskly, watching for Ben's food store and the Couronnes metro station. Soon they found it, Ben's in fact was two store-fronts side-by-side thus was a good landmark. Next to Ben's, almost unnoticeable, was #39 Boulevard de Belleville, a narrow weathered-wood door set in a pale green frame. In a panel beside the door they saw the schedule and notices for the *Mosquée Abou Bakr As Saddiq*. Jamel tried the door handle and was disappointed to find it locked.

"Well," Jamel said, "tomorrow is Friday, the schedule shows *Salat al-Jumu'ah* at noon. It is a congregational prayer, nearly all of the men will be here. We can be here to watch them arrive, maybe we will see Lakhdar. If not I can go inside and ask."

"Good," said Piet. "Let's walk up the boulevard and make our way back to the boat. If we just go straight north we will go right to the basin."

They walked in the paved median so they could look around more easily than on the sidewalk, where crowds of pedestrians made it difficult to watch for a heavy-set elderly man with white hair. They did see a few that matched the description, but when Jamel approached them they weren't Lakhdar and didn't know the name. North of the main intersection at Rue de Belleville they stopped at a pleasant place in the median, with tall trees and small bushes on both sides, to sit on a bench and watch the people passing by.

"It's nice here," said Jamel, "but not as nice as Toulouse."

"You're right," Piet replied. "Of course this is just one part of Paris, there are certainly plenty of beautiful boulevards, but I know what you mean, this just doesn't have the *gentil* feel of Toulouse. This is the big city, Toulouse is more like a large town. I'll be glad to get back there."

"You'll probably be glad to get back with Zaki, I think," said Jamel.

"You're right, I do miss her," Piet admitted. "But we've got work to get done."

At 10AM the next morning they took the train from Stalingrad to the Couronnes metro station and emerged into the daylight to be surrounded by a small sea of men, nearly all of them dressed alike, in an unofficial uniform of blue jeans and black nylon windbreakers. They milled around on the boulevard median and on the sidewalk in front of Ben's store or the corner cafe *Le Métro*. Many of them were watching a very attractive young woman dressed like the men, but in a much more attention-getting way. Her faded-blue jeans were skin-tight over thin legs and nice round buttocks, the sleeves of her windbreaker pulled up to her elbows, showing beautiful chocolate arms with multiple silver bracelets, her hair tied in a leopard-skin scarf; even though he was thirty years older than the girl, even Piet took careful notice. Traffic kept her there for several minutes, until she was able to cross the street and the men could return to their wait for the mosque to open.

Jamel and Piet took a sidewalk table at the cafe and ordered coffee, but their main purpose was to watch the men on Boulevard de Belleville, hoping to spot Lakhdar. Most of them were in their 20s to 50s, so an older man with white hair would stand out.

To their great surprise, within a few minutes there he was: "…a heavy man in his seventies, with white hair and a knitted cap." He had come from behind them, walking east on Rue Jean-Pierre Timbaud. Piet tapped Jamel's arm and pointed discreetly as the man turned the corner toward the mosque. Jamel quickly followed and stopped him just as he turned into the mosque entry.

"Bonjour m'sieu, pardon, may I speak with you?"

The man was startled but stopped and stepped away from the busy entrance. "M'sieu, pardon, are you Lakhdar?" Jamel asked.

"Yes, I am," he replied, with surprise. "What do you want?"

"My name is Jamel, I have been looking for you after talking with Ramon, the plumber, he knew you from the Hotel du Nord."

"Oh yes, I know Ramon, but I haven't seen him in years."

"Ramon told me that you worked at the hotel fifty years ago. I am trying to find someone who knew my father, in 1960 and '61. His name was Majid Hammad, he had just come from Algiers and found work at the hotel."

"I did work there then, I started in 1955. But I don't remember him, and I must go in now for prayers."

"Yes, I am sorry to delay you, you must go ahead. Can you talk to me afterward? I will be sitting at that table with my friend," Jamel said as he pointed to Piet.

"All right, but I will be some time, I won't hurry," Lakhdar said.

"That's fine, I have been waiting a long time, we will be there." Jamel returned to the table and said to Piet "It's him, he will talk to us after the prayers. He said that he doesn't remember my father, but maybe he will when he has time to think about it."

"Good," said Piet, "I didn't think we would find him so quickly." They ordered lunch and stayed at the table, with no intention of leaving it until they saw Lakhdar again. Passing the time, Piet said to Jamel "Look at that scooter wheel, securely chained to the lamppost, but all the rest of the scooter is gone. It's the kind of sight that you see in a big city."

"I saw that wheel," Jamel replied "that's why I'm glad to have a garage to store my moto at my apartment. I wouldn't be able to sleep if I had to leave it on the street, even though thefts are not common in my neighborhood."

"Yes," Piet said, "I haven't been in Toulouse very long but I do feel safe there. And when my boat is tied up in the countryside, I don't worry about it at all."

The time passed slowly, with Jamel fidgeting in anticipation. After all of this time getting ready, he hoped that soon he would find a good result. Eventually men began to leave the mosque and Jamel moved to stand on the curb in front of the doorway, to be sure that Lakhdar didn't leave in the other direction. Jamel waited there more than a half-hour, then Lakhdar emerged.

"I didn't forget about you," he said when he saw Jamel, "and I do remember a man that might be your father. In fact I have thought about him often over the years."

They sat down at the table, Jamel introducing Piet as his 'Dutch friend'. Lakhdar ignored him, now in his retirement years comfortable only with his fellow North Africans. He spoke directly to Jamel:

"I do remember Majid, he came to work at the hotel after I had been there a couple of years. I can see the resemblance of your face to your father. And I remember Doriane, a chambermaid, who must be your mother. I went with them to their wedding, I was the witness."

Jamel was stunned by this, he had never expected such good luck. "I never knew my father, or my mother. My father had disappeared before my mother moved from Paris, in October 1961, to be with her sister in Toulouse. I was born there, but she died before I knew her."

"I am so sorry to hear this," Lakhdar said. "I liked your father very much and I thought your mother was the most beautiful girl I had ever seen. She was very young, I think maybe only nineteen when they married."

"Thank you for those words," said Jamel. "I only have a photo of her when she was about sixteen, before she went to Paris. I think she was there less than a year, a year in which she married Majid and then she returned to Toulouse in fear after he disappeared. She died a few years after I was born. There were no pictures taken of her during that time, I suppose that she did not want her unhappy face to be seen."

"I will tell you my story, and what I know about Majid and Doriane," Lakhadr said. "I came to Paris when the FLN became violent. In 1954 the Front de Libération Nationale was demanding independence for Algeria. I wasn't political, I was practical. I wanted to have a good job and to live a peaceful life, so I came to Paris with a few friends. We found a cheap apartment in Belleville and went out looking for work. After a while I was lucky, I walked into the Hotel du Nord on a day when the toilets were all backed up and the regular maintenance man was at his mother's funeral in Bretagne. I fixed the problem and the owner of the hotel was so happy that he kept me on, and told the Breton that I was to be his assistant. A few months later that man decided that he would go back to live in his mother's house, he had had enough of the city, so I was in charge.

"One day Majid walked in, just as I had. I don't remember when, it was several years after I started to work there. The desk clerk sent him to see me, and I did need a helper, so I hired him. I think Doriane already worked there, I'm not sure, she didn't work for me. But of course it didn't take long for a young man to spot a pretty girl. Sometimes I had to tell them both to stop spending time together and to get back to work. I often saw them leave work together to go to the metro, I think they went west on Rue Lancry to the Jacques Bonsergent metro station. Majid told me that he lived on Rue Marx-Dormoy, in the 18th arrondissement, and that she lived in the 19th, near the Jaurès metro.

"It wasn't long after that when Majid told me that they wanted to get married and that she would move in with him. So one day he and I walked from the hotel to the *mairie* of the 19th and I helped him fill out the necessary papers. I don't think I was much help, I was never married myself! A week or so later we all went there, Majid, Doriane and me. It was a simple wedding but very elegant, I remember that the impressive white-haired man who presided wore a wide *tricolore* sash across one shoulder.

"They lived together in Majid's room, which was in an apartment with three of his friends. They had all fled Algiers as a group. Majid told me that his father, Yacef, had been executed by the French authorities in Algiers, by guillotine, for 'subversive activities'. Majid had himself been part of the FLN, a courier, even though he was young. He said that he could get past French patrols for just that reason, he looked young and innocent. But after Yacef was executed Majid was afraid that they would arrest him soon, so he joined with a small group to cross the Mediterranean by boat. I think they landed at Marseille and made their way to Paris.

"Majid was able to get the job at the hotel soon after he arrived in Paris, but the others weren't so lucky. They spent most of their time on the street and became involved in the activities of the FLN. Their apartment was in the Chapelle district, where most of the residents, as well as the cafes and shops, were Algerian.

"Majid told me that his friends took part in beatings and killings to eliminate opponents of the FLN, such as the rival organization MNA, the *Mouvement National Algérien*, during what was called the Café Wars. There were bombings and assassinations by both sides, acts of terrorism, usually done at cafés. Majid wasn't directly involved but there must have been plenty of talk about it in the apartment, with guns and bombs part of the newlyweds' home life. He wasn't sure what he should do, part of him wanted to have a job and a family but another part wanted to be active with the terrorists.

"At that time there had been many attacks on Paris police stations, usually targeting the stations of the Muslim auxiliary police, manned by *Harkis*, because the FLN had a special grudge against them. The station most frequently attacked was the Goutte d'Or, on the north side of the Boulevard de la Chapelle, just west of the rail lines going into Gare du Nord. That is a street of two separate lanes, with an elevated metro track in the middle, so they could attack from a car or escape quickly on foot, on the metro.

"One night in the summer of 1961, when Majid was at home with Doriane, the three others went to attack the nearby Goutte d'Or station, armed with knives and grenades. I guess they weren't very good at this work, because they didn't manage to get past the guards at the door. They threw their grenades, which exploded harmlessly outside the building, then ran. But, because of the frequent attacks, a policeman with a sub-machine gun had been stationed under the stone abutments of the metro. He stepped out into the street and shot all three, killing them immediately.

"Majid heard the shots and the sirens afterward, so he left Doriane in the apartment and walked to the scene, in time to see the bodies of his friends still laying on the sidewalk and in the street. He told me that this left him conflicted, he wanted to revenge his friends but he also now had a wife to think about, who of course wasn't Algerian.

"The bombings of police stations were common in August and September of 1961, there were a lot of troubles, what we call a *fitnah*. More than a dozen policemen had been killed. The police were rampaging, arresting or beating immigrants. They were after Algerians but didn't care if they also included other Maghreb people and even Spanish and Italians, just because they looked like they might be Algerian. The leaders of the police gave them free rein and promised to give their officers cover for whatever actions they might take.

"In early October the chief of the police, Maurice Papon, announced a curfew for all Algerians, even those with a French identity card. I can still remember reading about it in Le Monde, just a few months after I saw Papon's picture in the news, receiving the Legion of Honour from Charles De Gaulle. The FLN organized a demonstration, which they wanted to be large but peaceful, for the evening of October 17 at landmarks around the city.

"Majid was excited about the demonstrations, he wanted to do something for the FLN cause, without violence. He told me that he and Doriane would be part of it and he asked me to come with them. I thought that would be good, I wanted solidarity with my own people in some way; I looked forward to marching with them.

"We met at Gare du Nord and took the crowded metro to Luxembourg Gardens, where thousands already lined the west side of Boulevard St Michel on the sidewalk along the fence. A car with a loudspeaker called out to the crowd, calling for justice for Algerians and saying that the curfew was racist and discriminatory. We had come out of the metro near the leaders of the protest, at Place Edmond Rostand. We were soon at the edge of the front echelon, marching eastward toward the Pont St Michel. The planned route was to turn left on St Germain so as to end at the Assemblée Nationale, for a protest on the steps of the parliament building. But the group we were with kept on going, straight toward the Seine.

"When we arrived at Place St Michel a group of young men decided to cross the bridge and protest in front of the Préfecture de Police. We were swept along with them and crossed the bridge, then turned along the river onto the Quai Marché Neuf toward the front of the police building. We didn't get there; a sea of dark blue was coming toward us, the street filled with officers of the CRS, *Compagnies Républicaines de Sécurité*, the riot police. These were the tough guys, not the gendarmes, and there were a lot of them.

"Worried about Doriane, Majid asked me to take her back and try to disappear on a side street and take her home, while he went to help the men at the front of the crowd, being beaten by batons. I told him to come with us, but it was already too late. I saw him go down under the batons of two CRS men, while another squad gathered us into a group of a dozen or so and swept us into the courtyard of the Préfecture. We were packed into a bus, maybe one hundred of us crowded into a city bus. We were taken to the Palais des Sports at Porte de Versailles and held there for days, without food or blankets. Considerable violence took place, prisoners around us were taken and tortured. Men were dying there. Doriane and I kept very quiet and passive, so they left us alone. Eventually they opened the gates and let us out. I took Doriane to my apartment, she couldn't return to Majid's apartment alone. A week later she left by train for Toulouse, to go to her sister. I never saw Majid again.

"We had seen officers beat protesters and thought that they had been taken to jails or other detention centers. But then I heard stories that they had dumped them into the Seine, from the St Michel bridge and also, at another demonstration, from the Neuilly bridge. It was confirmed when bodies were washed up on the banks of the river. Some of them were identified but many more were not, perhaps their bodies were never found. The Seine is a strong river, it could carry the bodies a very long way.

"There was nothing I could do. I went on with my work at the hotel, never hearing from Majid or Doriane until you found me today. I am very sorry, I have thought of that terrible day often, now for over fifty years. I didn't know that Doriane was pregnant but I am glad that she was, as now you are here and I can feel that Majid has been recovered, in a way."

Jamel and Piet had listened attentively to Lakhdar's tale, and now the three of them sat there in silence, each with their own thoughts. Jamel's thoughts were of revenge.

During Lakhdar's telling of the story he had refused offers of coffee or tea, and afterward he refused their offer to have lunch. He said that the story had been with him for fifty years but now that he had told it, he was done with it. "I have told you everything that I know," he said. "There was nothing that I could do then, and now I have done everything that I can do to help you. I will go to my home relieved. Please don't ask me again."

They thanked him profusely but didn't press him any further. He rose slowly and walked away.

"Well, that was amazing." Piet said. "I never thought that we would find a witness, but here we have the story from a man who was directly involved. He has told us everything, except to confirm that Majid was thrown in the river."

"Yes," Jamel said, "I would still like to find what happened to his body, if it was ever found. Was it buried somewhere, if so I would like to know where. The police kept records, I read in Einaudi's book a list of 140 names, about half of them confirmed killed but the others were listed only as *disparu*. But Einaudi thought that there may have been twice as many killed, with no record kept."

"It doesn't seem that Lakhdar would have reported Majid as missing, he was too terrified," Piet said. "And there was no one else to look for him, Doriane had left and his roommates were killed earlier… Let's start to walk back to Villette."

They walked silently, each thinking of what they might do next. As they neared Rue de Faubourg du Temple, Piet suddenly had an idea. "Let's cross over to La Vielleuse and see if Jacob Soumokil is there. He has been a businessman here for almost sixty years, maybe he can give us advice."

He was there, as he said he would be on most afternoons. He greeted them warmly and invited them to sit down. "Did you find the mosque yesterday?"

"Yes, we did," Piet said "and today we returned to find Lakhdar, who was exactly the right person to help us. Now I came here to look for you, perhaps you could help us also?"

"Certainly, if I can," Jacob said.

Piet told the story in brief and asked Jacob "Do you know if we might be able to look through archived documents, perhaps at the Préfecture de Police?"

"Ah, you were right to ask me, I have personal experience in that terrible event," Jacob said. "As I told you, I have lived here since 1954, I came when I was a young man. So I was here in October 1961, I can remember it well, in fact I remember that the demonstrations were on a Tuesday evening. I have always been interested in the news and current events, so I had read what was available about this in Le Monde. A few days before the massacre it was reported that Maurice Papon, the Prefect of Police of Paris, at the funeral of a policeman killed by the FLN, promised that "for every one of us killed, we will kill ten of them!" And that is exactly what came to pass a few days later.

"The provocation came in the form of a police order that Algerian Muslims should be subject to a curfew from 8:30PM to 5:30AM, on the pretext that there had been a significant increase in the number of attacks on policemen. At that time I was living in a small apartment on the 4th floor of a building on Quai de Valmy, where I could look out on Canal St Martin near the pont tournant at Rue Dieu. I was awakened early on the morning of Wednesday October 18th, by splashing sounds and the low voices of many men. I opened the window very wide so that I could lean out and suffered the immeasurable horror of the sight of three bodies being fished out of the canal, then five, then seven, and finally forty. When the bridge is closed it is very low, and the police had put a net there so that the bodies couldn't pass under, and they were lifting them onto the bridge, then immediately into the back of a covered truck.

"It wasn't unusual for a body to be found in the canal occasionally, some people said that the éclusiers, if they saw a body in their lock, would open the lower gates to send it downstream, rather than have to fill out a report. But that was always just a single body, from an accidental fall, a suicide, or a murder. This was entirely different. I suppose that these bodies were thrown into the canal at Place Stalingrad, after demonstrators had gathered on Boulevard de la Chapelle and then walked eastward to block the important intersection and metro station at Stalingrad. Policemen had been brought by buses to stop the marchers at the spot where the street is narrowed by the stone structures of the elevated metro track, before they could fill the square. After stopping the march with batons and guns, there

151

were bodies to be gotten rid of, I assume by dragging them to the canal, just a few meters away.

"Most of what happened that night was covered-up for many years. The official statistic was two dead. Papon himself said that 'only' 15 or 20 protesters had been thrown into the river Seine by police. The real figure is not known, maybe it is in the hundreds. As I said, I counted 40 bodies myself, in the Canal St Martin."

Piet stopped him to say "Jamel asked me to read Einaudi's book 'La Bataille de Paris', it includes a list of the dead and missing. The name of Jamel's father, Majid Hammad, is not on either list. Do you think we could find some other records?"

"I never read the book," said Jacob, "but I did read a magazine article by Einaudi, about ten or twelve years ago. He described how he had done his research, to come up with an estimate of more than 200 victims. I can remember his statement almost exactly 'The pages for October and November 1961 are full of names of Algerian-French Muslims followed by a rubber stamp saying *mort* . . . against some names there was an indication that bodies had been recovered from the river Seine'. I don't think that you could find anything more than he has reported."

"No, I'm sure you're right," Piet said, "and there were certainly victims who were never identified, or even their bodies found."

"Yes," said Jamel. "I now am certain that my father was killed by the Paris police at the Pont St Michel. I wish there was a grave that I could visit, but I'm sure it doesn't exist. Thank you, Jacob, for helping to fill out the story."

To Piet, Jamel asked "I would like to see the scene at Pont St Michel, will you go there with me tomorrow?"

"Certainly," Piet replied. "And I thank you also, Jacob, you have been very helpful, I'm glad to have met you."

"Please come back to visit with me," Jacob said, "I enjoy your company."

Piet and Jamel took the Metro, just as Jamel's parents had done years before. They emerged at the corner of Boulevard St Michel and Rue Gay-Lussac, which they understood to be the meeting place for the demonstration in 1961. In front of them was a broad intersection with the arc of the tall iron-spike fence along the Luxembourg Gardens stretching out of sight in both directions and forming the long west-side leg of a triangle. Piet had looked at the map of Paris the night before and had noticed that this intersection was one of the largest open spaces, with good Metro access, on the Left Bank. "This was a good choice," Piet said, "you can gather a lot of people here if you take over the streets."

But today the streets were filled with vehicles, not marchers, and on the sidewalk by the Gardens there were only tourists and a few fathers pushing babies in strollers. The two of them couldn't take over the streets, and no one took notice of them on their march toward the Seine. Piet stayed quiet, he thought that Jamel would want to imagine that day, with first hundreds and then thousands of marchers joining behind him, pressing the leaders on.

As they passed the Place de la Sorbonne, Piet was reminded of the event that had been mentioned in one of his college classes, the student riots of May 1968. Again the Paris police had reacted with violence, using batons and tear gas on students and their supporters. He thought he remembered that the police won the battle, but only in the short run.

Walking toward the Seine on Boulevard St Michel meant walking with traffic; it is a one-way street and traffic flows toward the river. This gave Piet just a bit of the feeling that they might have had that day in 1961, the press forward, especially when four huge white tour buses roared past in a long line. He felt a rush to get there.

Soon the street widened into the open plaza at the fountain, the Fontaine St Michel, with hundreds of people walking, taking photos or just standing to watch the rest of the crowd. They dodged through the crowd and quickly crossed to the east sidewalk on Pont St Michel, where they stopped in the middle of the bridge to survey the situation as it might have been on that day.

"That's the Préfecture de Police," Piet said, pointing to the building ahead and to the right. "The one with square towers on each corner, I guess you would call them a mansard roof style. The block that we're looking at must be where Lakhdar saw the police encounter the marchers."

"Look at that wall along the quay, straight down to the river for the whole block," Jamel said. "It must be a ten-meter drop, it's a vertical stone wall, with only a narrow walkway along the river. If the police threw men over that wall, the river would just have swept them away. Even worse, some might have hit the edge of the concrete walkway, injuring them before they went into the water. And it's more than a meter from the walkway down to the water, no one could have reached up to save themselves. It's a perfect killing field."

"You're right," Piet replied, "that's a good name for it, a killing field. All a policeman had to do was get someone over the edge and it was done, the men were disposed of. It makes me sick to see it." He started to go but saw that Jamel wasn't ready; he was staring down into the Seine, watching the water rush past.

Piet let him stay there for several long minutes, until a tourist boat interrupted the scene as it passed under the bridge, the huge barge filling the view before it passed out of sight beyond the Pont de la Cité. When the rectangular basin between the bridges was again empty, Jamel again looked down and quietly said *"Salamu alaykum"*. He saw Piet watching and said "It means 'Peace be upon you'."

They walked on across the bridge and turned right, headed toward Notre Dame along with dozens of tourists. But while the tourists were excitedly looking ahead to see the cathedral, Piet and Jamel were looking at the long rows of police vehicles. On their right, backed up against the wall of the quay, were a long row of bland white or gray cars, unmarked but obviously official vehicles, certainly there for the use of detectives and others who worked from the PdP. On the left, backed up to the wall of the building, a row of tall blue vans marked Gendarmerie. Piet and Jamel had seen such vans often in Toulouse, but never a row of dozens, all the same and all looking ready to transport hundreds of police to any incident.

At a gap in the row of vans they saw an entrance to the building, but when they walked into the short foyer they saw that the closed wooden doors were controlled by a card-swipe reader. A policeman pushed past them to use his card, gruffly telling them "En face Notre Dame" and pointing vaguely around the corner. They followed his suggestion and turned the

154

corner, but they immediately found themselves in a narrow path between temporary barricades; the face of the building was under repair and covered by scaffolding, including what must be the main entrance. They walked until there was an opening in the construction barricades and a tunnel through the wall of the building, protected by a steel gate and two police guards. Beyond the gate they could see an interior parking area, in the courtyard of the four-sided building. If they were to go inside the offices of the police, they would have to pass through that gate.

But it would not be allowed, as made clear by one of the guards. Men in uniform passed through a turnstile, swiping their ID card to release the swinging arm. But passage was not possible for ordinary citizens. Jamel protested, saying "I must see the records of the police" but Piet took his arm and led him across the street to the plaza in front of the cathedral.

"That's hopeless," Piet said. "It was fifty years ago, and even then the records were either destroyed or stored someplace inaccessible. Einaudi was able to see some of the records when he researched his book, decades ago, but they will never let us find anything. We'll only get in trouble if we try it."

"You're right, I know that," said Jamel "but we are so close to the heart of the event that I wanted to see it for myself. Now I can imagine what happened that day, probably men were thrown into the river and washed away, without anyone knowing who they were. So now I understand that the records couldn't have been complete anyway. We can go, I have told myself that my father went over that wall, into the river, and no one ever saw him again."

Piet slept late the next morning, feeling a sense of accomplishment and completion. He heard Jamel moving about and, when he pulled back the curtain of the forward cabin, saw Jamel putting the shoebox back under his berth.

"Just adding to my notes," Jamel said.

"Do you want to go over it with me today?" asked Piet.

"No, I'm going to the mosque today, to pray. I'm leaving in a few minutes."

"Okay, I will go out later," said Piet, "I want to visit Jacob Soumokil, if I find him in his usual chair at La Vielleuse"

"You probably will, guys like that have a regular routine. After I leave the mosque I'll come by to see if you are there."

After Jamel had gone Piet made coffee for himself and decided that he would look around the neighborhood for a good boulangerie; they had been busy since they arrived and had never settled in and found nearby shops. He drank the first cup quickly, then set off on Rue Riquet, headed for the major shopping street Avenue de Flandre. It was a good choice, for just around the corner he found a *Traiteur-Charcuterie* and a *Boulanger-Patissier* side-by-side, both very nice-looking shops. He bought pâté and a traditional baguette and went back to the boat for another coffee and open-air breakfast, sitting on the stern.

He was enjoying the sun and the food when he heard a shout from across the water. "Hallo, it's Waldo Quarry." Piet looked over, puzzled for a moment, then he saw the barge Le Roy moored along the quay on the east side of the basin. Oh no, he thought, it's that obnoxious little man.

"Hallo, I recognize your little barge from when I saw you at Toul, remember me?" Waldo called out. "Come on over and have a tour of my Luxemotor."

"Oh, I can't, I have to meet someone down in the city," Piet said. "Maybe some other time."

"Well come over anytime, I'm not going anywhere for a long time."

That's bad news, thought Piet, I don't need to be harassed by that guy. Feeling pressed, he hurried to finish his breakfast and get away. It was still early, so he decided to walk to Belleville and see some sights along the way, maybe go by way of the Buttes Chaumont park. "If I go across the lifting bridge on Canal de l'Ourcq I don't think he'll see me," Piet said to himself.

He walked quickly to the northeast end of Bassin de Villette and found the bridge over the canal raised for a tour boat, the *Canauxrama*. There was an arched steel footbridge alongside so he used that rather than wait, pausing at the top to marvel at both the tourist-packed barge and at the ancient bridge mechanism, four vertical posts each with a pulley wheel at the top, cables lifting the roadbed straight up.

Still wary of Waldo, he didn't stop long and strode briskly up the slope of Rue de Crimée. In less than ten minutes he came to the park and walked in through some relatively dense woods of tall trees, emerging to a broad view of the city. In the distance he could see the hilltop Sacre Coeur dome and tower, just as he had seen it in tourist guides. This is a great view, he thought, I didn't know It would be so high above the rest of the city. And right there in the park he looked down on spires of rock alongside a lake and several grassy fields. He realized that the lake was actually a large horseshoe with a rocky island in the middle.

"What a surprise to find this wild, natural place in a dense part of the city," Piet said to no one in particular. I never would have imagined it, he thought, I'll have to come back here on my bike and ride the trails. He walked across a short bridge to get onto the island, followed a steep path up and then left the island on a suspension bridge high above the waters of the lake. It was a thrilling experience, somewhat like a commercial theme park but entirely real and natural.

He left the park at its southern tip, onto Avenue Simon Bolivar and in just a few minutes came to Rue de Belleville. He walked down the hill, past many shuttered shops but also a full range of the services of a city: butcher, baker, coiffure, insurance, cell phones, fruits and vegetables, pizza. He happened to glance up at just the right place, 72 Rue de Belleville, to see the plaque for the birthplace of Edith Piaf, an appropriately seedy and run-down building. Then, at a small open corner, the flat side of a four-story building was the canvas for graffiti, primarily filled with an excellent drawing of a kneeling man in a brown suit, wearing a tan fedora hat, holding a paper with something like an X drawn on it; perhaps a detective at the scene of a crime?

Piet knew he must be close to La Vielleuse when many of the food stores and restaurants became Asian, mixed with other ethnic cafes like *Le Celtic*. And then he was there, at the Belleville intersection, Jacob sitting at his usual place. Piet sat down beside him.

"Bonjour Jacob, I'm glad to see you again," said Piet. "As am I," Jacob replied. "Jamel is not with you?"

"No, he has gone to the mosque. He is not a practicing Muslim, he was raised as a Catholic, but he does identify with North Africans. Even though he and I have become close friends I'm sure he wants to be with men like himself. In Toulouse his friends went to the mosque but they also rode motorcycles together and some of them drank alcohol."

Jacob laughed, "Yes, there is real life, isn't there? Most of us don't follow all the rules, even when we are participating in the formalities of a religion."

"I guess I have followed most of the rules," Piet said, "except that I never participated in any religion. And now that I feel like I have my freedom I don't worry much about the rules."

"Did you and Jamel have success at the Pont St Michel?" Jacob asked.

"We did," Piet replied. "We saw the spot on the Seine, alongside the Préfecture de Police, where Jamel now is convinced that his father was thrown into the Seine, after being beaten by the police. Jamel could picture the scene and saw that there would be no escape, and that the body would most likely be washed downstream and probably never seen again. So I think he has found resolution on that terrible memory. Maybe we won't be staying in Paris much longer."

"Well, I hope that you stay a bit longer, you could sit here with me every day," said Jacob.

"I'd like to," Piet said, "but to tell you the truth I found a woman in Toulouse that I like very much, and I'm getting eager to be back there with her. I'm not sure why I got this involved with Jamel, probably it was because I made the long trip down from northern Holland alone, with no one to talk to, and I spent a lot of time thinking about injustice… You said you are Indonesian, do you know about the South Moluccan boys who were killed in the *treinkaping* event in 1977? I visited that site early in my trip."

"I do remember that, even here it was on French TV for several days," said Jacob. "That was early in the time when television news went to the scene, although all I remember is the continual circling of helicopters over a train stopped in an open field. I did feel some attachment to their situation, even though I was by then a quite successful businessman and in an entirely different position."

"I was also quite different from them, at the time," said Piet. "I had just turned 18 and my life had been so normal that it was boring. My parents weren't wealthy but we had a very comfortable life, I guess you would say I was spoiled by having everything taken care of for me. I couldn't comprehend being in such difficulty that you might want to hijack a train just to make a point. It was an exciting thing to watch on television but I don't remember it having much effect on me at the time. It had a much greater effect when I was there last April, and I thought about it a lot. So when I met Jamel I was a bit of a sucker for his story, it made me want to do what I could to help. But now I think I've done that and I'm ready to go back to what already feels like my true home."

"Bonjour," boomed Jamel, giving Piet a start, as he had come quickly around the corner and they hadn't seen him coming. There wasn't a chair for him to sit down, but he obviously had little interest in that, he was excited and on his way to go somewhere or do something.

"Bonjour Jamel" Piet and Jacob said in unison.

"Have you been at the mosque all morning?" Piet asked.

"Yes," Jamel replied, "I met some guys that were pretty friendly. In fact I asked one of them to come and see me at the boat tomorrow morning, is that okay with you? His name is Kassa Dalouche."

"Sure, you're welcome to treat the boat as you would your own apartment. But I probably won't stay around long, there is a guy on a barge across the basin who wants to be friends with me, but he's a creep, I might have to go be a tourist just to get away. I don't think he'll bother you, I'm sure he is not interested in hanging around with a couple of black guys," Piet said, with a bit of a smile.

"Well that would be fine with me, you're the only white guy that I'm friendly with. Jacob is okay, he's a nice shade of tan," Jamel joked.

Jacob smiled, used to such banter in his neighborhood, where there is a mix of skin colors, enough to scare off a guy like Waldo Quarry.

With just a perfunctory "Bonne journée" Jamel was off, north on Boulevard de la Villette towards the boat. "He seems different, very excited all of a sudden," Jacob said to Piet.

"Yes," said Piet, "he was quite subdued until he worked through what had happened to his father. I think he still wants to do something about it, but I can't guess what it will be. But I think I've done my part, he'll have to decide if he wants to go back with me or stay here somehow."

"I'll be right here, as usual, if you need any help from me," Jacob said.

"Thanks, I appreciate your advice, and to have someone to talk to. I'll still be here for a few days, I want to do a bit of sightseeing before I leave. In fact I want to go to the famous part of the Left Bank right now. I looked at the Metro map, it looks easy."

"It is," said Jacob. "Take the metro right over there, head for République and Châtelet, change at Châtelet for the number 4 line to St-Germain-des-Prés. That will put you right in the center of the well-known places. You will come out next to the church, walk straight ahead to Les Deux Magots, Café de Flore and right across the street is Brasserie Lipp. That's certainly the center of left-bank tourism. If you want to visit a museum, I recommend the Musée d'Orsay, not too many blocks west along the river."

"Thanks, but I think I will skip museums, I just want to walk around and watch all the other tourists. See you tomorrow, I mean *à demain.*"

Piet spent the afternoon wandering the blocks of St-Germain-des-Prés, amazed by the sheer number of sidewalk cafés, not only on the boulevard but also crammed onto the narrow sidewalks of Rue de Buci and many other short streets leading in various directions. His good sense of direction and occasional glimpses of the sun kept him generally aware of where he was, so eventually he ended up back on Boulevard St-Germain. He took the metro back to Villette, wanting to get through the city center before the trains became too crowded and to find Jamel for dinner.

But when he arrived at the boat there was no Jamel, just a note saying to go ahead and have dinner, he would be back late. Piet was surprised but not concerned. Anyway, he had noticed the bistro *Le Bastringue* just across the street from the dock, so he dined alone on a delicious lamb dish, with garlic and thyme.

Piet wasn't entirely alone, even though most of the tables were empty. He had a clear view of an attractive woman who reminded him of Zakia, probably because of her long black hair, he thought. This woman was more slender than Zaki, but with just the same breasts. He tried, with not much success, to keep from staring at her cleavage, formed by a tight blue v-neck tee shirt. She also ate alone and Piet had some thoughts of speaking to her, perhaps inviting her to join him, but couldn't get the nerve. She finished before he did, so he saw that her behind was just as attractive as her breasts. He lingered a bit after she left, thinking of what might have been if he only was more brave, and if he didn't feel guilty about Zaki.

It was well after midnight when Piet heard Jamel come into the boat, but he had already been asleep for a while and didn't say anything as Jamel quietly set up his bed. I'll find out where he was in the morning, thought Piet.

But he was still asleep at 6:30 when Kassa Dalouche arrived. Piet heard them talking at the stern of the boat and got up to meet Jamel's friend. When he did, he was surprised to see Jamel's shoebox on the bench between them.

"Piet, this is Kassa Dalouche," Jamel said. "Sorry to wake you up, Kassa is here early because he has just finished his shift at work, at Charles De Gaulle airport. He's a baggage handler there."

"Bonjour Kassa, I'm glad to meet you," Piet said, as he glanced at the shoebox. Jamel saw the glance, hesitated a moment, then decided to go ahead.

"Piet, now I am ready to tell you," Jamel said. "Kassa is going to help me with my plans to get revenge on the French police for my father. I was just going to show him what I want him to do for me, and I think I have to tell you about it now. I do have some documents in this box, but I also have this…" he said as he took a small plastic box from the shoebox and spoke to both Kassa and Piet.

"This box has an altitude sensor, a switch and a battery. Kassa will take this to the airport with him and attach it to Air France flight 990 to Johannesburg, while he is loading the bags into the hold. Kassa, here is the button to press just before you place it, that will sense the actual atmospheric pressure and set the electronics to the runway elevation at the airport. The switch will trip at 1,500 meters above the airport elevation. You must place the trigger box on the inside hull of the plane and connect two wires, you push each wire into one of these small holes. They are very tiny steel wires, near the top front corner of the baggage compartment door. Use the width of your closed fist to measure from the edge of the door opening, 45 degrees up to the left. You'll be able to feel the wires if you slide your fingers around that spot. After you connect the wires, remove this paper strip; underneath it is contact adhesive which will hold the box tight to the skin of the aircraft. That's all that you have to do, but of course be sure that no one is watching you."

"That will be easy," Kassa said. "There is one other handler there, but he will be at the baggage trailer. He puts the bags on a conveyor belt that comes up to me, I grab the bags and place them in the hold. I will have a minute or so free when he is moving the conveyor to the next trailer."

Piet interrupted and asked "What are you doing? What does this box connect to through those wires?"

"It connects into the wiring bundle that I made, a few years ago." Jamel replied. "The aircraft on this flight is an Airbus A380-800 that I helped build. I made the wiring bundle that circles the inside of the aircraft's skin, just ahead of the baggage compartment door. I built into that bundle two extra wires - one of them is a wire that Airbus keeps in a storeroom but no longer uses, because the Kapton insulation is not safe, it may allow arcing to other wires. The other is a wire that has been made for me, it looks just like the Kapton wire but instead of copper wire inside, there is a thin line of plastic explosive. When the Kapton wire is connected to the battery it will carry voltage that will break through some small slices that I made in the insulation layer. That should be enough to trigger the explosive."

"Wait a fuckin' minute," Piet exclaimed. "What are you talking about? You are going to blow up the plane!"

"Yes," said Jamel, startled by Piet's sudden change in demeanor. "That's the idea! I am expecting that it will blow the nose of the plane off. And I am expecting that the plane will break apart and scatter all over Paris. You probably know that the A380 is a double-decker, the largest commercial plane in the world. There may be hundreds of passengers onboard."

"Oh my god, Jamel! What are you thinking? This can't happen."

"It will happen, I'm going to make it happen. I have been waiting and working on this for years. I don't need you to help me now, but don't try to stop me."

"Well I am going to stop you, you're crazy!"

Kassa stood up and quickly left the boat, saying "I'll leave this to you two, I'm going home, to sleep. See you later, Jamel."

"Jesus Christ, Jamel," Piet exclaimed. "You can't kill all those people! And if you do, they'll catch you and you'll hang, or whatever they do to terrorists in France. You'll hang if you're lucky, first they'll do to you what they did to Algerians fifty years ago!"

"I don't care what they do to me, there's just me, no wife, no kids, just my aunt Marie-Christine, and she'll be happy that I got revenge for her sister. She was broken-hearted to see how Doriane lived in fear after she came home to Toulouse. Now I'm going to make it up for them and for all of my countrymen who died in Algiers and in Paris because of French brutality."

"I can understand how you feel, I guess, just a little," Piet said. "My own life had no tragedies like yours. But you'll just be continuing the tragedy."

"No, I'll be ending it," Jamel replied. "This will be a lesson that the French can't ignore, the way they ignored the deaths in the Seine. No one was ever really punished for that, now I have to deliver the punishment."

Jamel closed the shoebox but dropped the plastic trigger box into the leg pocket of his cargo pants. "I'm going to the mosque now, to pray."

"Well I hope that you pray about this and come to your senses," said Piet.

Jamel put the shoebox back under his bunk and left before Piet could think of anything more to say to him. "My God," Piet thought, "what can I do to stop this?"

He sat on the stern rail of the boat for a while, until he was hailed by Waldo Quarry. "Hallo, come on over," Waldo called. Piet didn't reply, just looked at him for a long moment, then he closed the cabin door and walked up the dock. Not to go to visit Waldo, but to go for a long walk alone.

Piet knew exactly where he wanted to go, to the peace and quiet of Parc des Buttes Chaumont, where he could be alone and think about what he could do. It didn't take long to get there, in his agitated state he took long, quick strides. He didn't yet know the paths of the park very well, but he had looked at a poster map and knew that he could get to the belvedere, on the rocky island, by crossing a bridge on the south side of the lake.

He found the "Suicide Bridge" easily enough; though it is only 12 meters long its stone arch is 22 meters above the lake and a paved path, high enough to do the job for a suicide leap. Piet paused in the middle of the bridge, looking down, and thought that perhaps he could solve the problem by luring Jamel here and throwing him off. But the bridge is now fenced-off with wire mesh to prevent jumps, and anyway Jamel is the bigger and stronger, it would probably be me instead, Piet thought, with a rueful grin.

He followed the paths that wound upward on the island to the Temple Sybille, where the view sweeps across several magnificent old seven-story apartment buildings to the dome and tower of Sacre Coeur. As he had anticipated, there were already some visitors enjoying the view from the temple so he carefully climbed the sharp rocks nearby and found a good seat on a spire at the very top of the island mound. He looked down around him and thought that this looked very much like the steep, wooded islands he had seen in photographs of the sea at Vietnam.

He stayed there for several hours, watching visitors come and go on the paths below him, or those stretched out on the grass at lake level. But although he had found the peace and quiet that he wanted, he hadn't found an answer to how he might deal with Jamel. He knew that he had to stop the planting of the trigger box, but he didn't want to simply turn Jamel in to the police. After all, the police are the enemy in this case, even though Piet had been a policeman himself.

He left his aerie and walked across the long suspension bridge on the west side of the island, again pausing for a while to look down on the lake; he was in no rush, for he didn't know where he was going.

But Piet should have guessed where he would end up, on a chair at La Vielleuse café, next to Jacob Soumokil. Jacob was not only friendly to Piet, he was wise in the ways of the world, and especially the ways of Paris. Piet knew that he could trust Jacob to give him good advice.

Still, he didn't want to reveal the whole story to Jacob. So, after they had both ordered coffee, he told him only that Jamel was headed for serious trouble, that he was intent on getting revenge for the murder of his father and the other Algerians.

"I can understand that," said Jacob, "but not from personal experience. I have never been interested in 'causes', I grew up in a comfortably wealthy family and got into business when I was still young. I can sympathize with Jamel, but he needs to be very careful, he could ruin his life without really accomplishing his goal."

"Yes," said Piet, "I am trying to find a way to stop him without involving the police. I don't think that I can just talk him out of it, I have to figure out how to thwart his plans."

"Perhaps I can help," Jacob replied, "but you'll have to tell me something about it, maybe leaving out the details."

"Well," Piet said, "basically he wants to blow up the largest Airbus, the A380, over Paris. He has already installed an explosive cable that would separate the nose of the airplane from the rest of the fuselage, just as it passes over the Stade de France, southbound over Paris."

"It seems like that would accomplish his goal," Jacob said drily. "Would he be onboard?"

"No, he has a small electronic box, a trigger, that would set off the explosive at a preset altitude. He has found an accomplice who works at CDG as a baggage handler, that man would install the trigger in the plane's baggage compartment."

"Well then, that's easy,' said Jacob, "all you would have to do is somehow disable the trigger apparatus before he puts it in place. And not let him know, let both Jamel and the baggage handler think that it will work. Where does he keep the box?"

"Right now he has it with him, in the pocket of his pants. I don't know where he is, he said he was going to the mosque. I think he is getting ready to do this soon… But of course you are right, that's what I should do, and I think there's a chance I can do it. I think he has more than one trigger box, there is probably one still on my boat, in the shoebox that Jamel brought with him. If I can disable that one, then switch them somehow, the trigger can be installed but it won't go off."

"I have a good electronics man, who maintains the computers at my office, and keeps to himself," said Jacob. "If you can get the box to me I can ask him to look at what's in it and prevent it from working. He won't ask why or what this is all about."

"That's a great idea," Piet said. "I'll go to the boat right now, can you contact your man to see if he can do it right away, before Jamel comes back?"
"Yes, his shop is on Avenue Jean Jaurès, near Place Stalingrad. You can meet me there, it's not far from your boat. His shop is named *Publiphone*, at number 11 Jean Jaurès, next to the restaurant Paris Istanbul."

Piet immediately took the metro to Stalingrad station and, not wanting to waste time making the connection to Riquet station, jogged along the north side of Bassin Villette to the dock. As he had hoped, Jamel wasn't aboard Margriet. Piet quickly found the shoebox under the dinette bench and was relieved to find a small black plastic box inside, which he hoped was a duplicate of the one that Jamel was carrying. He took it, then replaced the shoebox.

Piet crossed the footbridge at the center of Villette, knowing that would bring him to Jean Jaurès just a block or so away from the shop. As he jogged down the steps on the south side, he ran directly into Waldo Quarry.

"Hallo," said Waldo. "I saw you leave your boat and thought I would catch up with you here. C'mon, come to my barge, we'll have a drink and I'll show you around."

"Sorry," said Piet, brushing past Waldo and knocking him back. "No time now, I have to do something right away." He left Waldo there, still talking, as he rushed across Quai de la Loire and onto Rue de la Moselle; he knew that would take him directly to Jean Jaurès. The broad sidewalk on Moselle was empty this time of day and he jogged quickly, almost hit by a scooter as it exited an apartment building parking garage; both the driver and his girlfriend behind him flipped off a rude gesture as they sped away. Piet ignored them and came to the corner of the avenue in just a couple of minutes. He passed a long row of new Citroen cars on display behind the showroom windows of Félix Faure Citroen, looking in vain for the street number. A bank and a supermarket didn't display their number either, but soon he came to a row of small shops and saw #49, and then #47 next. Okay, he thought, not far. He hurried along, watching for numbers, until he saw the red awning of Paris Istanbul. He slowed to catch his breath and turned in at the doorway of Publiphone. Jacob was there, sitting calmly as usual, in a white plastic chair.

"You have been quick," Jacob said. "I have spoken to Jean Louis, he can do this right away." A short man, typical Frenchman, Piet thought, stepped out from a doorway and beckoned him into the workshop.

"Bonjour, merci pour votre aide," said Piet. The man smiled a bit at Piet's obvious foreign accent, but put out his hand for the box. He turned it over in his hand; both of them saw that the box had been assembled with glue and would have to be cut open. "Pas de problème" Jean Louis promised with a grin.

Piet watched as Jean Louis carefully used a heated knife blade to cut along the glued seam. When he held the two halves open, he looked at the electronics and wiring, then pointed to the wires leading to the two sockets for connecting other wires. "Oui," said Piet, "couper."

"D'accord," Jean Louis said, cutting the wire from each socket. "C'est fini." He ran a tiny tube of glue around the edges of the box and resealed it. It looked just as it did before, and Piet thought for the first time that this might work.

Jean Louis handed the box to Piet, who used the still-hot knife to make a tiny scratch across the seam of the box, so that he could identify the disabled box later. Piet reached into his pocket to pay Jean Louis, but Jacob, who had been watching this whole process, stopped him; "I will take care of Jean Louis," Jacob said. "You go and deal with switching the boxes."

"I will," said Piet. "Merci, Jean Louis" And he was off, back to the boat, where he again took out the shoebox and replaced the disabled trigger.

"Now how do I switch them?" Piet thought. "I'll just have to watch for a chance." He had decided that he should cooperate with Jamel and seem to be helping him, but actually with an eye out for an opportunity to stop him. Perhaps if I talk Jamel through the details I can see a way to stop him, Piet thought.

Piet left the boat and walked across the promenade and Quai de la Seine to an outside table at Le Bastringue, where he could watch for Jamel to return without being watched himself, by Waldo. He sat at one of the outside tables and ordered a Heineken beer. Along with pondering the situation with Jamel, Piet thought perhaps he might see the young lady with whom he vicariously had dinner the night before. Those thoughts took him to Zaki, who he was now missing greatly. He knew now that he needed her and wanted to be back in the more welcoming city of Toulouse. "Let's get this mess resolved and get out of here," Piet thought.

And just then Piet saw Jamel crossing the bridge over Bassin Villette. He waited as Jamel walked along the promenade, then waved him over to the sidewalk tables.

"Hello Jamel," Piet said, "have you been at the mosque all day today?"

"No," Jamel replied, "I walked through the city to Pont St Michel, and stayed there all afternoon watching the river go past underneath. Then I took the metro back to Stalingrad."

"And did you come to your senses? I can't believe that you would do this."

"I'm doing it! I've been getting ready for years, and I'm not just giving up now."

"All right," said Piet, looking around to see that they were alone in the row of tables. "Let's talk about what you are going to do. First of all, how do you know that the cables that you installed will work? Will the fuse wire actually ignite the explosive wire, and will that provide a large enough explosion to crack the aircraft structure?"

"I've tested it," Jamel replied. "I went up in the Pyrénées by myself and rode my moto on an old road that went to the top of a mountain. Up there it was wide open, no trees, only flat stones. I laid out a circle of the two cables, in the same oval shape and size of the fuselage. There was a large rock that I could get behind; I ran wires from the cables to a trigger box that I held in my hand. My supplier had made a test box without the altitude sensor, just a switch that would send the battery voltage to the cable. I got down behind the rock and turned the switch. There was a loud blast, then tiny pieces of stone rained down on me. When I walked over to the blast spot, there was a circle cut into the rock about 2 centimeters deep. Not much, but plenty enough to cut through the skin of the airplane."

"I was told that this explosive material has great *brisance*," Jamel continued. "That is a measure of the speed with which the explosion expands, not the overall strength of the explosion. The small amount of material in the cable might not be enough to blow up the plane if the bomb was in a small package hidden in luggage, but when it is laid alongside the skin of the fuselage it provides a shattering effect, tearing a line through the skin of the plane. There is already plenty of stress on the structure at that point, just ahead of the wings, so it won't take much to separate the nose."

"Okay," said Piet, "it does sound like it will work. But what about the trigger box, you said it will sense the altitude but it will be inside the cargo compartment, isn't it pressurized in there?"

"It is," Jamel replied, "but the pressurization doesn't start right at takeoff, it comes up slowly and is set to only maintain the equivalent of only about 2400 meters. The trigger will activate at 1500 meters."

"Well, it does seem that you have this well planned. But what about Kassa, it depends on him to do a proper job, and not get caught at it," Piet asked.

"I asked my friends at the mosque and they told me that there is no one better than Kassa at being focused on a job and doing it right," Jamel said. "And he is just the man that I need, he works the shift on the flight that I want."

"He will certainly be investigated after the event, he can tell them about you and even implicate me," Piet said.

"No, he is an Algerian, and his father was a revolutionary in Algiers, who was captured and beaten to death by the French paratroopers in 1957. He was just a baby then, but his uncle was able to bring him to Paris, on a small boat across the Mediterranean. He feels the same way that I do and was very happy when I approached him, to have a way that he could do something to revenge his father. He will never talk."

"Well he'd better not!" Piet said gruffly as he stood up and walked quickly to the boat. Jamel followed, a little startled; Jamel realized that he never seen Piet anything but calm and even-tempered.

When they got to the boat Piet turned to Jamel and asked "What about that trigger box? Are you sure it will work? I saw you put it in your pocket, let me see it."

This was such a sudden demand that Jamel reacted without thinking and handed it to Piet. Piet took it, turned it over in his hand several times, then threw it as far as he could into the middle of the boat basin.

Jamel leaped up on the stern of the boat, only to see the box float for a few seconds before it went out of sight. "Why did you do that?" he said angrily to Piet.

"To stop you from this crazy scheme," Piet said calmly. "I can't let you ruin your life, not to mention the lives of a few hundred innocent people."

"You can't stop me! This is what I have lived for, for the past five years. Now I'm ready, I've got it all set up and I'm ready to put it into action."

Jamel went into the boat and took out his shoebox; taking the other trigger box, the one Piet had disabled, he said to Piet "I'm taking this to Kassa right now, he is ready to install it on tonight's flight."

Realizing that his plan to switch the triggers had worked, Piet saw that he should work along with Jamel. "Okay," Piet said, "I guess I can't stop you, so what can I do to help?"

"I was hoping you would say that, you can help me. I am going out to the airport tonight, and then I am going to take the RER train to St Michel so that I can be there, on the bridge, when the plane explodes overhead. But I can't stay at the airport long enough to find out if Kassa can successfully install the box. You can help by relaying that information to me."

"I guess I can do that, without getting directly involved. What do you want me to do?"

Jamel reached into another of the pockets of his cargo pants and came out with two cell phones. "These are burner phones, one for you and one for me. They aren't registered in our names and we will throw them away when we're done. I have programmed the number for each one into the other phone. What I need you to do is to go out near the airport tonight, right at the spot where the Concorde crashed into a hotel will be about right. You can rent a car at Gare du Nord, then first go to Le Bourget airport, there are shops there where you can buy a cheap radio that can receive the signals used at the airport. Here's a note, Kassa wrote down for me the channels that the tower air traffic controllers use, and the channel for ramp communications from the baggage handlers to the terminal. At a little after 11PM Kassa will say, on the ramp channel, 'Okay, all bags are in the right place'. When you hear that use this phone to call me and say 'The box is in place'. I will be on my way to St Michel, and then I will know that everything is ready to happen. And you can then listen to the tower channel to confirm the takeoff; listen for 'Air France 990 Super', that's the flight to Johannesburg. Super means that it is the A380, a super-size aircraft."

"Okay, it sounds like I can do that without anyone knowing that I am involved," Piet said. "Shall I call you when I see the plane take off?"

"Yes, that would be good. Just say 'It's in the air'. I have checked out the RER schedule, when you call I should be standing in the middle of the Pont St Michel".

"And then what?" asked Piet. "Should I come find you?"

"No, you have done plenty for me, and I appreciate it. I think you should return the rental car, come back to the boat, and leave as soon as the locks operate in the morning, to go back to Toulouse. You won't see me again, I don't want you to get into trouble."

"All right," said Piet, "but if you can, come to the boat during the night and we'll leave together."

"No, I'm not going back," Jamel replied. "The investigation will probably lead back to the wiring that I installed, so I will need to disappear as soon as I am sure that my goal has been reached. But thank you for all that you have done for me. I hope that you can go back and find a good life in Toulouse with Zakia. Now I'm leaving, I'll hope to hear those messages from you."

And with that, Jamel quickly left the boat and walked to the footbridge. Piet watched as he crossed, then was surprised to see Waldo Quarry intercept him as he descended the stairs on the south side. "Now he's after Jamel, just like he kept after me. What a pain-in-the-ass," Piet thought. "Oh well, Jamel can brush him off like I did."

And Piet thought that now he could relax, as he was sure that the plane wouldn't blow up. He decided that he would go through with the things that Jamel asked him to do, then try to find Jamel afterward and take him to Toulouse. He closed up the boat and walked to Gare du Nord, to get the rental car.

"Hey there boy," Waldo called to Jamel as he saw him coming off the footbridge.

"I'm not your boy," Jamel shouted, irked at this dwarf trying to stop him just as it was all coming together. He jogged down the stairs to get away, but Waldo was fast enough to meet him at the bottom. "Wait," Waldo said, "I think I have something of yours."

Jamel stopped and turned to look; he was surprised to see the trigger box in Waldo's hand. "I saw Piet throw this, I couldn't help noticing the two of you arguing on the boat," Waldo said. "It floated near my barge and I scooped it up with a long-handled net that I keep handy for the times when I drop something overboard. Looks like it's waterproof, it should be okay. It was only in the water for a few minutes."

"Wow, thank you very much," Jamel said. "I appreciate it, this is very important to me."

"Well you're welcome," Waldo said. "Tell your partner to come and see me, I want to talk about Dutch barges."

"Okay, I'll tell him, but right now I've got someplace to go," Jamel said.

"Sure, I'll be here," Waldo replied and turned to go back, while Jamel looked at the wet trigger box. He shook it to get water out of the wire sockets and then carefully wiped it dry. He took the other box from his pocket and compared them by eye; he noticed the scratch that Piet had put on the side of that box, which made him suspicious. He turned the box over and looked at each side, noticing a tiny drop of glue on the seam. "This box has been opened," Jamel thought. He thought about it for a moment, then decided that it may have been tampered with, and so he should use the box that Waldo had just retrieved.

Jamel hurried on to Belleville, for the last planned meeting with Kassa, outside the mosque. As Jamel exited the Couronnes metro station, Kassa was there, leaning against the railing. The Belleville street market had been in operation earlier that day; the mess from that was still being cleaned up by a large crew of men in green suits, so Jamel beckoned to Kassa to walk with him down the side street, Rue Jean-Pierre Timbaud. They stopped behind a van, which blocked the view from the cafe across the street.

"We're ready to go tonight, if you're still with me," Jamel said.

"I am," Kassa replied, "I can do this. I already looked for the wires on the plane that I loaded last night, and found them easily. But you did a good job, no one would notice them without knowing just where to look."

"Good, here is the trigger box," Jamel said. "You can see the sockets for the two wires, on this end. Just push the wires in there, it doesn't matter which wire goes in which socket. Then pull off this cover and stick the box on the hull of the plane. I have talked to Piet, he will be listening on the ramp channel. When the box is in place you should say 'Okay, all bags are in the right place'. Piet will call me and relay that message."

"Where will you be?" Kassa asked.

"I will be in Terminal 2E while the plane is being serviced, I want to see it for myself," Jamel replied. "But I can't stay there to see you install the box because I want to be at Pont St Michel when the plane flies over. I have to take the RER-B at ten minutes before eleven, and you won't be loading the plane till after eleven, right?"

"Yes, we usually start out on the ramp right at 23:00, and we finish by twenty minutes after," Kassa said.

"I'll be on the train when Piet calls and I will have enough time to be standing on the bridge just before the plane takes off," Jamel said. "Afterward they will certainly interrogate you, it will be easy for them to find the place where the bomb was installed and see that it was near the cargo door. So you will have to be strong and not tell them about me or Piet."

173

"Don't worry, I am Algerian, and as strong as you are. I don't think they will do torture now, but they may knock me around just because I'm an immigrant. I can take it, I will tell them that I know nothing about it. They may not get a chance, because if it goes as you say it will, then after the explosion and crash I will disappear. I'm ready to go back to Algiers. Even though I was taken from there as a baby, I grew up feeling like that was my home."

"That's good," Jamel said. "I may do that too, I haven't decided yet. You're on your own, if I see you again I will be happy, but if I don't, good luck to you."

"And to you," Kassa said. "Allahu akbar".

"Allahu akbar," Jamel repeated.

Jamel arrived at the RER-B station St Michel just as he planned, at 23:28. He wanted to be in the center of the St Michel bridge before 23:35; he easily had enough time to get there, the stairs up from the RER platform come out right at the western end of the bridge. Crowds were light so he took the stairs three at a time, walked quickly to the center of the bridge and leaned back on the stone railing, watching the clear sky to the northeast. He thought it was ironic that he would be watching right over the Palais de Justice, the same place where his father and the others had gotten no justice.

Earlier, at seventeen minutes after 11PM, he had gotten the call from Piet, just as the train left the airport grounds and turned south, past Piet's location: "The box is in place." Exactly what he wanted to hear, his plan was in motion. He had watched from a window in Terminal 2E as the plane landed at CDG over two hours earlier. As he had anticipated, with the wind coming in from the west, from the English Channel and over Normandy, the plane had landed to the west on runway 26R. The forecast was for the wind to remain strong and from the same direction, so the takeoff of flight 990 should be to the west, on 26R. That would give him the takeoff path that he wanted.

Jamel had purchased a one-way ticket to Johannesburg, but only to be able to be in the boarding area and watch the airplane and the passengers.

Then he planned to leave so that he could take the RER train to St Michel and watch the event from what he considered to be 'the scene of the crime', the Pont St Michel over the Seine. He stayed as late as he could, pacing back and forth, keeping an eye on the airplane. Walking time from his viewpoint to the TGV/RER station at Terminal 2 would be 6 minutes; he had tried it earlier, clocking the time. The scheduled departure of the train would be 22:51. He was disappointed that he couldn't stay to watch Kassa at the cargo door, but there wasn't time to do both; anyway, Kassa would be working out of sight.

Jamel noted the airplane's identification, F-HBJB. He had worked on all A380s but it was good to confirm that he knew this one, he had been there when its delivery flight was accomplished. He sat for a while in the boarding area, watching the early-arriving passengers for flight 990. The business travelers weren't there yet; he noticed two separate French couples, probably off for a safari holiday. And a black family, father, mother and two boys, impeccably dressed, probably they now live in France and are going back to South Africa to visit relatives. Too bad about them, he thought, but it couldn't be helped. There were plenty of Algerian families that had suffered, including his.

At 22:40 he stood up and took one last look at the plane. It was being serviced for food and cleaning, but he knew that it would be too early for baggage loading, so he began his walk to the RER station. He wanted to walk slowly and not draw attention, even though it was common to see people dashing to catch a train. In ten minutes he boarded the train and found a seat. As soon as the train pulled out, he would be watching his mobile phone for the call from Piet. And it came, just as he passed through the Parc des Expositions: "The box is in place."

Jamel looked out the side window of the train, in the direction of where Piet must be standing, in the field. It was just a few kilometers away, but of course Jamel couldn't see anything except the face of the Hotel Ibis. He thought about all that Piet had done to help him. "I know that I have used him," Jamel said to himself, "but I needed someone thoughtful and steady like Piet to get me to this point. Sorry Piet, I hope that you can safely get back to Toulouse without anyone knowing that you were involved."

As the train continued into Paris Jamel watched the passage of stations, impatient to get to the 'killing field' on the Seine at St Michel. The Stade de France passed by on the right side, brightly lit for a football game.

"That's the place," Jamel thought, "the explosion should happen right about here, about 1,500 feet over the stadium." There were no delays and, when the train left the Châtelet station, he rose and waited at the door, stepping from the train two minutes later as it stopped at St Michel.

Watching from the Pont St Michel, Jamel expected to see the lights of the plane coming toward him over the corner of the Palais de Justice, but for several long minutes there was nothing. Then he got Piet's call: "It's in the air." In a few moments he saw a flashing light which he thought was too low to be the plane, passing to the west behind the square tower of the Palais building. "That's not it," he thought, but he watched it anyway because it was the only airplane that he could see. "Maybe it's gone farther to the west than I thought."

His eyes followed it westward, towards La Defense, and then it turned, in his direction, coming right over the Seine. The flashing lights now became clear, on each wingtip, and a bright white landing light still lit on each wing. He was transfixed as the plane came straight along the path of the Seine. It was climbing at a steep angle and soon Jamel could vaguely see the underside shape of the plane; he thought that it was an A380.

Then it erupted; a ring of fire between the flashing lights, ahead of the wings, a flash bright enough to show the oval shape of the aircraft's nose. "That's it!" Jamel immediately identified the bulbous shape of an A380. He watched as it came closer, slowly tipping downward until he was looking straight at the point of the nose. Behind it he saw the burning shape of the fuselage and the two wings, still together but arcing off toward the ground.

The nose continued straight toward him, aimed at the Pont St Michel as if it had been programmed into the autopilot. Jamel couldn't move, this was the moment that he had been waiting for. And he realized that he had not only blown up the airplane, but that it had happened perfectly. The plane's nose will crash directly on the scene of the murder of his father, right here where he is standing. He knew that he should run, probably best to run to his left on Boulevard St Michel, but he couldn't move. He still leaned back against the stone railing, watching the nose come closer. Within another second he could see only a great white whale filling the sky. Now he could make out the row of six cockpit windows; the two in the center seemed like eyes, aimed at Jamel, looking right into his soul.

The nose came down into the canyon of the river, between the tall concrete walls, passing only a few meters above the Pont Neuf, then filling the width of the Seine in the narrow passage leading to Pont St Michel. In a second it had swept across the bridge, taking away cars and pedestrians, most of whom hadn't seen it coming. The debris and the bodies were dropped into the Seine, stretching from St Michel to Notre Dame. Then all was quiet.

Piet had watched from the plowed field, identifying the plane as it passed over him then watching until it made a turn over the city, soon bursting with a ring of flame. "*Merde*," he thought, not noticing that he had now been in France long enough to be using the French term for dismay at the event which he thought he had prevented. "Oh my god," he said aloud, "how did this happen? I got rid of one trigger box and disabled the other."

He watched the burning fuselage and wings fall nearly straight down, to him it appeared to have struck right in the center of Paris. It hit the ground with a huge burst of flames and smoke, the plume of the rising smoke illuminated by the lights of Paris. "The 'City of Light' is at its best tonight," Piet thought for an instant, before he realized that his whole body was trembling. He watched the glow of the flames until he became sick, throwing up his steak dinner.

Piet had never made a plan for what he would do now, but he realized that he could get a room here at the hotel and watch the reports on television. He found the night auditor in a room behind the desk and paid for a room, in cash, and registered with a French name; he was glad that the bored clerk didn't bother to check his identification. He went quickly to the room and pulled a chair in front of the television. The first reports were just coming in, with very little known, but already they were calling it an *attentat*, a terror attack. There was a live view, from the rooftop camera of station TV3, of dense smoke rising from the Bois de Boulogne park. Then a report from a street camera crew of the plane debris in the Seine; Piet recognized the Préfecture de Police building in the background. The entire row of blue police vans in front of it had been swept into a single pile. The camera turned to the roadway of Pont St Michel; there were no stone railings, no lampposts, in fact nothing but the paved surface, swept clean. "If Jamel was standing there as he planned, he has either run to the side streets or was taken away in the crash," Piet thought. He tried to call Jamel's mobile phone several times, but each call went straight to voicemail.

"Either turned off or destroyed in the crash." He wasn't worried, it was a burner phone with no personal records and his call to Jamel couldn't be traced.

An updated report on television showed the fuselage, burning fiercely, in one of the open fields of the Bois de Boulogne. The reporter said that people on the ground have been killed; Piet thought that, because of the late hour, they must have mostly been prostitutes and their customers, who cruise through the park in cars looking for entertainment. "Not the kind of entertainment they had been expecting," Piet thought.

He watched carefully as cameras scanned the St Michel area. One cameraman had even gotten to a location high in one of the towers of Notre Dame; from that angle Piet could see the tip of the plane's nose, wedged under the bridge called *Le Petit Pont*. "My God," Piet thought, "It fell right into the basin of the Seine between the two bridges, right where Jamel & I were just looking down to see the spot where his father must have died. Jamel has achieved his goal, but I don't know if anyone will ever know it. And I wonder if Jamel knows it, is he there watching or is he under that debris?"

The scene on television moved to Pont Neuf, where the inflatable boats of the Brigade Fluviale darted under the stone arches retrieving bodies floating downstream, drawn by strong currents in the narrow channel. Some, still strapped into their seats, floated into the spaces between moored barges and the concrete wall, to be pulled out by police and firemen with long poles and ropes. A camera crew on Quai de Conti filmed as several firemen onboard the 'Sapeurs-Pompiers' barge, permanently moored just west of Pont Neuf, used the crane intended for launching the inflatable boats to lift seats and bodies onto the deck.

Piet decided what he had to do: first, get out of Paris. He would watch for Jamel but if he got back to the boat and Jamel wasn't there, he would immediately leave without him. Then, somehow, he didn't know how yet, he would put out information about why this terrible thing was done.

He watched the television through the night, then left the hotel just as dawn began to break. He retraced his route of the previous afternoon, the straight-line highway N17 past Le Bourget, later becoming the N2 in Paris, knowing that it would take him on the shortest route to Gare du Nord, where he returned the rental car just after 6AM. The young female clerk asked "Taking the early fast train to Amsterdam?"

"Oh... yes," said Piet, realizing that had rented the car on his Dutch driver's license. "I have to get back to my office before they close everything down in the Paris area. I hope the train is running."

"I think the early trains north are okay," the clerk replied. "But you're right, they may close them down soon. I hear that the A1 north is closed already, it's a good thing that you're not driving."

"Yes," said Piet. "Well thank you, and good luck to you here in Paris." And a good thing that I didn't try to drive in on the A1, he thought.

He went up several flights of stairs to the city bus terminal on the roof, then walked east to Rue du Faubourg de St Denis and then on a zigzag of minor streets to Bassin de la Villette. He certainly didn't want to try the metro and thought it best to stay off the major streets. He was surprised how quickly he got there, but he was glad that he did. He wanted to be at the first lock at 8:00, hoping that it, and the others down to the Seine, would be operating.

Piet quickly packed the boat and made it ready for the voyage south. He kept an eye out for Jamel but thought that, if he was alive and wanted to travel on the boat, he would have arrived during the night. Even on foot, as he surely would have done, it would take less than an hour to get to Villette. Besides, Piet really wanted to have nothing further to do with Jamel. The investigation would certainly lead to the mosque, whether or not Kassa revealed anything, but no one at the mosque knew Piet; he had asked Jamel about that and he had replied that he never spoke of Piet, the boat or Villette.

Piet motored away from the dock at 7:50 and went straight to the Canal St Martin top lock, idling the boat in front of the lock gates. He was glad to see the lockkeeper arrive at 8:00, hoping that meant that the locks would be operating normally. Since the attack had obviously started at the airport, he thought that there might not be any effect on the canals. At least that's what he was hoping.

He watched the lights on the lock wall: two red lights showing, so he must wait. Then one red light turned to green; Piet was elated, that means the gates will open soon. And in another minute they did, the gates beginning to swing open as both lights turned to green. His was the only boat ready to use the canal, so as he put a line on the right-side wall the gates began to close behind him. The water level went down, the gates opened to the lower lock chamber and he repeated the process. "Whew, first locks done, three more double locks then a single lock into the Seine; let's get this done and get of here," Piet said to himself. "I sure don't want to be stopped part way down."

Despite a few delays at the locks because of inattentive lockkeepers, probably glued to a television or radio, Piet finished the canal by noon. He stopped briefly at Arsenal Marina to tell them that he would be leaving his slip early, before the end of the paid month. He avoided conversation and asked for an immediate opening of the last lock, #9, from the marina to the Seine.

As he came out into the Seine he looked to his right, downstream; only a kilometer away he could see on the left-hand side of Notre Dame that the southern channel was closed by debris, with the flashing lights of emergency vehicles still plentiful on both banks. He turned his view and the boat quickly upstream, to the south, away from the site. Now he was away, returning to Toulouse and Zakia. "That's the place for me," he thought, "a Dutchman in Toulouse."

SOURCES

Alex Patterson: *Aircraft Electrical Wire Type*,
www.vision.net.au/%7Eapaterson/aviation/wire_types.htm

AZF: l'enquête assassinée   www.azf-enqueteassassinee.typepad.com/

Canal du Midi, Éditions du Breil,
Chemin Notre Dame, 11400 Castenaudary, France   www.carte-fluviale.com

Jean-Luc Einaudi: *La bataille de Paris: 17 octobre 1961*, 1991,
ISBN 2-02-013547-7

Francis Fytton: *War in the 18th Arrondissement*,
Paris Letter, The London Magazine, December 1961

James J. Napoli: *The 1961 Massacre of Algerians in Paris:
When the media failed the test*
Washington Report, March 1997
www.fantompowa.net/Flame/algeria_napoli_article.htm

Maurice Papon, Wikipedia   wikipedia.org

Paris massacre of 1961, Wikipedia   wikipedia.org

Hakim Sadek: *"Battle of Paris": When the Seine was full of bodies*
Liberté, 17th October 1998
www.fantompowa.net/Flame/algerians_liberte.htm

Printed in Great Britain
by Amazon.co.uk, Ltd.,
Marston Gate.